Fly Away, Pigeon

THE
SEAGULL
LIBRARY OF
GERMAN
LITERATURE

Fly Away, Pigeon

MELINDA NADJ ABONJI

TRANSLATED BY TESS LEWIS

LONDON NEW YORK CALCUTTA

This publication was supported by a grant from
the Goethe-Institut, India.

Seagull Books, 2022

Originally published in 2010 as *Tauben fliegen auf* by Melinda Nadj Abonji
© Jung und Jung Verlag, Salzburg, 2010

First published in English by Seagull Books, 2014

English translation © Tess Lewis, 2014

Published as part of the Seagull Library of German Literature, 2022

ISBN 978 1 8030 9 048 1

British Library Cataloguing-in-Publication Data
A catalogue record for this book is available from the British Library

Typeset by Seagull Books, Calcutta, India
Printed and bound by WordsWorth India, New Delhi, India

Fly Away, Pigeon

TITO'S SUMMER

As we finally drive up in our American car, a dark brown Chevrolet, chocolate brown, you might say, the sun is beating down mercilessly on the small town and has almost completely swallowed up the shadows thrown by the houses and trees, in other words, it's noon when we drive up, craning our necks to see if everything is still there, if everything is still the same as it was last summer and all the years before that.

We drive up, gliding along the road lined with majestic poplars, the avenue that announces the small town, and I've never told anyone how these poplars that reach up into the sky make me dizzy, a feeling that wires me directly to Matteo (it's the same dizziness I feel when Matteo and I spin without stopping in the middle of the most beautiful clearing in the forest near the village, the two of us alone, his forehead against mine, then Matteo's tongue, strangely cool, and the black hairs on his body hugging his skin as if they had yielded completely to its pale beauty).

As we drive past the poplars, their shimmer confuses me, our chocolate-brown ship glides from one tree to the next, and between them the air of the plain becomes visible, I can see it, the air, now immobilized by the pitiless sun, and my father says to the air conditioner in a small, quiet voice that it's all still the same, nothing's changed, nothing at all.

I wonder if my father would like a team of professional gardeners at least to prune the branches—to counter this wild growth with civilization!—or to cut down once and for all the poplars that announce the small town! (And we'd sit on one of the trunks, gazing regally out over the plain drenched with the midday heat, and my father would feel compelled to climb up on one of the stumps and turn around full circle, then proclaim with the bitterness of a man who has finally been proven right, still, better late than never: Those goddamn dusty trees are finally gone.)

No one else knows what the trees, or the air so clearly visible between them, mean to me, and nowhere do the trees seem to promise as much as they do here, where the plain gives them space, and I wish once again that I could stop here, lean against one of the trunks, look up and let myself be captivated by the leaves' small, rapid movements, but this time, again, I don't ask my father to stop because I don't have an answer to the question 'why?' because I'd have to explain too much and would certainly have to tell them about Matteo to make them understand why it is I want to stop right here, so close to our destination.

As if drawn by some occult force, our car drives on, almost immune to the potholes in the road, and before we finally arrive we have to go through one more *nothing's changed*, civilization has to suffer one more setback, or at least

4

a standstill, and the two of us, the children, press our faces against the left-side window which is surprisingly cool, and we look, incredulous, at people who live in a mound of refuse—nothing's changed, my father says—we look at shacks made of corrugated sheet-metal and rubber, and scruffy children playing amid broken-down cars and household waste as if it were completely common. What about the broken glass, I want to ask, what about when night falls and the shadows start to move and all those things lying around in a complete mess come to life? And in the blink of an eye I forget the poplars, Matteo, the shimmer, the Chevrolet, and the black night of the plain envelops me in all its destructive power, and I don't hear the gypsy songs, so often evoked and admired, I see only greedy shadows in the dark without a single street lamp to chase them away.

My father peers out the window, shakes his head, coughs a dry cough and drives so slowly you'd think he were about to stop the car at any moment. Just look at that, he says, tapping his index finger on the windscreen (I remember a fire and its spreading smoke) and I, taking in the faces caked with dirt, the piercing eyes, the rags, the tatters, the light glinting off the heaps of refuse, I take a broader view, as if I were meant to understand it all, these images of people who don't have mattresses, much less beds, and who probably dig themselves into the dirt at night, into the pitch-black plain that now, in summer, is bursting with sunflowers but in winter is so bare it's nothing but earth, pitiful earth, crushed by a heavy winter sky, and when the sky lifts the plain turns into a sea, unruffled by the merest breeze.

I've never told anyone that I love this plain, the way it thins out to a desolate line and has nothing to offer; when you are utterly alone on this plain you can't expect anything from it, at best you can lie on it with your arms outstretched, and that is the only protection it offers.

If I had told them that I love Matteo (a Sicilian boy who suddenly showed up in our class a few weeks before summer vacation, *Ciao, sono Matteo de Rosa*! and immediately became everyone's favourite except the teacher's), then most of them probably would have understood me, but how could I tell them that I love a plain, the dusty, proud, indifferent poplars and the air between them? In summer, when the plain has grown a storey higher with fields of sunflowers, corn and wheat as far as the eye can see, rumours spread that someone has disappeared again into the endless fields—if you're not careful, the plain will swallow you whole, they say, but I don't believe them. I believe the plain is an ocean with its own laws.

The poor things, my mother says, as if we were watching television, and instead of changing the channel we just drive on, we drive past in our icebox that cost a fortune and makes us so imposing, we seem to own the road, and my father turns on the radio so the music can transform the shabbiness into a dance tune and heal reality's club foot for a moment: 'Come to me, don't go so far away, my darling, come to me and give me a kiss . . .'

With a sound so slight it's not even worth mentioning, we drive over the tracks and past the rusted, crooked sign that for ages has had to bear the small town's name; we're here, my sister Nomi says, pointing towards the cemetery where obvious injustice runs riot, untended graves, simple wooden crosses, barely recognizable behind their screens of weeds, the dates and letters almost indecipherable, we're here, Nomi says, and in her eyes you can see the fear she'll have to visit the cemetery sometime in the next few days and stand helplessly at the graves, ashamed of her parents' tears, wanting to cry too, picturing our father's father lying in the coffin down below, our mother's mother, whom we, Nomi and I, never knew, our great-uncles and great-aunts, our hands always in the way at times like these, the weather never right for times like these, if you did cry, at least you'd know where to put your hands; gladioli and delicate roses next to graves covered with stone slabs, the dead, whose names are engraved in the stone and will remain legible for all eternity. I don't like those slabs because they crush the earth of the plain and keep the souls underneath from taking flight.

The worst that can happen to our family on our mother's and our father's sides, lying under their stone slabs, is that there are no flowers for them, none of the yellow and pink roses or gladioli, but the graves themselves, covered with those stone slabs, don't get run-down even if no one ever comes to visit, not on All Saints' Day either, not even on All Saints' Day, my mother says, when one of her cousins telephones

7

and, in a choked voice, tells Mother that except for her, no one had gone to the cemetery to light a candle for the dead. At least the gravestones aren't falling apart, my mother says then, and this sentence holds the profound sorrow of a life spent too far from her dead to care for them properly, to visit them even only once a year and bring them flowers on All Saints' Day.

Since death rarely gives advance notice, we're almost never there when someone in our family dies in the Vojvodina, and when Aunt Manci or Uncle Móric call—because they're the only ones with a telephone—to tell us that today, unfortunately, they have bad news, then our living room becomes eerily quiet. We might have something to say about the dead if we were there where all of our family still lives, or at least we could listen to what others have to say about the deceased, and we would certainly be moved when Mamika, whose voice reaches into the deepest corners of your soul, sang, but we aren't there, where they need three days to take leave of the dead before the mortal remains, as they say, are consigned to the earth, and since we only have a telephone over which a distant voice informs us that something irrevocable has happened, we move around like ghosts on days of bad news, we even avoid making eye contact with one another, and I remember that, on a day in October 1979, Father brusquely swept into the waste-paper basket the yellow chrysanthemums Mother had placed on the living-room table when we heard that his beloved great-aunt had died. No funeral flowers, Father said, the remote control still in his hand and the nape of his neck flushed red. Since then, Nomi and I call chrysanthemums forbidden flowers because we were no longer allowed to put them on the table and when we finally visited the cemetery in our hometown to decorate the graves of our dead, we certainly never brought chrysanthemums, not even in autumn, so then we've come too late again, I think, so now, for a second time, we're alone with our grief.

At the time, we had no idea that in a few years the headstones would be knocked down, the granite slabs defaced with pickaxes and the flowers decapitated, because in wartime killing only the living is not enough, and if we had known, we probably would have stood by the graves of our dead, heads lowered, praying that our quiet singing would harden into a magical shield that could protect them undisturbed in their eternal rest, as they say, but we might just as well have prayed that the earthworms, grubs, springtails, millipedes and beetles of all kinds not be sent scrabbling and scuttling about wildly when startled by the sudden change in the light, only to escape after their frenzy into the shelter of darkness.

Our brand new Chevrolet turns left onto Hajduk Stankova, tracing an elegant curve before my father has to brake because the street is unpaved, just hardened mud covered by a thin layer of dirt that turns our Chevrolet into a dusty monstrosity; here too, civilization is brought to a standstill.

We're here, I say. Our car sits outside the main entrance in front of a wall, maybe six feet high and nine feet wide, made of warped and dried-out wooden planks that offer more than one promising gap for curious eyes to peer through, my father cuts the engine, we squint at the little white house, starkly illuminated by the sun, the home of Mamika, my father's mother; for me it's the archetype of a house that encloses what is most essential, one's deepest secrets, and we sit there for a long moment before Father opens the front gate and our Chevrolet slowly rolls into the courtyard, scattering the ducks and chickens with a short blast of the horn.

The Lord has brought you, Mamika says this phrase in her soft voice without a smile or tear, and strokes our cheeks, one after the other, even my father's, her son's, it's God's will that brings us into her living room which is also her bedroom, His grace; she serves us Traubi Soda, tonic, Apa Cola and, in between, a drop of schnapps, as always Pope John Paul II smiles down at us from a colour photograph, and I anxiously inspect the room down to the smallest details, my eyes seeking out the credenza, the framed blessing, the rag rug; I always hope that everything is exactly the same as before, because when I return to the place of my early childhood there's nothing I fear so much as change—seeing these familiar objects protects me again from my fear of becoming a stranger in this world, of being shut out of Mamika's life; I hurry out to the courtyard as soon as I can to continue my anxious inspection. Is everything still there? The two wire-mesh silos in which the corn is stored and the cheeky mice frolic, the blue water pump that to me was always a living creature (a dwarf? some undefinable animal?), the roses and damask violets my mother adores, with their scent that can make your head spin at night, the paving stones from which urine evaporates quickly in summer and onto which the chickens' blood sprays when Mamika skilfully cuts their throats not long after they've pecked grains of corn off the very same stones. Everything still there? I secretly ask myself and only much later do I understand why this particular anxiety grips me in the first few moments of each return, and that I am not the only one who suffers from this unpleasant feeling; Nomi does too, but she deals with it differently.

And after I've inspected the courtyard, the chicken coop, the manure pile, the garden and, of course, the attic—which holds the most fascinating secrets—I have to climb back down the rotting ladder, taking care not to crush any of the glowing ice-plant flowers that grow in the gaps between the stones, I have to get back to the front gate as quickly as possible, push down the latch and stick my head out to see if she's still there, the crazy woman with her dishevelled hair and eyes that believe everything they see and forget it all immediately, that ask before her mouth does, do you have something for me? a little something sweet? for my heart, something sweet? I have to see if Juli is still there, Juli who still has the mind of a child, as they say, although for a long time now she's had breasts and frizzy hair under her arms, Juli who sits a stone's throw away, up against the wall or on a folding chair and does nothing but watch the day go by, Juli, are you there? The lunatic we children fear and constantly mock, Juli, whom we love because she believes everything we say and tells us things that hint at foreign worlds (hey, Nomi and Ildikó, Juli says, you have a sister, yes, yes, yes, you do, Juli giggles, I know it, look here, Juli points to the large orange flowers on her dress, these are my eyes, yes they are . . .).

Traubi Soda! Nomi and I shout in chorus after we've washed our hands and sat down at Mamika's table on which a plastic tray with little bottles awaits us. Traubi Soda! That's the name of our homeland's magic potion in a slender bottle with no label, just glowing white letters on green glass; Mamika, who has bought a ton of Traubi for us, just for you! And naturally, Nomi and I are spoilt brats from the West who make fun of the way they try to imitate Coca-Cola in the East and end up with nothing better than a brown, undrinkable brew called Apa Cola (Apa Cola, what a stupid name!), but we love Traubi, we love Traubi so much that we consider bringing a few bottles back to Switzerland to show our friends that back home, where we come from, we have something that tastes unbelievably good—but so far we haven't.

Mamika, who serves chicken goulash with dumplings, breaded pork cutlets with fried potatoes and squash, sun-fermented dill pickles and tomato salad with red onion, Mamika, who lets us drink all the Traubi we want and lets us get up from the table during dinner to get our fill of kissing her soft cheeks, Mamika is the only one who doesn't annoy us when she tells us we've grown at least the width of two fingers, my big girls, she says, soon you'll be young women! One after the other, Nomi and I put our hands on Mamika's bun because her braided hair is so soft against our palms and I, who already that summer have the feeling that my legs are too long, my hands too big, there's always some part of my body that's no longer the right size, I've definitely grown more than two fingers' width, but I'm still far from the world of adults. This is especially clear when Mother and Father start talking about life in Switzerland, about our laundry and dry-cleaners store—*WÄSCHEREI, GLÄTTEREI, BÜGLEREI*—the black-and-white sign announces the services we offer—washing, folding and pressing—and Father paints the letters in the air for Mamika, and gives the numbers—how much it costs to have a shirt pressed, a tablecloth, an undershirt, how much of a discount they give for ten shirts—and Mother describes what complicated fabrics the rich have, your fingers have to learn how to iron them properly, because at that price you can't leave the tiniest wrinkle, she says, and I listen to my parents with one ear while talking almost inaudibly with Nomi about how our friends would react to Traubi Soda, Betty would certainly say, not bad, but nothing special, and Claudia would turn the little bottle this way and that and not say anything or just shrug her shoulders, it's not easy to admit something else is better than what you have, Nomi says, yes, that's true! It wouldn't be fair to force our friends to lie to us, we decide, it's better if we just tell them how great Traubi Soda is and wait for the day when it's much more famous than all the other soft drinks, more famous even than Coca-Cola, yes, of course! and Nomi fills our glasses again, Father and Mother, in the meantime, are telling Mamika that we also deliver the pressed laundry in large baskets to our customers' homes, usually in the evening, for an extra charge, of course, we have to follow hairpin turns on the way up those hills, they like to live up high, the rich, Father says and laughs, and while he tells of the dogs that have attacked him or almost attacked him during his deliveries, I think of how we're stuck in a basement with the two washing machines, the detergent, fabric softener, special cleaning solutions, countless plastic baskets in all colours and sizes, cloth bags filled with clothespins, along with a cupboard full of dishes, spices and a cooking plate, how we sit at the small wooden table that Father had found on the street, and there, where it's always cold and the freshly washed clothing hangs on a line, that's where we eat lunch in silence, because Father doesn't like it when we talk during meals. When we're alone, Nomi and I measure the baggiest underwear with our fingers, imagining how many times our thighs and bottoms could fit in those parachutes! rich people have to go to the toilet too, and sometimes they're downright fat, we say giggling, but I feel ashamed when the owners come to pick up their bundles and I have to look them in the eye while running the cash register, and no one knows about my shame, not even Nomi.

That sounds like hard work, Mamika says, cuts a thick slice of bread and hands it to Father. But we earn our keep and no one tells me what to do, he shows his teeth and refills his glass, but tell us, Mamika, now that the king of all partisans is dead, do you still have to get up in the middle of the night to stand in line for what they call bread? or can you now buy bread in the afternoon or any time you want . . . ?

It won't be long before Father starts in on the basic differences between East and West, the most fundamental differences in the whole universe, and he will toss back one schnapps after another, the pear schnapps Uncle Móric made this very year, the year Comrade Josip Broz Tito died and the year when what everyone has always known—at least anyone intelligent—would be proven true, namely, that it will take several generations to fix this socialist mess of an economy, if it's at all possible! (We've already heard all this and more during the trip.) And just as Father is hitting his stride, Nomi unexpectedly says in the relentless, high-pitched voice she usually uses to beg for sweets, I want Mamika to talk to me now, I want Mamika to talk now. And she asks our grandmother how many babies the pigs have, asks about the geese, the chickens, asks if we could go collect eggs later, she wants to know if Mamika still forces food down the ducks' throats, if Juli still goes to the market for her and what Mr Szalm's garden looks like. And Nomi hangs from Mamika's neck, talks on and on, until Mother puts her hand on Nomi's feverish face and says, we've only just arrived, you have a few days to ask Mamika all your questions.

But I want to know now, Nomi says, I want to know everything right away, she says again and presses her face against Mamika's cheek, almost in tears, her voice cracks, and Mother shakes her head, confused, and Father says, after that long a drive, I'm in no mood to listen to this nonsense, and slams his hand down on the table, and since there are no flies to swat, we all jump, except for Mamika who says, welcome to my home! Welcome with all you've brought with you, my dear Miklós! I'm going to take Nomi and Ildikó on a quick tour and you take a rest while we're out, then we'll have dessert!

My grandmother's soft sing-song, the frogs' croaking at night, the pigs squinting their little piggy eyes, the excited clucking of a chicken before it is slaughtered, the damask violets and apricot-coloured roses, colourful swearing, the pitiless summer sun and, above it all, the smell of braised onions and my strict Uncle Móric who suddenly stands up and starts dancing—the atmosphere of my childhood.

That was my answer, after a long pause, when a friend asked me years later what 'homeland' meant to me. At the time, the most important things didn't even occur to me— first, Traubi Soda, the relatively unknown but, in fact, most delicious drink in the whole world which has surely been blessed by Pope John Paul II and which I associate so completely with my native country that I forgot to include it in my answer. And second, something that's not so easy to capture in words because it's my memory of Nomi, how her whining got on Mother's and Father's nerves back then, in the summer of 1980, when she started, soon after we got to Mamika's, demanding that Mamika tell her everything and tell it right away; my sister's whining, I suddenly realized, was comparable to my secret, frantic inspections. We were both afraid of being cut-off from our home country, we wanted to recover the time that had passed while we were away, and in our race against time it was immensely comforting to be able to orient ourselves with banal, mundane things—the chopping block that fortunately is always in the same place, next to the pigsty, near the outhouse, Mamika, who hasn't bought any cows or pheasants in the meantime but still makes do with her pigs, chickens, geese and ducks, the tiny pigeon loft that we find in the attic, just as we left it—and Mamika has told us that she only keeps the pigeons for our mother's sake, because Mother loves her pigeon soup more than anything else and looks forward to it every year just like a child, as she herself admits. We're happy when we make the rounds with Mamika and see that she hasn't turned her flower beds into a vegetable garden and that the plum tree stands exactly where it always has, near the corn silo, and some of the fruit falls in the garden and the rest drops onto the paving stones where it soon falls prey to the ants, beetles, wasps and the chickens who are always pecking stupidly at everything they see. When Mamika shows us her world, stops by the wooden fence that surrounds the chicken coop and says, yes, Mr Szalma's courtyard is still a mess, see for yourselves! when we peek through the gaps in his fence at the giant squashes, some already burst open, and the weeds crowding out the beautiful roses, when we hear Mamika say she just doesn't understand dear Mr Szalma, why does he repaint his house every year but let his garden go to seed, just look how the ivy is devouring the raspberry bushes! we're reassured, Nomi and I, that our homeland is not allowed to change, and if it has to, then only very, very slightly (and when we turn eighteen, when we're of age, we'll come back and creep under Mamika's thick, warm quilts and we'll dream that we were only gone a few years over there in Switzerland).

Yes, we're finally here, only after we've finished our tour of inspection do we feel we've arrived, that we're here now, where our grandmother lives, Mamika, who, incidentally, has visited us in Switzerland twice for Easter and once for Christmas and otherwise has only ever been out of the country once, when she went to Rome to kiss the Pope's hand, and

Mamika chuckled when she told us about the exhausting bus ride to see her beloved Pope, about Rome, which seemed infinitely large to her—that she was always leaning on her cane or on her friend's arm. My big little girls, Mamika says when we link arms with her and slowly move towards the car because Father has called us to help him unload it, and only once we've started pillaging the overloaded Chevrolet, setting our suitcases and bags down next to the well, do I notice that the heat hasn't changed even though it's now late afternoon.

What a car! Mamika says holding one hand in the other behind her back, how can you drive an enormous thing like that, Miklós, do you even know where it begins and ends? In America, everyone drives one of these, Father answers. It's a fact, he adds when Mamika looks at him, eyebrows raised, come, sit in it, and Father opens the passenger-side door, brushes his hand over the leather seat, it's even more comfortable than sleeping in bed, and Father lights a cigarette, Mamika hesitates, says, I'm too old for something this modern, and Mother says that tomorrow's another day, but Father already has hold of Mamika's hands, he helps her gently but firmly as she lowers herself into the car, lifts her legs and settles herself onto the broad leather seat. Father, who shuts the passenger-side door with an elegant flourish, and Nomi and I, sitting on our suitcases, watch Mamika as she looks out the windscreen and tries to smile, Father, who is already sitting behind the wheel and surely explaining how everything works, the automatic transmission, the windows with electric controls, the air conditioning, the *comfort*, a word he doesn't pronounce quite right in German but still likes to use.

Nomi, Mother and I know we will see more of these displays over the next few days, and when we drive over to Uncle Móric's the day after tomorrow to celebrate his son Nándor's wedding, all the men in their Sunday best will be gathered around our Chevrolet within minutes as if they had come to honour the car rather than the bride and groom; we can see them already, the men, how they circle the car, slowly, thoughtfully, caressing the gleaming metal, because any contact with the car must bring good luck, and not just anyone, but only the bridegroom, Nándor, is allowed to raise the hood and reveal the machine's core, its heart, the motor, and Father will start it and the men will stand around the car with its engine running, they will talk, talk, talk, and point out the important parts necessary to make up the whole, a beautiful whole that doesn't just roll or move forward but creates a perfect driving experience.

This, or something very similar, is what will happen, and Nomi, Mother and I, our aunts and cousins, we'll stand a little off to the side, pointing at the men and, within acceptable limits, make fun of the stamina and gravity they bring to mechanics; at such moments we really are no better than foolish hens clucking and cackling to distract ourselves from what we all fear, that this unanimous enthusiasm will suddenly degenerate into an argument because one of the men might contend that Socialism does have its advantages after all, we foolish hens know that all it takes is one sentence and suddenly the men's throats are taut and bare—yeah, sure, Communism's a good idea, on paper . . . ! And Capitalism! The exploitation of man by man . . . ! We chatterboxes know that it's one small step from mechanics to politics, from a fist to a jaw—and when men tip over into politics, it's the same as when you start cooking and you know from the very beginning, for whatever reason, that it will go wrong—too much salt, not enough paprika, overcooked—it's all the same; politics is poison, says Mamika.

In Mamika's courtyard, the Chevrolet looks like it's from another world, I think, as Mother puts her hands on Nomi's and my shoulders and we wait for the men's drama to play out, a little owl perched somewhere in a tree accompanies us with its shy call, we can take our bags in now, Mother says, you know this could go on for a while, and she grabs two bags and heads off towards the house, but Nomi and I, we keep sitting on our suitcases, slip off our shoes, the paving stones are so hot, we can only brush our toes over them, insanely hot, Nomi says, yeah! and we look out of the corner of our eyes at the car, at our Father, busy behind the steering wheel, his incisors gleaming occasionally through the windscreen, and only later, when we remember this strange scene, do we understand why we stayed there, seated on our suitcases, even though it was unpleasant to watch how helplessly Mamika swivelled her head from Father then back to us, her dark scarf had slipped down low over her forehead; we would surely have jumped up so as not to be upset by Mamika's helplessness much longer, but Father, our father, despite his cigarette, his impenetrable moustache, his gold teeth, the wrinkles on his cheeks and brow, our father all of a sudden looked years younger, like a boy telling his mother all about his new accomplishment with a child's excitement, hungry for her gentle praise, her acknowledgement (and Mamika will offer him what he so urgently needs, she will understand what he needs from her even though she feels completely out of place); Nomi and I, we stay there, sitting on our suitcases, because we want to watch this boy for as long as we can, so long that we'll never forget him.

Uncle Móric and Aunt Manci's house is surrounded by clunkers—Trabbis, Skodas, Ladas and Yugos, so we can't get near it, and, because we're so late, we have to turn into a small side street, we're bounced up and down, the slightest movement makes our new party dresses rustle and Father yells because everything makes him nervous, the rustling, the stupid *gyik utca*, Lizard Street, where our car is bound to get stolen, the sun that beats down through the windscreen, the bride and groom are going to melt away today, he says, and we laugh, Mamika, Mother, Nomi and I, but not Father, he loosens his tie as he turns off the engine and wipes his face and the steering wheel with his handkerchief, and Father is sweating not just because it's hot but also because he realized

22

last night that the bride and groom, Nándor and Valéria, are getting married on 4 August 1980, exactly three months after Tito's death! and Father can't help but milk this fact for all it's worth. It's a coincidence, Mother says, and we sit around Mamika's kitchen table, Nomi and I eat crêpes while Mamika recounts how much poultry was killed days and days ago for the wedding banquet, along with a pig, a calf, two lambs, the many buckets needed to collect the blood, how many pounds of peppers were stuffed with ground meat, how Aunt Manci must have forgotten her infamous stinginess since she so mercilessly ravaged her pantry and provisions for her son's wedding, and Mamika tells us that they are expecting two hundred and fifty guests, which means at least three hundred will show up, Mother says, and as the grown-ups discuss how weddings bankrupt the bridal couple's parents, that's what it takes to throw a proper cele- bration! and as Mamika reports that there will be at least five different meat dishes, stews, roasts, and the lamb will be grilled right in the courtyard, Father smacks himself on the forehead and calls out, my God, why didn't I think of it before? my nephew is getting married on such an important historical date, and Nomi still has a piece of the crêpe in her mouth when she asks, a historical date, what's that? Father goes off on an endless tangent, doesn't even notice he's filling his water glass with schnapps, give it a rest, Mother interrupts him at some point, it's pure coincidence that the wedding is being held on this particular date, surely you know how far

23

in advance you have to plan these events. Coincidence, maybe, Father answers, but that's some coincidence, I, at any rate, will congratulate the bride and groom for getting married on such an important historical date, and Father emphatically tosses back the schnapps, sets the glass back on the table, fills it again immediately, looks at us, probably annoyed by our clueless faces, Mother certainly irritates him when she says that he'd better leave the congratulations be, and Nomi and I share the last crêpe, cinnamon and sugar, those are the best, Nomi says and looks at me questioningly, chocolate with nuts, I answer, cinnamon! Nomi counters, sugar! I answer, shaker! We automatically start playing our word game in which we trade words that start or end with the same sound—baker! we play because we know what will come next—back! and Mamika joins in—book! cook! says Nomi, but Father's already in his bunker, as Nomi and I call it, he moves his lower jaw back and forth, shows his gold front teeth that have a freshly polished shine at moments like these, once or twice we've been able to distract him—could! but not this time. He ignores us, waves his shot glass in the air as if he were holding a flaming torch, to Nándor's marriage! he calls, to 4 August 1980! and throws back the schnapps, slams the glass back down on the table, you don't want to toast with me? he asks, is my nephew's marriage not a good enough reason to drink a little schnapps with me?

Nomi and I are silent, we squirm in our chairs, both of us search for an acceptable reason to leave the room, so that we don't have to watch Father crouching in his bunker, not letting anyone near him, I have to go, Nomi says, I'll go with her, and Nomi and I quickly lock fingers, Mother begs us to stay with a piercing look, but we don't want to, we're almost out the door when we hear Mamika say in a quiet voice, you know what, I'm going to pray for you tonight, that you don't get yourself blind-drunk at Nándor's wedding! and when we're in Mamika's garden, peeking through the gaps in the fence into the neighbouring courtyards, Nomi asks me, what do you think, how long will it last this time?

It won't even last an hour before the bottle is empty and Father's head is resting on the table, all his cursing and swearing blended with the fruit brandy and Father has happily disappeared into a deep, dreamless sleep, Mother, in any case, believes that Father goes on these binges to escape his nightmares. What nightmares? Nomi and I asked after Father had drunk himself almost unconscious well before midnight one New Year's Eve. Nightmares from before, Mother said, because of history. History, what history? Mother hesitated as if we'd asked one of those difficult questions children ask: What's behind the sun? Why don't we have a river in our garden? The communists destroyed his life, Mother said in a tone of voice we had never heard her use before, but maybe your father will tell you the story himself when you're older. Older, when is that? Someday, when it's the right time, in a few years, when you can understand the whole story.

We get out of our car, Nomi and I hang on to Mamika, Mother on to Father, and our heels click against the paving stones, our dresses aren't rustling any more but swishing in the hot air. It is so hot that I say to Nomi, look, the sky is white, yes, but kind of a dirty white, Nomi answers, and we match Mamika's slow, steady pace and when we turn the corner, Father glances over at us and says that the welcoming committee is already waiting for us, Juli, who stands in front of Uncle Móric and Aunt Manci's house, waves to us, yes, our little Julika also wants something from the wedding, Mother says and waves back. Is she invited too? Nomi and I ask, and Mamika laughs, Julika is invited to every celebration, or, to put it another way, it would be a bad omen if she didn't show up at a wedding even though she's still not allowed in the tent, and although we don't understand what exactly Mamika means, we don't ask her to explain and Juli, who keeps waving until we're just a few steps away from her, calls to Mamika, *panni néni! panni néni!* I have a carnation, look, a red carnation! and Mamika greets Juli affectionately, gently strokes her greasy cheek, says, you look pretty today, my little Julika, our grandmother actually says, you've got all dressed up for the wedding! and Nomi and I, we look at each other because she really means it, we certainly also have a guilty conscience because we had just been telling each other, in a language inaudible to everyone else, a language only siblings share, how ridiculous Juli looks in her crooked pinafore dress with her freshly cut bangs and the pathetic red flower stuck behind her ear, but when Juli suddenly plants herself right in front of us, with no manners whatsoever, when she blurts out right into our startled faces, I'm the secret bride! with an expression that reminds me, in its solemnity and gravity, of the saints' portraits that Mamika keeps in her credenza, when Juli pulls the carnation out from behind her ear and whispers, look, this is the tired little witness to my marriage and both of us really need something to eat right now, then I no longer find Juli ridiculous but instead strangely comical and alarming. You'll bring us both something to eat soon, right? a little bit of everything! she calls after us as we close the door to Uncle Móric and Aunt Manci's house behind us.

Nándor and Valéria, a true celebration in a shimmering heatwave, and the celebration had, in fact, already begun that morning in Mamika's living-room-cum-bedroom when we unwrapped our party dresses from the tissue paper and laid them out on Mamika's bed; Nomi, Mother and I spent hours in front of the mirror and were advised all afternoon by dainty women on whether our taste was up to the event and we let them convince us that dresses should be judged in their entirety, we bought dresses that, at our cousin's wedding, would look as good from the back as from the front, and for Mamika, Mother had chosen a black dress with a discreet pattern, Mamika, who since her husband, Papuci, died has not worn anything but black or dark blue, but definitely not anything with a pattern. Do you think I can wear that? she asks and gently caresses the fabric, and Mother helps Mamika out of her everyday dress, you shouldn't always spend so much money on me, Mamika says as Mother casually hands her a purse after straightening her collar and doing up the zipper. I think you look very beautiful, Nomi says, and you can barely see the pattern.

Nándor and Valéria, the memory of a boiling hot tent set up in Aunt Manci and Uncle Móric's courtyard, a tent we children decorated the day before the wedding with crêpe-paper streamers and red carnations, Nomi and I, sitting a little awkwardly at the table, getting tangled in the crêpe paper, having to let our very serious second cousin show us how it's done, nothing easier! Lujza's short fingers (in Swiss German we call them sweaty sausage fingers) wound the rolls one over the other so fast, it seemed that she wanted us to decorate not just the tent but the entire courtyard including the house. I think it's amazing you can't get the hang of it, Lujza says without looking at us, to be honest, I thought all of you in the West could do everything, naturally Nomi and I continue ridiculing her in Swiss German for her Coke-bottle glasses and her naive excitement about being one of the maids of honour who get to carry the bride's train. We're out of crêpe paper, I say loudly, and Nomi and I wink and nudge each other with our knees, then you won't be able to decorate the tent, Lujza says, stretching out the streamers woven together in accordion folds and gesturing, with a tilt of her head, towards the red, green and white garlands, Lujza, who flies up and down the ladders, fastens the garlands to the tent with agile movements of her hands, it will be a brilliant party, I'm telling you, a wedding people will talk about for a long time, and she points at the tent almost completely decorated with the colourful paper garlands and the red carnations woven into a heart shape, embellished with a few, chosen saints' portraits hung over the bridal pair's seats; and I am almost ashamed for Lujza, who is so proud and excited about a few decorations made of paper and flowers, she doesn't even know what real excitement is—boys with fashionable, well-fitting jeans and terrifying roller-coasters—I feel sorry for her that she has probably never seen a proper shop-window in her life.

And I, always looking for new things that will show up Lujza's naivety, I sit a little off to the side with Nomi while Uncle Móric and a few other men instal the strings of lights and we watch the men hang and rehang them because Lujza always knows better, but when we see the tent, fully decorated and lit up, with the long tables set with white tablecloths, with many glasses and plates, with napkins folded into fans, we are speechless after all, because it doesn't look rustic but festive.

And us? How do we look to them as we stand in front of the tent and are greeted by the master of ceremonies—Mother, in her grass-green, ankle-length dress, Nomi, with her passion for the 1950s, is wearing a dress of pink tulle, Father, who always looks so elegant and serious, at least I think so, has on a light-grey suit, a white shirt and an iridescent tie in three colours, and I am wearing a fitted, white, knee-length skirt and a light-blue, off-the-shoulder blouse (if I didn't know it was you, I wouldn't have recognized you, Mamika said after we'd changed our clothes). As we stand there in front of the tent, the master of ceremonies says something about how we've come from so far away, the wedding guests stop eating, soup spoons frozen in mid-air, mouths full of bread paused in chewing, and for a moment it feels like we should back out of the tent for everything to start up again without us, but a second later Aunt Manci and Uncle Móric, laughing, invite us to the table and give us big, smacking kisses, the bride and groom hug us and shake our hands, telling us insistently how pleased they are, you came from so far! for us, for our special day!

Steaming bowls of soup have already been set down before us, chicken soup with impressive drops of fat, feet, hearts, livers, and whoever gets the brain will be as smart as Einstein! people call out to one another; waxed-bean soup with vinegar and sour cream, a green-pea soup with pigeon meat that everyone thinks exceptional, Aunt Manci never shares her secret soup recipes, but this much I will tell you, I only use meat from very young pigeons! and naturally, fish soup with whole heads of carp, simmering in the summer kitchen.

On it goes with light meat dishes—crispy roast chicken and fried potatoes, pork cutlets pounded paper-thin—and the musicians sing and everyone joins in, 'We'll meet again, we'll meet again soon in another land . . .' Veal with fresh mushrooms, then sour cream and dumplings, enough! someone shouts, or we won't make it to the church, then you'll have to cancel the wedding! Yet, we're still served *fasírt* because Aunt Manci can't resist recipes with ground meat— we eat so much at the luncheon that Nomi swears she won't be able to eat another bite all day long, just wait, Mamika says laughing, the celebration has only just begun!

In the early afternoon, the wedding party staggers to the church (all of them praise the pigeon soup or the delicious ground meat once more or debate what will be served after the ceremony), a fat, lazy animal squats in the church, a few uncles whose wives won't let them sleep, let us pray, says the priest and just when everyone is sitting comfortably, his voice booms out Amen! right in the middle of the strenuous process of digestion, and finally, finally, it's time for the main event, the ceremony. Isn't the bridal pair lovely, don't they look almost transparent with joy, Mother asks emotionally and at the word yes, half of the guests burst into tears as if on command (Mamika whispers in my ear, what a flood! now they can all drink even more), and as everyone congratulates the bride and groom and kisses them with gusto, the fat lazy animal is transformed; the two violin players, the two singers, the cimbalom player and the double-bass player play songs in eighth note triplets rhythm and get even the biggest bellies swaying, the teeth are all laughing because they have a part in this joy, and Uncle Móric leads them all in the dance, the father of the bride sways, teases, emphasizes his jokes by shrugging his shoulders and eggs everyone on: Go on, get moving, then you'll have more room in your stomachs! and I remember the damp patches spreading under the men's arms, the glistening foreheads, strands of hair stuck to the napes of their necks, dance! in this heat! enormous, large-busted women, constantly dabbing at their throats and their cleavage but, most of all, I remember that Nomi and I stand out because of our dresses though not in the way we'd imagined, and the term 'mark of shame' occurs to me (from that point on shame and party dresses are forever associated in my mind). Did someone really say, how can we tell which one is the bride? Don't pay any attention, Mamika says, you both look simply lovely!

So we don't pay any attention—I'd like to know why the Swiss dress their children like that, as if they were something special, just not children!—and we head back with the other guests, singing, laughing, swaying, shouting and clapping to the tent where the real wedding feast is about to begin with the lightest *pogáscha* ever, a savoury yeast dough made with lard or curd cheese, accompanied by schnapps, Uncle Móric's pear brandy or the apricot brandy made by Mr Lajos, the most famous distiller in the region, for the children there's Traubi Soda, Apa Cola, Yupi and tonic water, for the teenagers a light red wine mixed with water, and as an appetizer the groom requests an outing, a short walk to America which today is luckily just around the corner, a few men start off towards the Chevrolet, so Nomi, Mother and I don't need to go along this time, there will be trouble, Mother says.

After a while, we're no longer certain whether what we'd eaten two or three hours earlier is what we're eating now, and more and more dishes are brought in, there is no end, just ever new beginnings and Nomi and I cannot believe how much our dainty Mamika can eat, Mother has long since given up freshening up her lipstick and Aunt Manci turns into an enormous hen as she recounts how her best laying hen had led her around by the nose a few days earlier when it began laying its eggs in secret hiding places, cluuuuuck-luckluckluckluck, and the guests laugh until tears roll down their cheeks, because Aunt Manci not only understands the chickens' language but can speak it as well, Aunt Manci, who kept on clucking until the hen led her to its eggs. The master of ceremonies keeps up a constant patter of clever remarks for every dish, goulash soup that will fortify you body and soul! goulash soup with hand-rolled noodles served as a first course and then probably again after midnight when all the soups will be brought out once more, along with the goulash soup there's bouillon fortified with Tokay, beef braised in mushrooms and sweet onions and on top of that a small serving of soup made with beaten egg and loads of parsley for all those whose heads are already in the bag, a figure of speech for someone who is completely plastered, stop yawn- ing so much or your head will fall right out of your mouth,

33

the night is still young! the master of ceremonies shouts, waving his hand for the steaming pots to be brought in, but the nimble, short-legged women with red kerchiefs and aprons carry in large platters which take two to lift, a little surprise before the soups! suckling pig in aspic, goose liver in schmalz, stuffed zucchini, tomatoes filled with fillets of fish, trout stuffed with goose liver, poached eggs with mushrooms and onions, savoury crêpes with veal ragout and sour cream; and the musicians play a fanfare for the surprise, for the bridal pair, for Nándor and Valéria! may happiness play its song for you and for us all! the master of ceremonies calls out while Nomi is annoyed by his endless effusiveness; Nomi and I, we slip out of the tents as everyone ooohs and aaaahs over the surprise dish, we ignore the men leaning against the side of the house, watching us out of the corners of their eyes and calling a few comments after us, we hurry to Aunt Manci's summer kitchen, quickly change clothes and don't need to say how relieved we are to be back in our everyday summer shorts and T-shirts.

Hey Ildi, look, Gyula's over there, Nomi says as we close the door behind us, Gyula, one of our cousins, the best looking of them all with his wild eyes, as we say, and if he weren't our cousin, then we'd be in love with him too for sure, but where's he going now? I ask and we cross the dark courtyard, past the pigsty, the occasional grunt blending in with the music, it's still hot out, Nomi says, is it ever! and we splash ourselves with water from the well. I want to know where Gyula's gone, I say and we head towards the chicken coop, a wide enclosure, empty now, look out for the chicken poop, Nomi calls, or you'll end up flat on your back, and we tiptoe carefully over the slippery paving stones, open the gate in the darkest corner of the garden and stand in a small scrapyard filled with old tires, bits of furniture, old toys, there's even a rusty exhaust pipe, it's a place we know well by daylight, pssst! I whisper, there he is, and Nomi and I, we duck behind a crooked old chest of drawers and hold our breath because we know that what we're seeing is not meant for our eyes.

Gyula's rear end looks like a full moon, Nomi whispers after a while, but, unlike the moon, Gyula's rear end is moving back and forth quickly and his pants look embarrassing bunched up around his ankles, but that's just what Nomi and I—the scene's only spectators—think, we really should look away! but since we're already here, I say, and luckily it's very dark and hardly anything is visible, just Gyula's moon moving back and forth and his hands gripping legs hanging down beside his hips, and the real moon hanging above us is not full but just a sickle. Do you know who it is? I ask Nomi. Teréz, she answers rather confidently, they were staring at each other the whole time. Who, Teréz, but she's married! exactly, Teréz is married and Gyula is engaged, and now and again Nomi and I hear a hen's solitary clucking, chickens probably dream too, Nomi says, but probably only of their corn kernels, they're too stupid for anything else. We have to keep whispering nonsense to each other to distract ourselves from what we're seeing, from the high-heeled shoes squeezing Gyula's thighs, the strained sounds each of them is making and Nomi presses up against me and giggles into my ear, come on, let's wake up the chickens, Ildi, I want something to happen!

And afterwards, afterwards the back wall of the tent, right behind the bride and groom, slips down so far that you can't see the giant heart made of carnations or the saints' pictures any more, only the dark courtyard. Bad luck! a few guests call out, that can't be a good sign on a day like today! Nonsense! That's enough! Air! Confidence! Freedom! the others call back, Aunt Manci loudest of all as she claps her hands, now the party can really begin! And the servers bring in stuffed peppers, veal with peppers, beef, lamb and pork stews—and I remember very clearly the few splashes of soup early in the evening, the bread crumbs that were swept under the table at the beginning of the banquet, a few broken glasses that had been knocked over inadvertently or because the young couple's beauty had to be praised one more time with an enthusiastic waving of arms, the cigarette butts that weren't yet crushed underfoot; it makes sense, of course, that suckling pig in aspic is slippery and will slide off a fork held in an unsteady hand and isn't the liver amazing if it can leave such a hefty stain on the tablecloth? I remember exactly how the tablecloth is already wildly spattered, how the mens' mouths hang open and how they wave for more beer even though their glasses are still half-full as Father leans heavily on the table; the musicians have just played the final measures of 'I Left My Beautiful Homeland' and Nomi pinches my arm when Gyula slips back into the tent, followed by Teréz a few minutes later, well, what did I tell you? Father, who, right before the song, had explained the state of the world to Great-Uncle Pista with a map that may well be imaginary but is still clear as day for anyone who's not as blind as a bat, Great-Uncle Pista, himself in such a state all he can do is nod, so I watch how Father, bracing himself on the table, slowly stands, lets go of the tabletop, sways and, when he's found his balance, straightens the knot of his tie and his light-grey jacket, reaches for a spoon, now what, Mother whispers because she knows what's coming, so do Nomi and I, and Father taps his spoon against two glasses, asks for quiet because he'd like to say something without wasting too many words, and quiet spreads through the tent, and I, looking around, see drooping heads, glazed eyes, holes in elaborate hairdos, smudged eyeliner, Nomi, I whisper softly, let's get out of here again—but it's too late.

Father who pulls it off, raises his glass and toasts the happy couple, to Nándor and Valéria, to 4 August 1980, to the fact that Tito bit the dust exactly three months ago! I wish for him, as I hope you do too, a good long roasting in a hundred purgatorial fires!

Nándor and Valéria smile politely but helplessly and someone yells out, not a hundred purgatorial fires but a blood-red one, and he raises his glass towards Father and stands up, but the rest, all the rest remain seated and one portly woman calls out, you lunatics, go outside if you want to talk politics, and she points energetically at the tent entrance and someone claps his hands, music! let's have some music! Miklós is right, someone else shouts, but the fiddlers and singers have already started, 'They are pretty, oh so pretty, those whose eyes are blue . . .' Listen everyone, another person shouts, making a megaphone with his hands, it was just a stupid prank with the side of the tent, listen, it was those two boys over there—but no one cares any more.

You want to get us all killed? asks Uncle Móric, who had come up to the table and planted himself next to Father the minute the musicians started playing again, so close that his blotchy nose was almost touching Father, do you want us in another war? Uncle Móric hisses, or did that just slip out? Mother is still beautiful in her grass-green dress but completely at a loss and no one pays any attention when she says, can't this wait for another day? Father and Uncle Móric spit words at each other, you want us in another war? Uncle Móric keeps repeating, Father shouts, give it a rest, just give it a rest, blowing his smoke scornfully up at the tent roof, has your sense of humour got lost in your fancy underwear? And the crêpe-paper garlands now look like tiny, colourful buoys bobbing in a sea of smoke and curses. I don't give a shit you didn't like Tito, bellows Uncle Móric, whom we've never heard swear before, but I'm not the only one who says this country has lost its rudder, and Uncle Móric's outstretched hand looks like it has taken on a life of its own. What happened to your sense of reality? Father asks and it takes him a few tries to say 'sense of reality', you don't really think a dead Tito could start a war?

A cluster has formed around Father and Uncle Móric, no one knows who yelled what or who was arguing with whom, even Juli, her mouth smeared with whipped cream, suddenly appeared next to Mamika yelling, it's snowing, it's snowing, the snow is falling! Nomi and I expected Mamika to put an end to the fight but all she said was, it's just two brothers having a disagreement, that's all, and the musicians kept playing even though no one was listening or dancing and it was so loud in the tent that the uneaten food on the plates warmed up again and Tito poked his head out of the fires of purgatory and into our wedding tent, stuck his tongue out, see how famous I am still! and the tip of his nose glowed with spite.

The hardest thing to explain is why Uncle Móric and Father didn't hit each other, there's barely an insult they didn't throw at each other, but after a while they swayed cheerfully towards each other, the fiddlers were sawing away with their bows, the double-bass player vigorously plucked the strings, and everyone egged Father and Uncle Móric on as if nothing had happened, and only Nomi and I were amazed.

THE KOCSIS FAMILY

Last year, Mother came home late one night, her radiant face at odds with the cold autumn day, and before even drawing a breath she said, I have a surprise for you, we're getting the cafe-restaurant Mondial, the Tanners persuaded the owners of the building, they actually wanted someone else but we won, and I'm sure Mother couldn't help laughing at that point because she said 'won'.

And that evening we linger at the dinner table longer than usual, Father even kisses Mother right in front of us, he holds her hands as we talk about what it means for us that now, after living in this village for thirteen years, we have an establishment in the very best location, right next to the train station, with an interior in perfect condition, affordable rent and garden seating. Nomi, Mother, Father and I celebrate, it's simply unbelievable, Mother says, it still seems unreal, as unreal as a fish that can fly. And I, who tell her there are fish that fly, take a cigarette from the pack, and that evening Father registers without a word that not only do I smoke but Nomi does too.

We'll need new carpeting, Mother says, that's very important, and maybe a lovely clock on the wall, Father adds, and obviously we won't change the brand of coffee, anything, but not coffee, we'll use the same baker too—

Father will be the cook, Mother will take care of some baking and all the paperwork, Nomi will work at the counter or wait tables as needed and I'll help out on days when I don't have class. We're sitting at our dining table, but only apparently because in truth we're speeding forward in years, with one jump we haven't advanced by a mere step, we've made an enormous leap, Mother says, and her eyes reflect images from past years, our mother as a cleaning woman, cashier, maid, laundress and presser and waitress, it wasn't always easy, her eyes say, but it was worth it! And because Mother finished her certification in a Food Service Management School five years ago, we'd already run a restaurant, and what a restaurant! in the city, on a side-street with horrific rent, inadequate ventilation and a kitchen on the second floor, back then, when Nomi and I always helped out after school and even on Sundays, our toughest time, Father says, for two years not one day off, that asshole of an owner made a good living off our backs!—but even this sentence no longer weighs us down because luck and the future are now a fair and logical continuation of the past, for Mother, who started working for the Tanners as a counter-waitress in the Mondial after that fiasco, it only seemed a step down, Mother says with a faint smile, I would never have dreamt that one day they would leave me their business!

The Tanners simply noticed you weren't thinking of your own interests but of theirs, Father says.

Oh come now, Mother answers, the Tanners wanted one of their daughters to take over but none of them wanted to and maybe they even felt a little sympathy for me, for our family. Doesn't the Hungarian word for 'family' sound like a nice warm dinner, I want to ask Mother. Father adds that it never would have worked out if we hadn't become Swiss! And if our reputation weren't top-tip! Mother points out. The other way round, Nomi says, why can't you keep it straight, Mama, it's tip-top! From today on I'll remember, Mother laughs, tip-top, tip-top, tip-top, tip-top, that's it, isn't it? And Father pops the cork from the champagne bottle. We came to Switzerland with one suitcase and one word and now we have red passports with a white cross and a gold-mine, *Isten Isten*! To God! To God! Father shouts and we clink our glasses cheerfully.

Workers in the grey market dress in black from head to toe, a thief has to wear camouflage if he doesn't want to get caught, only his eyes, quick and bright, move here and there in the night. The best loved of the black-clad workers are the clergy, unlike the thieves, they don't wear masks but they wear a white collar and their faces look as innocent as fresh bread. The other workers have to work with black things, carry sacks of coal, for example. Or, like a washing machine, they have to work and work until the black things turn white again . . .

At some point I picked up the term 'grey market' from my parents, I could barely speak German at the time and some words I forgot almost immediately, others I couldn't get out of my head, like 'grey market'. I was glad that even though I couldn't use it—as opposed to sleep, eat, drink, lake, woman, man, child, yes, no—it still evoked many things for me, whereas other words piled up in my head like useless odds and ends: identity card, settlement, waiting period. It was a long time before I understood the meaning of these words and part of the reason it took me so long was that my parents gave them their own particular intonation or changed them unintentionally. Identification card was *identation card*, waiting period was *wedding peeled*, and in their mouths settlement sounded something like *seddlemin.*

Father had worked on the grey market for almost six months without knowing it. No problem, Father's boss at the time, the master butcher Fluri, said, your papers are on the way. A co-worker who liked my father tipped him off, hey, Mik, Fluri makes a lot more money off you when you work without papers, get it? At the end of the month, Father had barely nine hundred francs in his envelope, room and board for a room above the butcher shop was deducted from his salary. His co-worker's tip was like a slap in the face, Father explained, he put two and two together, gathered all his courage and said to his boss, *if no papers, Miklós go.* And Father was floored to see that his short sentence could have such an enormous effect. Indeed, a few weeks later, he received a work permit and a small raise he hadn't even asked for, he didn't know at the time that his co-workers earned more than twice as much as he did—why not? We don't talk about salaries here, was one of the first sentences in German that he understood, Father told us.

Another thing Father didn't know at the time is that working without papers delays the 'family reunification permit' to bring family members into the country after you've had residency and work permits for three years.

And then Fluri wrote good letters to the immigration authorities for us—and for that I'm grateful, Father said. It's his fault that we had to wait an extra six months until our children could join us, Mother railed; my parents fought in secret and I sometimes eavesdropped on them, as I had that night; I hadn't been in Switzerland very long and I remember many sleepless nights, and often, after I'd eavesdropped on my parents, the words swirled around my head like leaves on a wet, blustery autumn day, Hungarian words for papers, police, letters, grateful, German words for family reunification, grey market, undocumented workers; my mother had probably been drinking on those nights, which she very rarely did, and I can still hear her voice, shrill with hurt, three years, ten months, twelve days until the children's entry permits finally came.

With which word did you come to Switzerland? I ask when the champagne bottle is empty and Father stands up to get a second one.

'Work.'

We took over the Tanners' entire inventory: canned beans, an unbelievable amount of gravy pouches, frozen ground beef, Duchesse potatoes. We took anything and everything even though we knew we wouldn't be able to use most of it: cans of ravioli, tinned meat with aspic, oxtail soup (what is this anyway, can you eat oxtails? yes, of course, Mother explained, you've had it yourselves, and she translated it into Hungarian for us, oh, that's what it is, we said and found that 'oxtail' didn't sound very appetizing). We took it all because with this cafe we'd hit the jackpot.

On 3 January 1993, we open the Mondial having spent the entire Christmas holiday cleaning and ironing, Mother had rolled and cut out two thousand short-bread cookies, covered them with home-made apricot jam and turned them into *Spitzbuben* sandwich cookies, Nomi and I made crescent-shaped cookies, *Vanillekipferl*, we worked hard all day because we wanted to surprise our customers all week long with home-baked treats, we wanted to give them the chance to get to know our best side first, to show them that we knew everything there was to know about handiwork—we, who had been kissed by a good fairy, it's as if we'd waited years for this opportunity, Mother says, there were any number of interested parties who'd lined up as soon as they heard that the Tanners were giving up their business at the end of the year, I saw it all while serving customers at the counter! Mother told the story over and over again, and again and again, Father and she speculated about what it was that tipped the scales in their favour, and now she's almost embarrassed when she feels the customers looking at her, working behind the counter, and the Schärers, who had a lucrative plumbing business, they knocked at Mrs Tanners door every day because they couldn't believe they weren't going to get the Mondial—and the whole time I am secretly picturing Mother walking through our village asking everyone she meets, did you know that I will be taking over the cafe Mondial! and as Mother says this, I picture her taking the other person's hand in both of hers and holding the stranger's hand for a moment, Mother, whom I imagine free and invincible in her happiness and pride.

We all get up very early to fix our hair, to dress up, outside it's still dark, we have circles under our eyes because we've infected one another with insomnia even through the walls, but we don't talk about it or about our cold sweats from exhaustion and excitement, we haven't conferred about what we should wear, if it would be best to wear colours that match and, mostly, when I'm this wound up, I think the day will never come, the day that's causing us all this anxiety, probably because the time leading up to the opening has been long and seems to be getting longer and longer until it expands into one sleepless night. In fact, I can't even tell what's going on in my head, I must be wondering if we've done enough to prepare but I'm also wondering if a day like this, awaited with so much nervous anticipation, won't also disappear into the black hole of days that are expected with such exaggerated levels of anxiety, I mean days like these weigh heavily even before they've begun—can it possibly go well, I ask myself, for us, for our family, with this cafe, in this community, one of the richest communities on the north-west shore of Lake Zürich, Nomi and me, who don't actually fit in at the Mondial? and me, I'm surely also thinking of how many things have gone wrong before this—all sorts of things—or not? important things, trivial ones? Here, we don't whistle like they do in Italy or Mongolia, one of the neighbours shouted at Nomi and me whenever we whistled through our teeth. Italy I get, Nomi said, but Mongolia? Since you all came here, everything's gone to pot! 'gone to pot' didn't sound so bad to me, but I couldn't get the 'since you all came here' out of my head. I burst into tears but I was also proud that Nomi and I seemed to have such an influence on our surroundings, and others, especially our customers in the laundry business, who always asked if we needed anything, who brought us bags of old clothes from which we learnt the names of expensive designers: Gucci, Yves Saint Laurent, Feinkeller, Versace, thanks so much, and we gave most of those clothes away in Yugoslavia or to char-ities—I've learnt there are Swiss people who believe they are fundamentally responsible for what's good, I'm sweating because I haven't slept, because I know and have known for a long time that you shouldn't think too much when you can't sleep.

It's perfectly obvious that not one of us has slept, so it would be pointless to say I didn't close my eyes all night or, as we say in Hungarian, my eyes were dreamless. Let's go in and win, Father says as we turn off the hall light, lock the door behind us and cross the silent car park to the garage where we get into our car, hardly making any noise, Father turns on the radio, almost backs into the snowblower, that idiot caretaker, Father rails, how many times have I told him to put his toys away, and all of us, Father included, know that it's about something else and with a mild, half-serious rant, the day can finally begin. We drive down the mountain, rolling inexorably towards our opening day.

I write 'warmest welcome!' on the blackboard and hang it near the entrance (and it occurs to me when I flip the light switches right behind the counter that our cafe is glowing brightly, you can't miss it, visible from every corner of the village, high-voltage current I think and laugh because I'm not even sure exactly what high-voltage current is).

We've not only taken over our predecessors' supplies of oxtail soup, frozen meat, gravy, canned ravioli and beans, but also their two waitresses, Anita and Christel and Marlis, the kitchen maid, our only new employee is Dragana, the assistant cook. From 3 January 1993, the Mondial will be run by the Kocsis family, with the menu and opening hours unchanged—is how the local newspaper reported the change in the cafe's management—we know the Kocsis family from the exemplary laundry service they managed here for seven years. The family, originally from Yugoslavia, is well integrated into our community and obtained Swiss citizenship six years ago.

Direct democracy, or my comic and capricious idea of it when I first heard this term in elementary school, we are the symbol of pure democracy, my teacher said and because he said 'we', I belonged, even though 'we' still had Yugoslavian passports at the time and so I wasn't yet 'Swiss on paper', as people would later say here and there. My elementary school teacher had nothing against foreigners, he once explained, the only thing that counted for him was accomplishment which was part and parcel of holding democratic ideals, equal opportunity for all! my teacher certainly contributed to my idea of direct democracy as an army, a mass of well-trained soldiers standing in rank and file, immune to bribes because they were defending something of fundamental importance—the idea of equal opportunity for all.

Today, exceptionally, we've double-staffed each station—Mother is helping Father in the kitchen, she coats the pretzels with butter and they debate how thick the coating should be, too greasy! Too dry! Father and Mother, who hand us samples to taste, agree on a compromise, Mother then divides one hundred croissants among the woven baskets. Nomi and I let the coffee machine run empty, make sure enough coffee has been ground, pour cream into the individual serving pitchers, slice lemons, fill the glass bowl with oranges and at a quarter to six we're sitting at the staff table, table number one, we quickly drink a coffee and when the waitresses arrive, Anita and Christel—sleep well? not too difficult waking up so early?—we're back on our feet, waiting for the first guests, who come in shortly after six, always the same ones, Anita says, a few early birds between six and seven, it hardly ever changes, and we scurry back and forth, Nomi and I, between the kitchen and the counter, constantly asking if there's anything we can do to help, but there's been nothing more to do for a long time, and sometimes the cafe fills up around eight but usually not before nine, even then in fits and starts, Anita says and Christel turns on the radio so that Madame Étoile can read this week's constellations for us in her breathy voice, Mother brings in the freshly baked cakes and sets them on the small table near the display case, homemade? Christel asks, yes! we'll bake fresh cakes every day, and this is my favourite moment, when Mother brings in the cakes with apricot and plum halves or grated apple drowned in a sweet syrup, Mother smiles at me, looks delicious, doesn't it? after she has carefully arranged the platters, and so far everything is going well, a few guests compliment our *Guetzlis*, our cookies, and find our new carpeting tasteful (our guests, so calm and relaxed, as if nothing had changed, I think, only once in a while do any of them, discreetly curious, look over the newspapers at us, the waitresses—but why would our guests be worked up, anyway?). Christel tells us that she's interested in astrology, the stars don't lie, Anita, who thinks it's all humbug, says, nonsense, they just do it to make money! We're able to chat with one another now and again because we didn't want to take any risks and, as mentioned before, are double-staffed, and now we're not sure what to do with so many arms and legs, Nomi says and we look at each other, pale and bleary-eyed, Anita, who now orders two medium coffees, corrects us, too much milk, not enough coffee, they're very important customers, she whispers, table seven, the Zwickys, they come every day and Saturdays they bring their grandchildren and then they even order breakfast; we try to remember a few things, above all the preferences of the more complicated customers, still they're very nice, Christel says, decaffeinated with a bit of cold water for Mrs Hunziker and table two, Mr Pfister, head of a moving company, he comes every day, sometimes twice a day, drinks very light coffee, usually, not always, and he likes it when you can lip-read what he wants, Anita says with a gleam in her eye, I'd like someone to lip-read my wishes too, Nomi says and makes us all laugh.

Just after eight all heads turn towards the front door, the two widowed sisters, Mrs Köchli and Mrs Freuler, pause on the doorstep, paper bags dangle from Mrs Freuler's hands, Mrs Köchli as usual is wearing one of her extravagant hats, wide-brimmed hats with ribbons, enormous bright-coloured flowers or animals (a snake flicking its tongue and encircling the brim or a bird that bobs with each step). Mrs Freuler puts her bags down and waves me over, me or Nomi or both of us, Mrs Köchli motions towards an empty table and Mrs Freuler, almost twice as wide as her sister, grabs her bags again and they both pass along the rows of tables, shaking hands here and there, and finally sit down at table three, right across from the counter. Mrs Freuler helps her sister take off her coat and scarf and heads to the coatroom with a brisk step, and I immediately draw a double espresso for Mrs Freuler and a light *café au lait* for Mrs Köchli. We'll serve table three, Nomi says to Anita and I prepare a small plate of our homemade cookies, call into the kitchen that the sisters are here, I'll be right there, Mother answers and before she takes off her apron and stops to chat with them a moment, Nomi and I greet and serve the coffee and cookies to Mrs Köchli and Mrs Freuler who shake our hands, congratulations on your opening and very best of luck! and hand us flowers like girls who have just fallen in love, Mrs Freuler bends over her paper bags and pulls out a yellow bouquet for Miss Nomi and a second yellow bouquet for Miss Ildikó, a third red bouquet for Mrs Rósza. Who are those two ladies? Anita asks when we're back behind the counter, what? you don't know them? Nomi asks with charming indignation, Ildi can tell you, and Nomi disappears into the kitchen to get vases and I don't feel like explaining so I just say that we've known the sisters for a long time, from when we had the laundry, and they were regular customers at our last restaurant, I see, Anita says and adds that she's never seen the two ladies before but then she doesn't live here in the village.

Mama looks much younger now, Nomi says to me, yes, it's true, and I glance over the coffee machine at Mother's face, the faint blush on her cheeks as she turns alternately to face Mrs Köchli and Mrs Freuler (and what difference does it make if Mother is fluttering her eyelids?), and Nomi places the flowers on the display case, a gorgeous sea of yellow, she says and we draw more coffee, heat the milk, pour hot water into teacups and check the receipts Anita and Christel hand us.

People say someone gives them a good feeling and there's surely nothing better than when someone gives you a good feeling (for no particular reason). Mrs Köchli and Mrs Freuler, whose husbands were still alive in those days, brought us their husbands' shirts to iron and I remember certain sentences—few can iron as well as Mrs Rósza and even Mr Miklós with his fat fingers!—the two sisters always came together and were never in a rush. Mrs Freuler carried the basket with the shirts, because she's stronger than any of the fellows around here, Mrs Köchli said of her sister who, in winter, would climb onto the huge, clunky ice resurfacer and smooth the ice in the skating rink and, in summer, would sit in the elevated chair under a sunshade; Mrs Freuler was a lifeguard at the largest public swimming beach in the area and no one made fun of her or her unathletic, unprepossessing figure—I'm an overripe pear, she'd say with a laugh— on the contrary, everyone respected her because they knew how fast the pear could move when it came to pulling someone out of the water. Mrs Köchli was known in our village because she was a librarian and had a sharp tongue, but mostly people said that she had lived in Basel during the Second World War and hidden refugees in her home. As soon as the sisters stepped into our laundry, Mrs Köchli with her striking headgear, Mrs Freuler with her short, salt-and-pepper hair, I got the feeling that the windows of our laundry stood wide-open, the two old ladies always seemed to bring something in from outdoors, the smell of apples or freshly mown grass, an argument they'd just had with their husbands or whomever, the joy that springtime was almost here, and I was impressed when Mrs Köchli told me that springtime feels exactly the same to her every year, in spring, I'm the same age as you, she said to me and her sister laughed, what are you laughing at? because it's true, Mrs Freuler answered; and the two sisters sat down on the chairs near the ironing board, it wasn't unusual for them to stay until the next customer arrived, but they stayed since Mother and Father bantered with the sisters as they almost never did here with anyone else; the sisters give me the feeling on our opening day that it was only logical to be excited, they communicate this with their warmth and fervour and my excitement finds a liberating echo in their bubbling congratulations.

* OPENING DAY MENU *

VEAL SHANK WITH PURÉED POTATOES

AND BABY CARROTS

DESSERT: SURPRISE

I write on the blackboard and set it outside the front door at eleven thirty and all morning Father and Dragana prepare salads, onions, garlic, carrots, Father shows Dragana how to cut the oranges and grapefruits for the dessert, we're not expecting an army, Mother says when she sees the largest pot filled to the brim with veal shanks, half of that will be more than enough, we'll see, Father says and retreats, offended, behind his pot, Father, who only relents after we tell him his veal is exceptionally delicious (but, of course, Mother is right, we'll be eating veal for a week at home because for Father cooking means filling pots, Mother says and it will take a few months for him to control himself, for Mother to teach him, more or less, how to gauge quantities, Father, who on top of that believes all the customers should choose his daily menu and if they don't, he wants to make them understand what's best for them—toast, bouillon, salad, does that count as eating? It's a debate we will have to have every day because Father is utterly convinced that we're to blame if the guests don't order his daily menu, his freshly prepared menu).

Where did you learn to write so well? Anita asks when we are sitting at lunch, I, with a piece of veal in my mouth, do you mean that seriously? I ask. Yes, I'm serious, Anita answers, no matter how hard she tries, she just can't remember words in a foreign language. Nomi says that she can relate to Anita, she can't remember either and always has to be careful not to write *veal* with two *e*s, no, really, it's true, Nomi says. Anita shakes her head because writing is very complicated but she would never, not in a million years, write veal with two *e*s, and Christel, who is on a diet and nibbling at her salad (she doesn't realize she's driving Father crazy since he thinks women who are always worried about their weight are almost as annoying as pampered dogs and politicians who bore everyone to tears), Christel says, some people have a photographic memory, maybe you have a photographic memory for letters, Ildi, and that what she would like most is to be able to remember faces, now that's what I'd like, says Christel. Marlis, sitting down with a healthy serving of veal and a *bon appétit*! focuses on her lunch, when she's not eating, Marlis murmurs to herself constantly and if anyone talks to her, she goes on about her 'groom' who will abduct her soon, and how she'll invite us all to the wedding, her 'groom' promised her they'd have a huge party; Marlis, with her blue eyes, lives in a parallel world, I think, she's been married for years but lost custody of her children, as the Tanners told us, a poor soul, Mrs Tanner said, but she does her work, and I find it touching the way she calls my Father *cheeehf*, drawing out the *e*, every day she pats him gently on the shoulder and says, *cheeehf*, you must cook for us, for me and my 'groom'!

Do you speak German? Anita asks Dragana, who's sitting a little apart and hasn't yet said a word, and Dragana takes her time answering, *speak German*, she finally says and tears up her slice of bread, drops the pieces into the sauce on her place, *not much, but she understands everything*, Dragana

56

says about herself, dunks the bits of bread and shovels them quickly into her mouth (I look away because I can't bear watching anyone dunk anything and eat it, the worst is watching someone stick a dripping croissant, all soggy with coffee, into his mouth), Dragana surprises me by raising her water glass slightly and saying, *Luck, for you, for open!* Marlis immediately drops her fork and calls out, good luck! luck wears a beautiful gown and from the side, you can't even see it, and we smile, Nomi and I, faintly irritated, and thank them for their good wishes, and Christel gets up to make us all coffee before the rush begins.

Because we're all double-staffed, except for the waitresses, we're only slightly rushed at lunchtime, Anita, in fine form, doesn't get tired of telling us that it's much slower today, that a few regulars haven't come (Christel claims that Mondays have always been slow), our salads are smaller than the Tanners' but just as expensive, according to Anita, and she's not giving us her opinion, it's what the customers are saying, she says and from the first day on, with her brisk pace and skirts always at least knee-length, she shares everything the guests tell her or want to know—Mr Leuthold says the coffee isn't as strong as when the Tanners were here. Who is Mr Leuthold? The gentleman over there, in the corner. The coffee is just as strong as it was before, Nomi says, you're welcome to tell Mr Leuthold (and her voice doesn't betray the smallest quiver). Mrs Zwicky says the new carpet is particularly attractive and cheerful, which is a question of taste,

Anita says. Thanks for keeping us in the loop but we don't need to know everything, Nomi doesn't avoid Anita's eye, remains friendly; I don't get it, you could learn something from what the guests have to say, Anita puts in, yes, of course, thanks Anita!

And that evening, at the end of the opening day, when we're sitting, exhausted, with Mother and Father at the staff table, going over the day, everyone agrees it went rather well, perhaps not as many customers came to eat cake as expected, but the sisters, yes, the sisters, they came a second time in the afternoon to have cake (we'll soon be fat and round—if we come here every day, but that's something we can afford—at our age! a quirk we love in Mrs Köchli and Mrs Freuler is that one begins a sentence and the other finishes it), on that first evening, when we still need a long moment to bring the day to a close, Nomi and I start making remarks about Anita, whom we call Hanuta, after the wafer-chocolate bar whose rear end isn't appealing but appalling, who starts every other sentence with 'When the Tanners were here . . .', Anita, a complete zero, who has to put on airs because she, unlike the rest of us, knows the business inside and out . . . We aren't yet able to recognize exactly what Anita is but over the following days and weeks, her comments become ever more unambiguous—I wish I were seeking asylum too, five francs a day, Ildi, that's the good life, right? Anita, who wonders out loud if we didn't bribe the Tanners because otherwise they wouldn't have handed the

Mondial to us of all people (she's not the one saying this, but the Schärer brothers and a few others). When Nomi, her eyes open wide, starts giving her absurd answers like, it's true, we must save Antarctica, or in winter there's nothing I like more than making candles, and me, I watch Anita, how she lingers at the table of certain customers, her back towards us, her head and ears a little too close to theirs, and the sight of her face always irritates me and reminds me of the synthetic fabrics you don't need to iron after washing. At the point we've almost got used to Anita, she gives notice for the end of January, which is possible because she and Mother had agreed on a one-month trial period during which she could quit at any time, and in the office Mother shows me the certified letter—Dear Mrs Kocsis, I hereby give notice that I will resign my position as waitress as of 31 January 1993. With best wishes, Anita Kunz.

A few days later, Christel gives notice and not a day goes by without her explaining apologetically why she quit—her boyfriend is so jealous, he doesn't want her to be waiting tables any more, she wants to start a new career in astrology, actually, what is your sign, Ildi, Gemini? That's what I thought, and she's always wanted children but has the feeling she'll never get pregnant because of this work, and to be honest, she also finds it more difficult to work at the Mondial now that the Tanners are gone, people ask her so many question that her head is spinning when she goes home at night, she can't help it but people make her so dizzy, grilling her like that, she doesn't even know what her name is, Christel, whom I liked.

Nomi and I only learnt much later what led to Anita quitting—Anita had said to Father that if he worked in the factory with that tempo, all the products would go tumbling off the conveyer belt and she tapped her hand several times on the board Father usually used to slice bread and when he didn't react but kept stirring his pot, she winked at him, laughed, Mr Kocsis, I wasn't serious, it was just a bad joke, Anita said, obviously alarmed that Father ignored her, then he finally held his spoon out towards her and asked, why are you still here, would you like to try my sauce?

Mother wanted to talk Father out of his decision to fire Anita, even though she knew it was impossible, but she did manage to persuade him that it would be better to convince Anita that she herself should give notice because then there would be less gossip in the village.

Father was indeed shocked that Anita had insulted him with her comment about the pace of his work, but that's not what tipped the scales, rather it was because Father fundamentally distrusts people who have no sense of humour when they say, it was only a joke.

BORDER POLICE, WEEPING WILLOWS

We wait at the border in our Mercedes Benz, Tompa is the border town's name and although the star of progress unmistakeably distinguishes us from everyone else, just like everyone else, we have to wait and wait until the cows come home, and my father simmers with rage, puts modernity to work with a soft whir and the window lowers obediently so that my father can lean on his elbow and blow his cigarette smoke out into the hot air and God, in His grace and mercy, suddenly changes our Mercedes into a dirigible and, in two or three blinks of an eye, we'll soar past everyone else, because we're the good ones, we live under the good political system, not only will we skip the queue, we'll spit on those godless communists below us, one day I'll be proven right, Father says and once again I have the impression that the sun has more room to bake, a continental climate, it's called, burning hot summers and freezing cold winters.

Mother forgets to let go of the door handle and Nomi and I play word games to pass the time because we're clever enough to know that it's better to ignore Father. Tompa—Pat—Tap—Top—Mop—Map—Moat—Ma—Pa.

Tompa, the small border-crossing between Hungary and Serbia, will be hopelessly overrun in a few years when the

61

embargo against Serbia and Montenegro is tightened in May 1992, and international air traffic is suspended so that here, at this tiny passageway to an almost completely inaccessible Serbia, bus and articulated lorries will fight ruthless duels day and night.

And if we had known what kind of chaos would reign at this border-crossing eight years later, in 1992—*tompa*, a word that means dull or muffled—we would probably have stopped our word game, but what could we have done if had we known what would happen here?

We forgot pot, yes, I answer, and Tom and poo. And we start to laugh, a soft giggle at first that gets louder and louder because laughing is infectious and then it turns into guffaws because Father blows his smoke into the air so seriously, because the sun beats on the white metal so pitilessly, and we're tired from the long drive. If you don't stop immediately, I'll hand you over to the communists, that's right, the ones over there who look like they're carved out of stone, and Mother begs us to be quiet with a pleading look.

And when it's finally our turn, Nomi and I turn our naive children's faces to the border guard's severe gaze, we show him we're innocent, and not just us, but Father too; the stony-faced communist turns us respectful again and wide awake as he leafs indifferently through our passports, taking the time now and then to pat his German shepherd, but this time we won't get through so easily, drive to the side please, the border guard says with a faint gesture that shows he means it. And this time we see for ourselves that there really are full-body searches.

When we finally drive into the small town, my father still hasn't calmed down, Nomi and I huddle in the back seat, as quiet as mice, and listen helplessly to the flood of Father's oaths and curses, and at the time we didn't yet understand that it wasn't really about Brezhnev, who can go fuck himself, or the Russian athletes who were stealing medals by the bucketload with their sophisticated doping, or about onion domes that were an expression of a lack of culture; only much later do we understand that an untold story lies behind all this hatred, a story etched deep in Father's heart, the story of Papuci, our father's father.

On this trip we're going to meet our sister, we glide past the poplars, the acacias and chestnut trees to meet Janka, who belongs to our father's earlier life, Janka, our half-sister, who suddenly appeared in our photo album as if she'd always belonged there, who's that, Nomi asked and Mother answered, that's your father's daughter, and of course it took a while for us to understand what that meant, your father's daughter, a child from his first marriage; Father's been around before, Nomi and I joked so we wouldn't feel the small, disconcerting pain hidden inside the word half-sister. Janka, then, in a black-and-white photograph with a stunning hairdo and a small but unmistakeable veil that seems to float from the highest point, the elegantly arranged curls that in contrast to the veil fall luxuriously over her shoulder as if to show that nothing can tame them, and that's supposed to be our sister, Nomi asks, Janka's index finger rests on the side of her large nose, as if she had just solved an important problem, and on top of that, she's wearing lace gloves, and Nomi's question founders on Janka's gaze, eyes that express a calm and confident superiority and show us that we, Nomi and I, are a long way from understanding life.

And I've heard that you can get out of a car with a light swing, with a gentle twist of your body, I'm sure I've seen it several times already, how your ribcage rises after you step out, how a self-confident mask spreads over your face in a way that is difficult to describe, that you can now enjoy your right to advance with slow, majestic steps and I push myself energetically off the white metal wing, to steal away from it quickly and escape the shameless, longing looks of the children who in a few seconds have gathered around this miracle of technology, admiring the star open-mouthed, as if it were more than a gift of God, and I have never told anyone that in such moments I feel particularly miserable and stingy and if God were standing next to me, I would ask him if he could explain this feeling to me, hey, Nomi yells, wait up, don't go so fast!

We don't meet Janka at Uncle Móric and Aunt Manci's house, or at Mamika's, but in a small restaurant near the river. And we see her already from a distance, how she stands there in a lemon-yellow dress, its airy cloth playing in the warm summer breeze, Janka, who is old enough to make herself taller with high heels, there she is, Nomi says, and, conscious of my small steps, I whisper to Nomi that, to be honest, I'm nervous even though I had sworn I'd be proud, but of what? But yes, of course, the sandy path, I remember it perfectly, the weeping willows that line the path to the left and right, and we had the feeling we were heading into a story we'd mistakenly believed we weren't a part of—our father's life before our mother's time.

Hello, we say, hello, hello (what do you say, the first time you see each other?), and Father introduces us—Janka, Nomi, Ildikó, Mother, who makes an effort, knowing we're all embarrassed she plays the role that Father should and tells Janka that we're happy to finally meet her so Janka can answer that she is happy too, Nomi and I hold tight to our drinks, unfortunately we don't have any straws, the waitress says and smiles apologetically, and I search desperately for a question but all I can see is Janka's picture, her full lips, they really are full! her thick hair which actually is a lot thicker! her eyes, lively and multicoloured, the way her teeth show when she laughs, so much so that the photograph seems to dissolve around them, and I wish we could all be silent for a moment, not saying a word, just sitting together, maybe not even looking at one another, I wish we could forget our fear of embarrassment and abandon ourselves to a silence that would correspond to the years that have passed when we knew nothing of one another, and I sit next to Nomi, whose smell is so familiar, whose ears I know well, her earlobes and bellybutton, who sticks her hands under her thighs and rounds her back slightly when she doesn't feel well, and Father is already snapping his fingers again to order something else, no, I don't want any more of the lemonade that is gluing my tongue and teeth together, but Father needs to drink the insecurity from his eyes, so they'll shine once again with the false gleam of I've got it all under control, and I remember the waitress too, scurrying back and forth in her orthopaedic shoes and, of course, Father has to tell the story of how we were harassed at the border, Mother who adroitly deflects all his complaints and accusations until they peter out, we smuggled a present for you across the border, Mother says and hands Janka a packet, we wrapped it for you, Nomi suddenly says, and I wonder if you're allowed to say that at a time like this, thank you so much, Janka replies, you shouldn't have risked your lives for me, and she laughs, she's laughing at her own joke, I think, and why is it so funny, anyway? Nomi nudges me with her elbow and naturally I notice that Janka's front teeth are huge, that she has gaps between them, abysses of hideousness, can you really laugh like that?

As for us, we've got used to laughing discreetly or not at all.

When will this finally be over, I think, when can we say goodbye, so that everything can go back to the way it was before, but I still remember the light breeze in the restaurant, how the warm summer air caressed our cheeks and seemed to encourage us to linger. What was it Janka talked about in that August of 1984? She must have told us about her school, told us that she had just graduated, she probably didn't say anything about her boyfriend and definitely didn't mention her mother. She must have talked about her plans, her dream job, she must have told us how much she liked our gift, a cassette recorder you can't even get here yet and, beaming, she would have said, in ten years maybe we'll be able to stand in line for something like this, that's how it would have gone; but the weeping willows sang a song for us, I heard them clearly, they dipped their wilted, dried-out leaves in the river so that we could understand one another in our small heartache that nonetheless is as big as the world to us, and even though I wanted to remember the willow's song, I've forgotten it, that too, I've forgotten.

May I come and visit you sometime? Janka asks as we say goodbye, I'd so much like to see you again, she says, and Switzerland, it's supposed to be the land of milk and honey, she says, I'd like to taste that famous special dish you have there, what's it called again? And none of us can answer Janka because we don't know which speciality she means, yes, we'll show you everything, Father says, you'll be amazed at all the things we have there, and Janka laughs, showing her impossible teeth, and packs the cassette recorder back into the squeaking Styrofoam box before hugging each of us, one after the other, and then she starts to bawl, she really can't hold back her tears, my sisters, she says softly, we'll see

one another again soon, won't we? And I would have preferred it if Janka had closed off her heart since Nomi and I
have to act as if we're made of stone because of her (and I
kept thinking of the lures that are thrown out to get the right
fish, the really big ones, to bite), Nomi and I have to be even
tougher than the border guard, or we'd probably have burst
into tears too, our hearts would have become so soft you
could have spread them on toast like butter and we wouldn't
have got back into our Mercedes and knelt on the back seat
and looked out of the rear window at Janka, standing alone
in her lemon-yellow dress waving goodbye with small
motions of her hand, she looks completely lost now, Nomi
says and we kneel for a long time, long after we can no longer
see our half-sister.

The same summer we met our half-sister, I'm pretty sure, or
perhaps it was one year later, Mother and Father are visiting
Uncle Móric and Aunt Manci and Nomi and I are helping
Mamika pick tomatoes and beans and dig up potatoes in her
garden. Tell us something about Father, Nomi says, we can
ask you but we can't ask Father; Mamika, who pauses for a
moment, her apron half-full with yellow beans, her worn-out
garden shoes covered with mud, what is it you want to ask
your father, my girls? and Mamika empties her apron into
the enamel bowl. About that other woman, what happened
then, and how he met our mother? And how God created
the world, Mamika laughs and straightens her kerchief, it's

not easy to tell that story, she says, come, that's enough for lunch, while you help me cook, I'll tell you about Miklós, I'll tell you what I know and that isn't much.

We stand around Mamika's tiny kitchen table, next to the gas stove, Mamika's kitchen is also her bathroom—a sink with a tiny mirror, a claw-foot tub Mamika never uses (such a waste of water) and under the tub is the blue chamber pot Nomi and I sometimes pee in at night when we're afraid to go to the toilet, and between the tub and the sink is a window almost always open in summer and covered with netting torn in the lower right-hand corner, through which mosquitoes slip in, I've got to put a stop to that traffic, Mamika says, her kitchen and bathroom window which I call my beautiful window, because early one morning I noticed for the first time how beautifully the light can shine on the rag rug. We peel the potatoes, wash the parsley and Mamika tells us about Father, about her Miklós, I don't know if it's right for me to tell you anything, since he obviously never mentioned his first wife, but why shouldn't you know? and while she speaks calmly and evenly, Mamika keeps looking at Nomi, at me, as if making sure she can continue her story.

And so Nomi and I learn that at some point Father became involved with a woman named Ibolya, but everyone had a different idea of his intentions. Uncle Móric claimed Miklós had taken her in his arms and kissed her after a dance one night and so had to accept the consequences and marry her, after our grandfather Papuci's early death Uncle Móric was the head of the family, which Father was never willing to accept, why should someone make decisions about my life just because he's my brother and six years older? Ibolya said that Miklós had kissed her, but she didn't want to make it into a drama, especially if Miklós didn't want her, she wasn't going to make any demands and the matter was settled as far as she was concerned. Miklós was beside himself, he raged, why was Móric butting in again, Móric probably didn't even know the difference between holding hands and kissing, despite being married for years, he, at least, knew exactly what happened with Ibolya, the cigarettes tasted good, the liquor even better, and she had beautiful hands, that was it (you know what a talker your father is), so it was never clear what exactly had gone on and the episode seemed over and done with but, then, a few months later, Miklós sat here in my kitchen and said that he wanted to marry Ibolya. Mamika, who asked Father if they'd reconciled and if he was sure of his decision, Father, who got up to wash his hands, he had come straight from work, sat down again, said that he and Ibolya had lost touch but then had run into each other again at the last village fair and, yes, he'd fallen in love with her, he'd made his decision. If you're sure, Mamika had said, I certainly don't want to get in your way.

A few months after the wedding, Father started coming home less and less often. He got drunk wherever he happened to be, with friends, after work, Uncle Móric went looking for him, beat him and made him go home, don't you know where a married man belongs? And Mamika did not get involved until Uncle Móric beat Father so badly that he lay in the middle of the street, his face covered with blood, and one of the neighbours woke Mamika in the middle of the night and brought her to her son who was still unconscious and barely recognizable. They dragged him to Mamika's house and she nursed him for days until he was more or less back on his feet; Mamika, who had both sons come to her and asked them in Papuci's name to talk over their differences, Mamika, who otherwise never interfered but now, after this incident, felt she had to intervene. But the two of them just looked at me stupidly, Mamika tells us while cutting the potatoes in two, she couldn't call it anything else, and neither said a word. They hid something from me, Mamika says, nothing trivial, something very important but I never learnt what it was. Your Aunt Manci met me by chance at the cemetery one day when the wind was unbearably hot and invited me for a cup of coffee, Aunt Manci poured the coffee and her tongue wagged so fast that I got a headache from her talking and from the weather, my head's going to burst, my dear Manci, then you can gather all your words up again, I said, completely worn out, and do you know what she said, just like that, out of the blue? Móric was in love with that Ibi, it's clear as day, but he was already married and that being the case, he rode in like he was defending Ibi's honour, however it had nothing to do with honour and all that, she, Manci, has her sources, and Miklós, when he finally

71

figured it out, wanted to get one over on his older brother, which she certainly understood, if you deal with Móric day in day out, sooner or later, you've got to teach him a lesson, she'd been wanting to do just that for a good while. I see, and what does it say about you that you're telling your husband's mother a story like that, I said to Manci, and her answer surprised me, it echoed in my head for a long time, namely, that when faced with their mother, the two brothers are as thick as thieves, but she, the wife, is a blind old thing you can tell everything to, the whole truth. Which truth? I asked Manci. Mamika, now you're asking me to betray a confidence and I won't do it. Besides, you just told me I talk too much, you won't learn anything else from me!

It's certainly true, Mamika says, that Ibolya, Móric and Miklós have some secret between them that I never learnt and sometimes I worried about it, especially since everything went on just as before, Miklós kept on working and drinking away his money, and when I say he kept on working I mean that he worked, but never at one job for very long, every time he got fired after a few weeks, three or four months at the most. At the chicken farm in Csóka, he did twice as much in one day as all the others, do you understand, my dear girls, and Mamika wipes her hands on her apron. His boss called him in, Miklós, have you blown a gasket? you know what the daily quota is, why are you working like a madman? I am a madman, my son answered, I work as hard as I can. Fine, then you can go. That's just one story among many and

Miklós was probably in his mid-twenties and no one wanted to hire him, no one in the area, and so your father started working by the hour or by the day. He helped in stores when someone was sick and people called Miklós in because he was known for making the best sausage and for being the fastest worker. He soon had a long list of customers, there wasn't anyone who didn't know Miklós, besides people were curious about someone who argued with everyone, that is, with all the authorities. Things went well for a while, Miklós earned a lot of money and bought himself a motorcycle, not just any motorcycle but one from the West, a German one, and no one knew how he managed to get one in such a short time, and once again Miklós was exceptional, and Mamika takes off her glasses and wipes them with her apron and Nomi says, yes, the motorcycle! we have a picture of it in our album, Father is sitting on a motorcycle in a stylish suit, his arms are crossed, he's holding a cigarette and laughing as if he were happy. Yes, Mamika says, that motorcycle was his great joy.

Then he was banned from working, those who wanted to hire Miklós were threatened with a huge fine, Miklós was accused of being a counter-revolutionary, some person from who knows where claimed he was distributing pamphlets, inciting others to sabotage Socialism. That sort of thing, Mamika says, can you imagine? and Nomi and I, we're speechless, we can't even manage a no.

You won't destroy me, was your father's answer and he started trading on the black market, I have no idea how he got the goods he was selling, and for a while things went well again. Everyone knew that Miklós only sold good products, many people considered him a hero, the motorcycle's coming, they'd say, your father on his motorcycle.

I'd almost forgotten Ibolya, with Ibi, as everyone called her, things didn't get any better, your father would sleep in the park, on a bench, on the riverbank, with a friend, anywhere, but almost never at home. Sometimes he came here, mostly very early in the morning, my son, I asked him, what's wrong, nothing, he answered, but once, it was February and there was at least two feet of snow on the ground, he sat next to the stove, rubbed his hands, said, Ibi's going to have a baby, without even looking at me. You'll be a father, I said, once I got over my fright at how unfeeling Miklós seemed, why are things so difficult between you and Ibolya? She lives in her head, Miklós said. I asked him to tell me more but he said nothing.

He didn't say anything else?

Not a word, and Mamika melts some fat in the frying pan, sautés the onions with a pinch of salt, we have to get the soup started or nothing will be ready when your parents come back, Nomi hands Mamika the bowl with the prepared vegetables, the beans, carrots, parsley, and I get fresh water and hand Mamika the pitcher, the hissing noise when Mamika pours the water over the sautéed vegetables, there we go, and now I have to sit a moment, Mamika, who says she's got lost in these events from so long ago, and now here they are again, as if they were ingredients for today's soup, then Mamika laughs and rubs her blue-grey eyes.

Janka was born on 1 October, it was an unusually hot day and, on that day, Uncle Móric broke a chair over your father's head because he was at a friend's house, dead drunk, he hadn't even washed, your uncle grabbed him by the collar, by the hair, by the ears, he talked and talked at Miklós, kissed him, pleaded with him, but your father had lost consciousness long before. Ibolya was in the maternity ward and Miklós in the men's ward, he had a serious head wound, I taught him a lesson Móric said, and do you know what I did to Móric? I slapped him, that's enough now, I shouted at him, you're acting like a vengeful Lord Almighty, but from now on you leave Miklós alone. Móric didn't speak to me for a long time and I was sure that Miklós and Móric would never be reconciled, and for a very long time they weren't.

I appealed to your father's conscience, I told him he couldn't leave Ibi with a baby, he should try to make it work with her one more time, and he looked at me, his head wrapped in bandages, I'll do it for you, he said, and he stopped drinking, he wasn't seen outside at night any more, and I asked God how long this would last, not long, I knew, it lasted a few months, then Miklós finally left Ibolya for good and filed for a divorce.

75

Now you must promise me something, and Mamika, who takes Nomi's hand and mine, our hands together, one in the other, says, you must never forget that you have a sister, I won't say more, my dear girls, one day you'll understand.

Miklós was the first one in our family to get divorced and, you know, getting a divorce meant cutting himself off from the entire community. Yet again. And I'd have liked to cut him into pieces, I was so furious with your father, especially since it didn't take long before I heard he was with another.

Our mother.

Yes.

Someone, they said, from the poor region. I never had anything against poor people, Mamika says, but this time I did, I was against her, against this woman who, they said, was a beauty with a bad reputation. Now this, I thought, if only she were ugly, Miklós lets himself get dazzled, and he has again already, I thought. It was a difficult time for me, I didn't know what to do, but then my Papuci came to me one night, he sat on my bed and, just imagine, he was wearing his best suit, the one we buried him in, Mamika, who makes the sign of the cross, in the name of the Father, the Son and the Holy Ghost; I didn't expect you, Vincent, I said, but he didn't answer, your grandfather, he held his hands out towards me, I hesitated for a moment, should I take the hand of a ghost? that's what went through my head, but I did and my Papuci's hands were so warm, I can't even describe it my dear girls, I may have sat up in bed all night, I can't say, but at some point I realized I was shivering and that Papuci had disappeared.

But you can't touch a ghost, when you try to touch one, there's only air, Nomi says grabbing at the empty air. I don't know what ghosts are like in general but Papuci came to me and he was very warm, maybe he was just warm air, Mamika says, that's not impossible, Mamika, stirring the pot, fishes out a bean and says, now we can add the potatoes.

In any case, I saw my shadow next to the well and I thought, Anna, what a big shadow you have, and you know what, I suddenly knew I had to take a step in a direction I didn't want to go.

Mamika, who invited Miklós, invited him and his lover; Father and Mother came, they sat at Mamika's table, Mother, Rósza, who had brought coffee, a voice and eyes, I liked her right away, Mamika told us. And a few months later, Miklós and Rósza moved away, to another town.

Because of Ibolya?

Perhaps because of her as well but Miklós and Rósza wanted to start afresh and that's easier to do in a new place. And the gossip was, well, how should I put it, that's when I learnt that some people provide the topics of conversation that other people need. How can you stand having such a son, I was asked, do you even speak to him any more? After questions like that, I always took off my glasses, waited a moment and then usually said, if it weren't for my son, what is it you'd ask me about? And Mamika dropped a large spoonful of lard in the frying pan, that's a good answer, don't you think? I think it's good that you know more about your father now, Mamika says, browning flour in the lard, taking the pan off the heat before sprinkling sweet paprika in it, I believe each person has more than one face and your father, he has five faces, maybe more, and Mamika stirs the roux slowly into the soup, as for me, in any case, there have been at least five times in my life when I've thought, now, once again, I don't recognize Miklós (and when I look Mamika in the eye, her eyes say to me, Ildi, you're wondering how many faces I have? I don't know, that's something you'll have to tell me), your parents ran a small grocery store and there they met Sándor who already lived in Switzerland with his wife, and Sándor is the one who gave your parents the idea of emigrating to Switzerland and not, as they'd originally planned, to Australia.

To Australia?

WORDS LIKE

We have to do better, Mother says one day in late February, above all we have to be faster, and now with the new team everything will go more smoothly, we'll start from scratch, all right? We talk about who will help whom during the rushes and the rushes are from nine to nine-thirty, at lunchtime from noon to one and afternoons from three-thirty to four-thirty; we're at home, sitting around the table in the living room, eating sour pickles, spicy salami, bread, yoghurt and, while we eat, Mother makes a list of the most important points we have to pay attention to when waiting tables, at the counter or in the kitchen, Nomi, who says we shouldn't get carried away, even if everything wasn't perfect, still, our first day went very well. Exactly, Nomi's right, Father says and cuts a paper-thin slice of salami with the big carving knife (and I'd like to tell Father that I love watching his hands when he works so calmly and quietly), Mother, who grabs a slice, looks at us in turn and says a sentence that she'll repeat more than once in the time that follows, a sentence I don't quite understand: We haven't got human status here yet, we still have to earn it.

And because Mother is the only one who has any idea of it all, of the business as a whole, she has to help out every-where, especially in the kitchen, Father, who is overwhelmed

79

for the first few weeks because he was never trained as a cook but still wants to make everything perfectly, not only prepares too much but makes it all fresh, from scratch, and now and then takes a sip of the cooking wine because of the heat, it's unbearably hot in this dollhouse kitchen! It's the beginning of the end if you start drinking, Mother says in Hungarian, you know that, it's fine in the evening, for all I care, but not in the kitchen, you promised me; yes, I did promise, Father says meekly, I just have to get used to it here; Dragana, who starts work at seven in the morning, leans her whale belly against the draining board, prepares the salads, chops vegetables (and always smells of garlic, which I find unpleasant); Dragana, who is always busy with something, who in the first weeks barely said a word aside from *yes, is good*, in answer to Father when he told her what she should do next, her taciturnity suddenly ended when Gloria started working for us, Dragana and Gloria talk to each other rapidly in Serbo-Croatian; and Marlis? she is the only original employee who stays with us, washing dishes, cleaning, the rhythmic clacking of her heavy white wooden shoes is as much a part of the kitchen as the buzzing of the microwave and the greedy sucking of the ventilator hood. And Mother, she's mostly the one who darts into the toilets with a scrubber, pail, rags and rubber gloves to wipe up the puddle that forms next to the urinal at least once a week—checking the toilets is at the very top of Mother's list, as frequently as possible!

On one unusually cold March day, so cold that you'd think it was still winter, I'm foaming the milk. I see my hands, how they hold the pitcher, raising and lowering it smoothly, not too quickly, so that the steamer wand moves slowly through the seething milk, I make sure the wand stays under the surface of the milk or it will spray everywhere, splatter the coffee machine, the counter, my hands and my blouse. And it always happens faster than you'd expect.

Because I need a lot of foamed milk and hot milk doesn't foam, I constantly have to change it, add cold milk to the hot, and I think about how there must be a chemical explanation for why hot milk doesn't create foam, but I don't know it. However, I do know the trick with mineral water, a tiny bit of seltzer water in the milk makes foaming easier; Mamika's the one who taught me to add seltzer not just to milk but to pancake batter as well so that the batter is lighter and doesn't burn as quickly in the frying pan.

If I concentrate on the milk too much, it's guaranteed not to foam. That's why I first put the pitcher under the steamer wand, then put coffee in the filter, place the saucers and spoons on the tray, I rely on my ear, it can tell exactly what stage the milk has reached. It's a particular sound that becomes more and more shrill the hotter the milk, and when it reaches a certain frequency, it means I have to take hold of the pitcher if I want foam—and I glance out the window in front of me behind the guests, through which I can see the bare chestnut tree showing its fists.

Even though I'd written 'Swiss applicants preferred' in the job listing, only foreigners applied (and I, who wrote it, think about what it means that we, the Kocsis family, prefer Swiss applicants. Nothing. It doesn't mean anything, that's just the way it is, I tell myself). Glorija, the most Swiss of all the candidates, speaks German almost fluently and so can speak in dialect, her eyes inspire confidence and, according to Mother her references are good, she starts working as a waitress with us in early March and Nomi and I, we share the second shift and work behind the counter. And your studies? Mother asked me. They can wait for a while.

Saturday is usually the nicest day, with a pink bow and special foam for your coffee, as Nomi says—but today isn't Saturday, just a regular Wednesday, and the sports club is celebrating its foundation day, so I'm making mountains of milk foam and I'm busy behind the counter, I, by the way, am wearing a black-and-white-striped blouse and a narrow black skirt that only lets me take little steps. I look at myself, ready to take orders in this indispensable disguise, and want to show that I'm a perfect counter-waitress, me, behind the counter like a cuckoo in another bird's nest, and it's a good thing too, because when waiting on tables, I feel like a fraud, everyone can see who I really am, but not today, today the army-green counter hides at least the bottom half of my body, yes, I'm always glad when I can switch stations with Nomi and she waits on the tables instead of me.

Great, darling, Glorija says to me in English, compliment-
ing me on my work, and if you're really *great,* you can whip
enough foam for three creamy cappuccinos from a half-litre
milk with steam and air. To finish, I sprinkle the mounds of
foam with chocolate powder and the movement of my hand
when I shake out the powder has to be gentle and calm, or
the fragile mountains will collapse; I wonder again which
chemical process causes this collapse. I only know that the
chocolate powder makes a slight hissing noise if I pour out
the right amount, in other words, not too much, and when I
talk about a calm hand-motion, I mean a careful tapping with
my index finger on the tilted shaker. Mother and her sister,
my Aunt Icu, have said that when you make things by hand,
your hands should move smoothly, like a gently flowing river,
whether you're kneading dough, making jam, embroidering
or darning, if you're hands are nice and warm, then everything will come out well, even the tricky dough for apple
strudel.

And that is what interests me most about this work,
making the necessary movements as efficiently as possible,
always more gracefully, that is to say, more smoothly, and
I'd like to be able to see my hands get better each day at
removing the filter, tapping it so that it empties, and drawing
a new shot so that the coffee I make is more than just satis-
factory, I'd like to perfect the interplay of my hands and the
Cimbali, a three-group machine with portafilters, electric
cup warmer and stainless-steel front—according to the

instruction manual—even though I know there are negative external influences I can't do anything about like windy, humid weather or a full moon. All of which means that I don't let anything distract me and focus solely on the tasks I've just described.

None of our relatives could work here in the Mondial, I think to myself on this cold March day as I steam milk for hours on end (or that's how it feels), neither Aunt Manci nor Aunt Icu could wait tables or work at the counter, no matter how skilled they are with their hands, and this thought has an unpleasant overtone, did I assume that one day they would work here with us? my uncles, whose especially dilapidated teeth would make our guests leery, and whom we could never teach to laugh discreetly and hide their gap teeth; Csilla, Aunt Icu's and Uncle Piri's daughter, now in her mid-thirties, suffers from a skin disease and doesn't have a single tooth left or any money for dentures, as Aunt Icu once wrote (Csilla's teeth are a constant topic of discussion, because when she worked with us one summer, in our first restaurant in Switzerland, Csilla swore to Mother on all that was holy that she would put aside some of the money she earned for beautiful new teeth, and then you'll be able to eat properly too, you're as thin as a rail, Father said. Csilla worked in the kitchen on the second floor where the guests couldn't see her, and whatever you do, don't open your mouth out on the street! Nomi and I said to her, or everyone will run away, the Swiss aren't used to that), and what about

Béla? I ask myself, it would probably be hardest to find something for my cousin Béla, Aunt Icu's and Uncle Piri's son, Béla's teeth are more or less acceptable but he is capable of starting an argument with anyone and everyone, he'd provoke those around him without speaking even a word of German, Béla, who becomes completely impenetrable for minutes at a time without even realizing, probably because he usually spends hours staring into the sky.

Glorija, who, incidentally, comes from Croatia and has perfect teeth (we noticed that right away during her interview), keeps handing me orders for cappuccinos, on a perfectly regular Wednesday! and I keep making mountains of milk foam and dusting the fragile peaks, occasionally make spiral designs of whipped cream on a *café crème*, and Aunt Icu bakes her marvellous, breathtaking cakes, I mean that with her enormous cakes with alternate layers of sponge cake and whipped cream, Aunt Icu would entrance absolutely everyone and, yes, it takes a while to work your way from the caramelized sugar decorations on top down to the bottommost layer of sponge cake, I'd be happy to tell them all, the members of the sports club and anyone else, that Aunt Icu, a confectioner and gardener who works in a hemp factory, should be flown in on a Concorde 787, so that with her hands that have souls of their own, as Uncle Piri says, she can whip up a cream made of natural sins.

My darling, Glorija calls, I need one more pressed orange juice, and I, in my black-and-white-striped blouse, rush to halve three oranges, lay the cut side onto the lower part of the press, pull the black lever down quickly, pressing hard until the juice squirts out of the orange, and my mother appears behind the counter, asks if she can help, yes, I need two more chocolate milks, three Rivellas, one sparkling apple juice, and I also need you to answer a question, I say. That can wait, though, can't it? says Mother and pours the cold milk and powdered chocolate into the blender, Glorija keeps handing in more orders and, in any case, the relatively loud hissing, gurgling and whistling of the concerto of steam wand, espresso machine and blender makes any conversation behind the counter impossible. Soon we can take a short break, Mother says.

And when we're sitting at the staff table, Nomi joins us and I ask, Mother, haven't you ever considered having Aunt Icu work with us in the kitchen? I mean, we could at least bring Aunt Icu here, and I speak very softly, almost in a whisper, because all of a sudden it's so quiet in the cafe—since there are no guests—you can even hear the discreet ticking of the clock, Mother looks at me, she looks at me for a long time with her large eyes and I don't know if eyes are the mirrors of the soul, maybe they really do mirror what's going on deep inside, but what good is that if you don't know how to read them? Even though I've learnt to read Mother's eyes, I'm confused because I've never seen her like this, the green of her eyes turning almost black, the soft gleam narrowing into a single point, what's wrong, I think, Mother, I say (and I look at Nomi), I was just wondering . . .

Do you imagine that I haven't already thought about what I could do for Aunt Icu? No, of course I don't, I say but Mother cuts me off, her eyes hit me like a slap, do you know how I spend my nights? do you have any idea if I sleep? you, Ildi, you're usually so sensitive and now? (Mother's looks hit me, not on the ear but on the cheek) And how do you think Uncle Piri and Csilla would manage without her? how is she supposed to come here, how on earth could we get her a visa? don't you think I agonize over how we could possibly help them? how many times do you think I've called the Serbian embassy since the war broke out in 1991? do you think I don't care about what our family is suffering? Nomi, who takes Mother's hands, says, no, she didn't say that, you're not being *fair*.

Fair? That's another one of those words you girls use, I'm using it, Nomi says, the English word *fair* means just. Well, good then, I've learnt something new, and now you two can learn something—I recently sent Icu a letter with money, German marks, she and Uncle Piri could have lived off it for at least half a year. Do you girls think the postman there goes from door to door on a yellow motorcycle like he does in Switzerland, bringing the letters with a friendly 'Hello'? Do you think letters actually reach their destinations? Do you think there's a single honest man in any of the public offices? How am I supposed to send a letter to them that doesn't have Swiss stamps on it, tell me, have you ever bothered to consider anything further than the tips of your noses? (This is usually Father's line.) Mother, who switched to Hungarian a while ago, had obviously forgotten that we're not at home, I don't want to talk about the war—*háború*—do you hear me, we can hope it will end soon, but that's all we can do. Ildi, I don't understand how you could ask such a question, how you could bring up a topic like this so thoughtlessly, and during work. Glorija, who turns her head towards us, asks if everything is all right, if she should bring us another coffee. The break is over, Mother says, and stands up, she doesn't look at me again, neither at me nor at Nomi and it's probably her dress, the way her dress swings out energetically to the side, which makes me realize it takes an almost superhuman energy to maintain normality here, to keep up the daily routine—a level of energy I would not be able to muster.

Nomi and I glance at each other and both stand up to get back to work.

Maybe it was thoughtless of me, I hadn't really considered the situation and so was completely taken aback by Mother's violent reaction, we actually never talk about the war at home, when the war broke out in Yugoslavia, all Father said was, this is a war that will end soon. Soon? how soon, I asked. In a few months, at the most. A criminal like Milošević has no future in today's Europe, and he sounded as convincing as an experienced news anchor. Since the outbreak of the war, Father has been watching the early morning news, the regular news at prime time and the late-night news, he switches from the German news to the Austrian to the Hungarian and back (our language has been coming into our living room via satellite for a few months), we sit on the sofa, Nomi, Mother and I, sometimes we watch too, we listen to the reports on ARD or ORF or MTV (Magyar Televízió) and wait to hear Father's verdict. It takes guts but it's the only right answer, he announces when Germany and Austria recognize the independence of Croatia and Slovenia. And we're sitting at the dining table when the United Nations Security Council imposes comprehensive sanctions against Serbia and Montenegro. They're finally doing something, Father says, it's perfectly clear that drastic measures are necessary to finally get rid of those goddamn communists and Serbs, in any case, they're all the same! And like every night, we eat our cold dinner of bread, ham, cheese, hard-boiled eggs and marinated peppers.

Perhaps we've forgotten that the Vojvodina is part of Serbia, that the drastic measures, as the newscaster calls them, Father too (though in Hungarian 'drastic measures' sound even more drastic), will impact our family as well, that the economic, oil, air traffic embargos may well have a drastic effect on the lives of Aunt Icu, Aunt Manci, Uncle Móric, Uncle Piri, Béla, Csilla and Great-Uncle Pista, or maybe we didn't forget at all, is anyone thinking of Juli or Juli's mother or Mr Szalma, Mamika's neighbour? maybe one of us remembers the tiny shop on Beogradska Street where Mother did her apprenticeship, remembers that this tiny shop, where Nomi and I bought salt sticks, sweets, tonic and Traubi Soda every year, is now completely empty, closed up, as Unclie Móric and Aunt Manci wrote in their last letter.

We eat, we keep eating, and talk about tomorrow.

Do you know what was wrong with Mother? I ask Nomi when we're eating lunch.

It's not that hard to understand, Nomi says, she's frightened.

Father and I, we're walking down the hill together, every time I'm surprised that we go at almost the same speed, my father has small feet, I think, not much bigger than mine, maybe that's why, and Father lights a cigarette, he almost always lights one at the same spot where there's a view of the lake, still dark below us and framed with lights ranging from yellow to orange, or is the sky the lake? At this time of day, it's not easy to tell things apart, I think, Father and I, we rarely talk, we keep walking, and the smoke from Father's cigarette tickles my nose, I don't know if Father is listening to the sounds of our swinging arms, our steps.

Mother told me you've given up your studies, Father says, in between our steps. No, I didn't give them up, I just reduced them for now, I answer. Won't they miss you there, at your school? Father asks and points his cigarette at a hedgehog disappearing under a parked car. I can manage it myself, I say and I want to ask him to be quiet, because I like this quarter of an hour when we walk together in silence, I like it because I feel free when we move through these dark tonalities, in fact, I could sleep in a bit longer and take the bus down to the village later but I don't want to, I don't want to face the atmosphere of the village bus, I don't want to have to look at faces so starkly lit this early in the morning, I can't bear it.

School is more important than anything else, Father says, we're happy when you help us at work but you've got to stay in school, and I don't answer, I don't say, Father, stop saying school, it's not a school, it's a university, I'm one of twenty thousand students who have no real idea of what they should pursue, who get lost in enormous libraries, until now I've only found one professor who's at all convincing and he's not even a professor, he's a lecturer in the university, ladies and gentlemen, he tells us with a straight face, you'll be buried alive, keep in mind that you are nothing more than employees in an institution that might as well be a museum, and only once you've accepted that, will you be able to think independently, to swim against the tide (I'd like to tell Father that I stopped studying law a year ago and spent a semester taking courses in philosophy, religious studies, literature and pedagogy, but the only subject that really interests me is history—modern history and Swiss history; it's hard to convince Father about liberal arts, especially history, because he has already experienced history and has an allergic reaction whenever I tell him something about the Second World War, did you read that in a book? he asks irritably, the Second World War doesn't fit in a book, he declares, and I even agree with him, that's why I haven't told Father yet that I'm studying history, because for him, that's as far as you can get from a useful field of studies. It's fine if you don't want to become a dentist, that I understand, there are more attractive things to look at than everyone's dental hardware, but why not a doctor, or even better, a lawyer! A solid profession, Father declares, people will always need lawyers because they'll always be arguing, you'll earn a ton of money and can have me chauffeured around the world in a limousine— Father's view after he's drunk a few glasses of schnapps.) Father stops suddenly, right before the stairs that lead to the train station and asks, why don't you answer me? and me, I've already gone down the first two stairs, I stop, turn towards Father, I'm going to continue my studies, as I've already told you, and I can hear how unconvincing my voice sounds. Find another reason if you want to quit, Father says, and comes up to me in his dark green suede jacket, his curly hair looks wild in the faint morning light (me, I can't tell Father that I'm still searching, because that word is a red rag to a bull, searching, you and your sister, you're always searching for something, everything's right in front of your noses, and what do you see? You see stars around you everywhere and you run in circles like stupid animals). Father stands on the same step with me, we look at each other for a moment and an express train thunders past. Father may have said something when the noise rolled over us and the cold air hit our faces blowing back our hair; we descend the stairs at the same pace, cross the underpass and walk the short distance to the Mondial.

Three happy-faced suns with rays beam at us from our cafe's front door, what is this? three large-format fliers have been neatly and carefully taped to the plate glass of our entrance door. An invitation to a *Puure Zmorge*, I say, it means farmer's picnic in Swiss German and it's free! What's that supposed to mean? why did they stick it on our door? and Father starts scraping the adhesive tape from the glass. Our presence is important to them, I say, to the Swiss People's Party, you get free *chäs* and *wurscht*, that's cheese and sausage, and all they want in return is a signature for some initiative, usually against peoples' interests. This right-wing populist party, the Democratic Union of the Centre, is well represented in this community and I look around to see if their messenger is still in sight. I couldn't care less who's represented here, Father says, better give me a hand, we don't have much time. Just leave it there, I say, we can tape another flier next to it, and thank the stranger who invited us to the farmers' picnic.

Hülye csíny, Father says. What? I ask. And Father translates because he thinks I didn't understand the Hungarian, a *plank*, a stupid schoolboy *plank*, he says. Prank, I correct him (but professionally presented, I think), and Father and I scrape and rub the various spots and because the tape sticks stubbornly to the glass, Father gets a kitchen scraper and surgical spirit, you can't take such a stupid-looking sun seriously, Father says (he has no interest in Swiss politics, politicians here are all half-asleep, Swiss politics is a hobby for retired people, he claims and watches the debates filmed in the German parliament), the Swiss People's Party, what is that supposed to mean? Father asks me in all seriousness, that sounds to me like hard-core communism, the People! the Party! Father has obviously forgotten everything he had to learn for his Naturalization exam, and I wonder if the experts on the Naturalization Board asked my parents about the Schwarzenbach Initiative as well, the so-called excess immigration initiative which was meant to limit the alien population in Switzerland. Not often, but occasionally, Mother and Father talked about the weeks leading up to this referendum, how they learnt about it even with their rudimentary German and only gradually realized that it concerned them and would affect their lives, that approximately half of the foreigners residing in Switzerland would have to leave the country if the Initiative was passed. They would be afraid of returning to the Vojvodina with next to nothing, of having to start again from zero, back into the Yugoslavian desert, Father said, back to those idiotic Titoists! but after that *Schwarzback*, he was left with a certain amount of respect. Respect? Yes, at the fact that you always have to remember they can deport you at any time. Father, whose boss, Mr

Fluri, invited him into his living room on 7 June 1970, to listen to the returns on the radio, his boss opened a bottle of beer in the middle of the afternoon as the results were announced—rather close, but rejected! his boss called out and added, *Proscht, uf ois*, Cheers, to us, Miklós! And they even had a smoke, Father carefully tapping the ash from his cigarette into the crystal ashtray. Seventy-five per cent! his boss kept repeating, that's something! Imagine, Miklós, three quarters of the pie turned out to vote! And Father chuckled to himself as he pictured a pie with a big slice missing showing up at the village hall to stick a ballot through the slot. *Big thank you to men of Swiss!* Father said the next time they clinked glasses, and his boss was very touched by the toast, yes, Miklós, cheers! *big thank you Swiss men!*

While we were checking the glass door one more time to make sure it was really clean and just as I'm about to tell Father more about the Swiss People's Party, our first guest of the day arrives, good morning, I'm a bit early, he says, I hope that's not a problem. Not at all, I answer quickly as if I were trying to hide something—the three fliers in my hand, we're already here too, I say, and the guest laughs, indeed, you are! and we all laugh together at my unintentional joke.

Today I'm waiting tables.

Even my back is jittery, I constantly have the feeling that I'm overlooking someone who wants to order or pay the bill (you have to keep sight of the whole picture when waitressing), and I hand in orders for five coffees, three espressos, two dark *cafés au lait*, Nomi, who usually handles the cash register, is working behind the counter today, lucky girl, I think (in a small business, a family-run business, you have to master every single position), Nomi, fast and efficient, helps me because I'm in danger of losing the big picture now, at nine o'clock with the door opening and closing continuously, office and construction workers who all take their breaks at the same time and want to be served as quickly as possible, Nomi, who knows how to reassure me with a look, a small gesture, hands me a glass of cold water. Being able to give every customer the feeling that you, the waitress, are there only for them, even in the worst rush, is an art and if you're a pro, you can still fit in an appropriate comment here and there, a discreet compliment (what a lovely brooch), and when you're such a pro that no one even notices just how good you are, then it all runs like a well-oiled machine, without a hitch, and each guest feels he's getting personal attention—no rushing—and doesn't notice that every seat in the cafe is full.

Nomi places my order on a tray—which is actually my job—and Nomi, who never turns on the radio when I'm waiting tables because she knows it makes me nervous, quietly tells me that Mr Pfister has got his egg and gives me a wink (Mother has forbidden us to speak in our secret language because it provokes the guests, they think we're talking about them), I head off with my full tray to soothe the customers, I think, and I like the construction workers, waiting impatiently with their famished eyes and tired faces, making no effort to look pleasant, six or seven men at a table, smoking, chewing or drinking coffee, but who mostly want one thing—not to talk much, good morning! and I place the coffees on the tables that have been pushed together, they all drink coffee, strong with lots of sugar, and that's another reason I like construction workers—they know what they want.

The noise level is high at nine o'clock, so no one notices that the radio is off and the only advantage of the nine o'clock rush is that in the buzz of voices, no one complains that we're in a graveyard (it's Glorija who says that without music it's a graveyard, you need music to feel good while drinking coffee or leafing through the paper, a lovely melody brightens your day), various pitches, dialects, shrill voices that cut through the general noise, and faint, mumbling voices towards which I discreetly incline my head, and it's precisely this chaos of voices that makes clear which ones have the strongest effect on me, sometimes it only takes two words in a strident tone, *Froilein zalle*! bill please! to send me retreating inside myself (there's nothing worse when you're waiting tables than letting your self-control slip, it's OK in the kitchen but never in the dining room, not even in the most stressful situations!), yes, Mother's right, I don't like waiting tables and the only thing that motivates me is the challenge of being a perfect waitress from six to two (so, it's not really a question of self-control, I tell myself).

Another ground rule—running is absolutely forbidden, no matter what happens, no matter how quickly the cafe fill ups, at the most you can walk briskly (you can be quick but not hasty, swift but never rushed), a waitress who's running has already missed something, she's already too late (we have to give our guests the sense that this work is easy for us, understand?), I do understand and I try not to lose sight of anything in the nine o'clock rush—to serve coffee with an elegant ease, to ring up the bill, to avoid hurrying the guests even when we no longer have any idea if we're coming or going—Nomi takes over the tables near the counter (my stockings are uncomfortably tight around my thighs), Nomi, who lets me know we've got everything under control, the nightmare will be over at nine-thirty, I glance at the clock, it's not true that time goes faster when you're busy, Nomi and I, we know that the time between nine and nine-thirty is divided into minutes that last hours and it's amazing how many looks, hands, ties, shirts, wedding rings, elaborate hairdos, bald spots, brands of cigarette, whiffs of perfume, front pages and headlines you can take in or at least notice in half an hour.

Can you believe how they're bashing heads in the Balkans, and those Serbs, what a pack of warmongers, they're like hyaenas (Mr Pfister, head of a moving company that operates internationally, even overseas, is saying to a friend), you ordered a light coffee, right? Yes, thank you, and who's leader of the Serbs in Bosnia? Ah yes, Mladić, exactly, thank you, Miss, he and Milošević, they're worse than real Nazis, believe me.

Mrs Müller, Mrs Zwicky, Mr Pfister, Mr Walter, Mrs Hungerbühler, Mr and Mrs Schilling, the teacher, the sales clerk, the gardener from the next village, the hairdresser who until now went to our competitors for her coffee, the post-office workers and the construction workers, they all want coffee and possibly a bite to eat too, would you like something sweet or something savoury?

And is it really true that Milošević's father was a shoe-maker?

It's not true that time goes faster—the harder you work the more it slows down, yes, Mrs Wittelsbacher, I'll be right with you, and it's an art to serve everyone without a hitch, like a well-oiled machine, tables two and three want to pay, Nomi says (right away, yes, I'm coming), a special order between nine and ten shouldn't derail you (why certainly!), the high collar on my elaborately designed blouse draws attention with every step (you think so? thank you! it's true, I don't usually wear this colour), Nomi hands me another glass of water, Mrs Hungersbühler who is looking for her second shoe hops up to the counter on one foot, says the children stole her other shoe, where are they, the snotty brats? I crawl under the upholstered banquette to find Mrs Hungerbühler's second shoe (all between nine and nine-thirty), the navy blue slip-on is waiting patiently for Mrs Hungerbühler's foot in the furthest corner, or for my hand that now holds the shoe out to Mrs Hungerbühler, thank you so much, many, many thanks, and what would you like?

(another ground rule you should never forget—never leave your hands empty, there is always something to carry between nine and nine-thirty: a plate, empty cups and bottles, crumpled napkins, don't forget the ashtray, who wants to sit at a table with cigarette butts?) how on earth did my shoe end up there? I simply can't understand it! Nomi asks if she should switch with me and Mrs Hungerbühler will surely press a *Fünfliber*, a five-franc coin into my hand (for getting down on my hands and knees, for searching, for finding the shoe, for getting all sweaty), no, it's fine, I've got it, I say and Mrs Hungerbühler takes my hands in hers, I don't live far from here, on Horn Street, stop and visit some day when you have time, that would be such a pleasure! and I am so surprised that Mrs Hungerbühler's eyes are shining with sincerity and that her invitation is heartfelt that I can't for the life of me think of an appropriate response and simply say, it's fine. Instead of being pleased by Mrs Hungerbühler's unexpected warmth, I get annoyed by Mr Pfister who brays with laughter, hugely amused by my scrabbling around on my knees to find Mrs Hungerbühler's shoe, and asks, tell me, miss, why doesn't Anita work here any more? she was good, an excellent waitress, so there I am, between nine and nine-thirty in the morning, suddenly looking into the eyes of Mr Pfister's dog, dark brown, skittish eyes in a black ball of fur cowering under the seat, and me, on my knees in a skirt and blouse, I've got a wet muzzle in my face, and one of these days I'm going to bite Mr Pfister in the leg, just like his dog would, and why? probably because Mr

Pfister bends down a bit to peer under the banquette and says to his dog and me, I'm an employer myself, you see, and I know that the Swiss have other aspirations, and when there aren't any Swiss left, you've got to make do with Albanians or people from some other country in the Balkans; Mr Pfister finally catches on, but with you it's different, he says, you've already got your citizenship and you know the customs and morals of our country, but those who've been coming here since the nineties, they're crude stuff, Mr Pfister says, and sits back upright, he's no longer talking to me and his dog, but to his friend again, certainly also an employer, you see, the *homo balcanicus* simply never went through the Enlightenment, Mr Pfister says, by the way, my dog doesn't bite, he calls down to me and his laughter shakes the seat, the comfortable upholstered mustard-yellow bench, and I think to myself that the view from under a banquette is surprising (especially between nine and nine-thirty), and as I stretch the tips of my fingers as far as I can and feel around for Mrs Hunger-bühler's shoe in the depths of the corner, I look at the dog's attentive face and think for a second that dogs should be rescued, they should be saved from shampooed rugs, from dog-training courses, from flannel-trouser legs and from funny jokes (by the way, do you know what my dog's name is? Mr Pfister asks gleefully), as I was saying, the view from here is surprising, it all looks completely different under the bench, legs, socks, stockings, croissant crumbs, Mr Pfister's incredibly thin calves, the dog's furry head that has nothing to do with the rest, do you have it, Mrs Hungerbühler's voice trembles, yes! and next time I'll stay longer, I may even lie down next to Mr Pfister's dog (thank you so much!) in my fancy blouse and support hose, that's what I'll do to see the Mondial from another perspective, an amusing thought, then the frightening thought that I might like to stay under the banquette next to the recessed radiator, me, all sweaty, drenched—it's more than sweating—the sweat is pouring out of me, table seven is staring at me: the Schärer brothers, two pairs of inscrutable eyes. Excuse me, Mr Pfister says, standing up and buttoning his jacket, I think you do your job very well (thank you, yes, have a lovely day, Mr Pfister, see you tomorrow!), and despite it all, I feel flattered, and am annoyed with myself for feeling this way.

What's wrong with you? Nomi asks when the Mondial is half-empty again, Nomi, who lights me a cigarette and tells me I should sit down for a bit. I put on the wrong stockings, the wrong blouse, I haven't slept, I haven't had anything to eat yet, today is Friday and Friday is a day I thoroughly dislike, although I'm not sure why, maybe because it's the day right before the weekend . . .

Cut it out, Nomi says, come on now, tell me what's wrong, Nomi looks at me closely and strokes my shoulder but, as so often, we can't talk because the door opens and closes, we put out our cigarettes, take another quick sip of coffee, we'll talk later, we're going out tomorrow night, right?

HEAVENLY

We drive up in the middle of the night, it's 1986, not to
Hajduk Stankova as we usually do to go to Mamika's, but to
Aunt Icu's, our white Mercedes stops just before our destination. A sudden rain shower turns the unpaved road into a
sea of mud, we are stuck, the wheels spin, my father starts
swearing, Brezhnev, you can go fuck yourself in the ass (and
none of us points out that Brezhnev's been dead for a while),
the windscreen wipers sweep back and forth hysterically,
Nomi and I stare at the yellow glow of a streetlamp, the rain
is . . . on a hunt! we say, but we don't laugh because Father
stomps on the pedal and curses the system, the two-stroke
engine and communism, this car isn't made for these roads,
Mother says softly, still gripping the door handle tightly, we
should go get help, she adds, Father pulls his jacket over his
head and his grey loafers sink into the mud. I hear the
swampy sound, the greedy, slurping sound of the wet mud,
my father, who finally takes off his shoes and socks, wades
through the mud, jumps over the drainage ditch, runs to my
aunt's house, rings the bell, and I can hear the dogs barking,
two German shepherds who do nothing but pace back and
forth in their kennel, keeping guard, only when our cousin
Béla lumbers up to the kennel do they start whimpering,
drawing through the air sharp, thin, whining sounds, like

string, Nomi and I usually stand at a safe distance near the well, and watch the dogs lay their heads submissively on the dusty ground as if Béla had drugged or enchanted them—which is the same thing—as if they were apologizing for having bared their teeth moments before. Béla opens the kennel with a practised hand, gives the dogs a few pats on their backs in passing (as if he'd never played with teddy bears), and just as routinely, sweeps up the piles of crap and hoses down the rest, Béla who doesn't just rule the dogs with the merest glance but heads towards us now with his father and ours, without the slightest hurry while the fathers run ahead, as if Béla had shooed them away, as if he were driving them forwards, he advances slowly, regally, his arms crossed, he triumphs over the mud by not paying it any attention.

Over the years, Béla will perfect his gift, his penchant for training animals, and will become one of the best pigeon-breeders in the country and his reputation among pigeon-fanciers will spread far beyond the borders . . . and while men are being conscripted for systematic killing and the destruction of the country, Bêla points out his meticulously arranged trophies with a gesture that seems utterly helpless and the men in their sober, earth-coloured uniforms laugh, almost embarrassed at first by the sight of the trophies whose showy gilt kitsch testifies to a brilliant career. And one of them feels compelled to click his heels and announce that these days everything's being blown to hell and where Béla's headed, he's going to forget a lot of things and first of all he'll forget his heavenly creatures or rather, his flying rats.

We'll say hello later, Béla says, grinning at us through the open car door when we try to hug him, first we've got work to do. He pushes the car with Uncle Piri while Father steps on the gas and Mother still keeps a tight grip on the light brown handle, my sister and I flop and twitch like two fish on dry land, longing for the warm summer rain that in a few seconds will completely drench our light summer trousers, our T-shirts with 'Hollywood' written in glittering letters, and glue our clothes to our bodies like a second skin, the car's wheels go around a few more times to the accompaniment of the men's curses before they finally decide to do what is expected of them, namely, to roll forward rather than spin.

Aunt Icu puts bread on the table with tomatoes, sausage, peppers—you must be starving—cream, cheese, fresh butter, my aunt, whose dry curls stick to her head this late at night, her sky-blue eyes filled with childlike joy, children, children, you're finally here! But the table is not yet full enough, the ham, I still have to get the ham, how could I forget the ham, and some schnapps! her plump body disappears into the pantry again and reappears a second later with an enormous tart to embellish the table, oh dear, I forgot the ham and the schnapps again!

And we gather around the table, we squeeze in tight together, a harsh cone of light shines on us, illuminating our eyes as they roam around the room, we want to look at everything, to see what the years have brought, how time has flown! how long has it been since we've seen one another? how many things have we done without you? how many feelings have we not been able to share with you? Time is a sack big enough to hold everything, the roses didn't bloom this year and the sow had twenty babies—piglets we had to rescue from the mother or she'd have crushed them—and the drainage ditch still stinks as much as it ever did, and those gentlemen up there whose lives are nothing but empty promises! but let's not talk politics, Uncle Piri fills the shot glasses with a practised hand and quickly raises his glass: In honour of this special day, may God forgive everyone, the layabouts and the hoodlums who stole my bicycle as easily as if it were a loaf of bread! Ah, children, God grant us a drop or two to warm our hearts, and not just our hearts, let us forget the troubles of the day, the politicians can piss one another off, we've got something to celebrate even if it's the last thing we ever do! Béla, who excuses himself after a few glasses, says, tomorrow I've still got work to do.

At moments like these, when Uncle Piri's and Father's eyes reflect the number of glasses they've downed, when the toasts, the pronouncements, the curses accompanied with waving arms and the lowering clouds of smoke coalesce into an evermore compact unity, when the mood is an emotional roller-coaster rising to heights of tenderness (arms and hands locked together, mouths rushing to meet) and plunging to the depths of voluptuous anger (a fist punishes the table), at such moments I wish night and day were one, so that this night won't be dispersed by the coming morning—and so that we can get even more drunk on the grown-ups' increasingly feverish mood, Nomi and I sneak out to the porch and huddle outside the window covered with green mosquito netting, we listen, amazed at our parents' transformation through our secret language in which our parents now express themselves fluently, talking faster and faster, using words we've never heard cross their lips before, and if happiness has a name, then it must also have a face, a face telling stories in a smooth, easy sing-song.

You certainly are spoilt over there in the West, when your parents complain that everything is so expensive, I call that a high-class problem, Béla says, sticking a toothpick in the corner of his mouth, when he sees Nomi and me the next day sitting on the covered porch in the midday heat because our parents are sleeping, there's no shade in the courtyard, the dogs have retreated into their kennels and the water in the bowls has evaporated, you've got to have something to start with before you can call it expensive! and Béla pushes the soda siphon with his thumb and water shoots into the glass, the stream is so strong it splatters the tablecloth, Nomi and I, all we can do is admire Béla, as if that were our reason for being, we hang on Béla's lips because there is something fearless and unsettling about him (his haircut reminds me of

Limahl, the British pop singer from the 1980s, whom Béla would certainly call a fairy if he knew who Limahl was).

What's more, you've always got the feeling you can live in security, Béla says, no one here could ever come to such a false conclusion, he puts on his earphones and pushes 'play', but the music doesn't seem to have any effect on him, he doesn't sway his body or tap his feet and instead of singing along he taps his pack of cigarettes and sticks a multifilter between his teeth. His eyes drift away from us, you girls! and up to the sky as he lights his cigarette, then casually slips the headphones down around his neck, those are mine, he says, pointing his cigarette at the cloudless sky, the walkman plays a song by someone who doesn't impress Béla, look at that, he says and we try to follow his gaze, his piercing blue eyes finally fix on the object of his fascination, he raises his surprisingly small hand and points the smouldering tip of his cigarette at a flock of birds, they're pretty but slow, Béla says, soon you'll see the real ones, and of course we know which are the real ones, they're his pigeons, the ones that have won almost every race for years now, you know what, people have come to see me from Germany and England, from the *United Kingdom*! I don't want anything from them but they want something from me, well, what do you think of that?

And because Nomi and I don't answer, don't know what to say, Béla says in English: *Business is international*—What? *Business is international*, real business knows no boundaries, remember that, if you really know what you're doing, then no one cares if your little house is in the East or in the West, our fathers are always swearing about the politicians, but what's the point? It's all bullshit, you'll see, we're young, we'll live to see it, freedom! and Béla props his elbow on his left hand, blows smoke rings into the air through his taut lips, and the next time you come, a whole lot of foreign business will have investments here and they couldn't care less about politicians, the *businessmen* will discover that we've got things worth having, you'll see!

Aunt Icu wraps up a few meatballs left over from yesterday, puts them in a basket, adds a slice of ham, a loaf of bread, at least a dozen potatoes, yellow and green peppers, what do you think, should I pack up some of the tart, too? she asks in a whisper and my mother answers, a little something sweet never hurts, does it? Aunt Icu laughs, pats her around belly, I'm carrying enough as it is! cuts a large slice, puts it in a plastic dish and covers it with a soup plate, she takes one more look around her pantry, asks, what else could I bring? takes the smaller braid of garlic from the nail, stows in the basket, so! and now some coffee, sugar and a little packet of paprika, now we can go.

　　Aunt Icu, Mother, Nomi and I have a plan while the men 'sleep it off upstairs' as Aunt Icu and Uncle Piri say, even though their house, like all the other houses in the neighbourhood, is only one storey (sometimes I really can picture them climbing the stairs arm in arm to flop down in the rooms on the second floor and I can probably picture them so clearly because I've heard Uncle Piri rhapsodize countless times about how he will renovate the house one day, you won't believe what all I'll do!). So the men are snoring in the back rooms where the blinds are never raised during the day in summer in order to keep the rooms nice and cool, and if someone does raise the blinds, like Aunt Icu when she wants to annoy someone who has a pounding head, her Piri, who guzzles the drink as if his feet were always dying of thirst, and when her husband shields his eyes with his hand leaving his mouth free to spew obscenities all the more vociferously, then Aunt Icu serenely says, every once in a while my little plants need a bit of light and besides, you promised to repair the wire mesh, the chickens are pecking away at my flowers! Yeah, yeah, and Uncle Piri pulls the blanket over his head and the narrow feet that appear don't give any sign that the person lying there downed more than a few too many.

It's just before six o'clock, we're standing in the summer kitchen drinking coffee when Aunt Icu points at the flies and says, today will be boiling hot, because the flies are already zig-zagging in a mad dance this early in the morning, and although I'm still groggy with sleep, I look at my beautiful plump aunt in her floridly patterned dress, as if the 1970s were still in full bloom, and I'm impressed that she can see the flies I merely find annoying within a much larger and, to me, incomprehensible context. Come, we need to get going so that we make it back here in time, and Aunt Icu grabs her basket which Mother immediately takes from her, I'm younger! and Nomi and I shoulder the bags we filled with clothes yesterday and before we open the gate, Aunt Icu makes a commanding gesture at the dogs so they don't dare bark and jump at the kennel fence but instead creep into their huts, their tails between their legs.

Barely out of the house, Mother and Aunt Icu, arm in arm, start conferring in low voices as if they'd been waiting for this moment for days and Nomi and I trot along behind them, trying to catch threads of their conversation, Nomi, who now seems awake, asks, can't you talk a bit louder? No, Aunt Icu answers without turning her head, you don't need to know everything and you'll learn what's most important soon enough anyway! Nomi is annoyed, whispers that their behinds are swaying so exactly in tandem, you'd think they were Siamese twins, and Nomi's laughter is infectious, but soon both women stop short and Mother calls over her shoulder in an irritated voice, you're too old to giggle like little girls! But too young to be told everything, I think, and Nomi and I imitate Mother's and Aunt Icu's walk, make faces and secret gestures at each other, in short, we behave exactly like silly girls because we really do want to know more about our cousin Csilla, whom Mother and Aunt Icu have definitely been discussing.

What, our Csilla? Mother had said into the telephone a few months before when Aunt Icu called from the post office, completely hysterical because Csilla had run off with some guy, she didn't take anything with her, not even a change of clothes, and no one knew where she was. Uncle Piri, who took it hard, stayed sober for days and didn't say a word, then on the evening of St Joseph's Day he sat down at the kitchen table, sliced off chunks of bread and ham in turn with his penknife, eating his way through half a loaf of bread and a big piece of ham, and after he had finished eating and drunk a glass of seltzer he announced that if Csilla ever showed her face here again in his house, he would wring her neck with his own hands, faster than he would any stupid goose. Through all sorts of back channels, Aunt Icu found out where Csilla was hiding, went to see her, begged her to come home, to ask her father's forgiveness, then everything would be all right. But she's as stubborn as a mule, Aunt Icu said, and Mother couldn't hang up even though all Aunt Icu could do was weep, Mother had to promise her that she'd talk to Csilla the next time we came, and that we would come soon, Csilla will listen to you, Rosza, that much is certain!

Csilla runs off with her lover. And? what's so bad about that? it's not the first time that's happened in the family, you told us that story not so long ago, Nomi and I answered in chorus while Mother gazed at the telephone, lost in thought, and pressed her hands onto the table as if she wanted to reassure herself that what was there, under her hands, really was a table, in the garden the forsythia was in full bloom, Mother turned her head towards the window and the yellow rain, as

112

Nomi and I call the flowers in Hungarian, and she said softly, you have no idea, not the slightest idea and I hope you never do, but how can I explain to you what it means when a father says something like that, that he's going to wring her neck, his own daughter! when he threatens her with the worst, that's something you can't understand. Nomi and I were used to having Father checkmate us with bits and pieces from his life story, but Mother often defended us, leave them alone, you too want them to have a better life than ours, and now Mother was letting us know for the first time that we didn't have a clue about certain things that went on in our native country.

We have to ask if we don't understand, Nomi said, or tell us if there's something else we can do? I looked at Nomi, both proud of her and surprised that she could come up with such a good answer. Mother's response was very odd, she said, fine, I'll tell you a story, but I'm talking to the plants outside. And because Mother was talking to the plants instead of us, she didn't look at us even once while she was telling her story. And as you know, plants never ask any questions, Mother added before telling the story that from then on was for us her 'yellow rain story' and we thought of it whenever we wanted to understand that everyone has a secret, even our mother, whom we had always believed we knew inside and out.

I don't remember how long we walked, probably an hour, and Nomi and I stopped giggling, became more and more quiet, because the neighbourhood wasn't familiar, the houses had no plaster or were run-down (I remember one roof in particular that looked like it had been pushed in by a giant's hand), as we walk, we have to watch our every step, the bumpy pavement ends in a dirt path, Nomi points to the drainage ditch filled with household waste and a dead cat, even the poppies and wildflowers look dirty, why is that? Nomi asks me, but I don't know. I have the feeling that we're about to see something we won't forget any time soon.

Houses made from boards, sheets of corrugated metal, car fenders, scraps of cloth, bits and pieces of just about anything, a few open fires and mud everywhere even though it hadn't rained for days, it smells of manure and smoke and burnt plastic and chicken droppings and pig shit. This is where my Csilla lives now, Aunt Icu says and points to a house with a dark red bicycle frame propped up next to the front door, should I be ashamed? Aunt Icu asks Mother and calls loudly, Csilla, Csilla, your aunt is here, your cousins too, come! And I don't want to look around, I don't want to see too much, I'd like to look somewhere, anywhere, up at the sky perhaps, where I wouldn't have to look at the filthy, half-naked children I'd only ever seen from a distance, a few women watch us with reddened eyes, stealing our clothes and smooth skin with their hungry looks; yes, here it looks exactly like the dump where the gypsies live outside of the little town, and because I already know a few scraps of English, the word *slum* comes to mind and the film our history teacher showed us before summer vacation about the outskirts of Sào Paolo, but this isn't Sào Paolo, my cousin Csilla, still looking half-asleep, hugs us and immediately lights a cigarette stuck in one of the gaps between her teeth. I knew you would visit me, she says and starts to cry, she gets all choked up, kisses Mother's hands, Csilla's hair looks singed, Nomi, Ildi, Csilla says, this is how it is when you fall madly in love with a man, but you can't even meet my Csaba, he left early this morning, Csilla says still weeping. It's fine, Aunt Icu says, make us some coffee, your Aunt Rózsa wants to talk to you.

Csilla, who then invites us into her house, I don't have any coffee, she says and sniffles to stop her nose from running, Aunt Icu puts the coffee on the table without a word, Csilla takes the coffee and the basket of food also without a word, sit down, she says, but where? Our cousin, who goes to borrow two chairs from the neighbour, how can she live here? Nomi whispers to me, but Aunt Icu has very sharp hearing, why don't you ask her? she says, takes a deep breath and wipes the table with a rag. It's hard to describe how it looks inside, hard because I can't easily identify the things I see as a wardrobe or a bed or a washbasin, everywhere tin cans hang from the ceiling on strings, that looks funny, I say, it leaks, Aunt Icu explains, looking for the coffeepot, there, Csilla says when she returns with two chairs, pointing at a wooden crate filled with dishes, a few glasses, cups, plates. Have a seat, Csilla says, sit down so I can admire you, and our cousin kisses Mother's hands again, my beloved Aunt

Rósza, you look younger and more beautiful every time I see you! What are you doing here, Csilla my dear? Mother asks while Aunt Icu puts the water on to boil and measures out the sugar, Nomi, whose eyes are glued to what passes for a window, namely a hole that is covered according to the season with either thick plastic sheeting or a thinner cloth of fabric patches sewn together, and a black-and-white photograph is pinned onto the wall next to the window, a picture of Aunt Icu, Uncle Piri, Béla and Csilla, which I'd like to take with me, I'd like to have the picture with me, always, wherever I go, I don't know why, maybe because I have the feeling the picture has captured a tiny bit of happiness, a moment when anything seemed possible—Csilla wearing a short, polka-dotted summer dress and a little hat, Csilla, who is the centre of the picture, embraced by Uncle Piri, Aunt Icu and Béla.

Mother, Aunt Rósza, who now tells Csilla the same story she recounted not to us but to the plants in her garden after Aunt Icu called her a few weeks ago.

I look out past the dangling plastic sheeting, past the ragged cloth out into the distance and listen, I listen to Mother's soft, gentle voice as she tells the story of a young woman who wants to be a teacher but can't because there's no money at home and anyway her father doesn't see any point in educating girls! besides she already has all the admirers a young woman could want, but she had sworn to herself that she would at least complete an apprenticeship if she

116

couldn't become a teacher and in the store where she's doing her apprenticeship, she meets a man who is different from all the rest (there's always one who's different, Mother said and laughed). Imre Tóth is his name and if you want to know why the young woman falls in love with him, there's only one answer—his sense of humour, which made him irresistible, you can't even imagine. Imre is called up for two years of military service and sent to Croatia, the young woman has a few days holiday for Pentecost, she takes the bus to Croatia and her father is outraged, of course she hadn't told him she's going to see her lover, her father rants and raves because she wants to travel so far, alone, he probably sensed what was going on because the young woman's face looks completely different, she can't hide it. Her mother takes the young woman's side, let her go, if you try to stop her, you'll lose her for ever. The young woman has a window seat and in the bus she feels free for the first time in her life. If my father beats me black and blue, I won't regret a thing, she thinks without any trace of fear, she has to change buses five times and every single second she thinks of her Imre, of the hours she would finally be able to spend with him alone. And Imre meets her at the bus station with a few flowers in his hand and the next three days are such that the young woman never wanted to tell anyone about them. She returns home with Imre's promise that they'll get married as soon as his military service is done, I'll be married and he won't be anything like my father, the young woman thinks, he won't beat me, he won't insult me, he'll be good to me every day. Her mother dies that same year, which is hard for her since she loved everything about her mother, even her bad moods, today I'm in a mood fit for an old dog, her mother would say and wrinkle her nose, or she'd say, today you'll have to manage without me (Aunt Icu places the coffee cups on the table and lays her hand on Mother's arm), there's a lot more to tell about the young woman's mother, she has 'my mother, beloved above all else' engraved on the tombstone, her father shakes with rage because it cost a lot of money, the headstone, the engraving, but she paid for it with her own money, and I'm only telling you this, Mother says, the young woman feels that with her mother's death she has also lost a protective shield. A few days after her mother's burial, she realizes she's pregnant. She tells her father about Imre but not about her condition, she wants to test him, to see how he reacts before telling him the whole truth. You're just a common whore is what her father says. A few weeks later he lets loose on her with a bronze pestle after an argument. After her mother's death she had cooked and cleaned for her father and taken care of the livestock and she'd asked him for some money to buy wood for the autumn and winter, Mother took a sip of coffee before continuing with her story, what? you want money, her father swears and goes after her with the pestle, she defends herself, evades him. A few days later, the young woman loses her baby. She can't confide in her father, he has called her a whore almost every day since their argument. She waits for the day when Imre will return from the military. Imre doesn't come back. Only much later does she learn that her father had gone to find Imre and had told him that his daughter had taken up with someone else, and no matter how much it pained him as a father, he had to tell Imre the truth, man to man. And Imre? The young woman cannot believe that he didn't ask her himself, he left her, slandered by her father, in the lurch.

If you do something against your father's will, you have the whole world against you, Mother says, you have to reconcile with him, at least give him the feeling that you're not making decisions without consulting him. And everything you do will stick to you, do you understand? (But Uncle Piri's completely different, he's not at all like the father in your story; Mother ignores Nomi's objection), Csilla answers that she respects Mother's story and thanks her for coming to open her eyes, but she doesn't mind living here and recently, when she was asleep, an angel came to her and told her it was her destiny to live in poverty with her Csaba, poverty, after all, is nothing to be ashamed of, and the angel assured her he was an angel even though he couldn't fly since one of his wings was broken, and that had to be a sign—Aunt Icu stands up suddenly, brushes her dress with her fingers as if something had spilt over her, Csilla, you're not going to talk to me about angels! Tell your angel he should explain the difference between poverty and squalor. You know that my door is always open for you, Aunt Icu says, but don't come to me with angels! and she turns on her heel without another word. Mother puts two more packs of cigarettes on the table, Nomi and I give Csilla a quick hug as if she has some contagious disease, come back, Mother says, please!

Uncle Piri, who doesn't believe us, that we were at the market according to Aunt Icu's elaborate account, not even when we pile honeydew melons, yellow peaches, Turkish honey and a bowl of raspberries on the table (distracting men is a skill you have to cultivate, Aunt Icu says), if you've brought so many sweet things, it means you've got something to hide, Uncle Piri says while Aunt Icu brews him a strong coffee (Father is still asleep 'upstairs'), ah yes, you're my clairvoyant, Aunt Icu says, it's a wonder to me you can't make any money with your gift.

Uncle Piri puts a second cushion on his chair, asks us to sit down and folds his hands together, waiting silently for Aunt Icu to pour his coffee and when his coffee is before him, steaming, and we're all seated around the table, Uncle Piri juts out his chin, rubs a hand over his stubble and says, in the last war I was shot through the shoulder, the bullet went in one side and came out the other; our handsome, loveable uncle unbuttons his shirt to show us the spot, his scar, since then my left arm is always a little bit colder than my right, he says and sips his coffee, since then I can feel it, right here on this spot, you see? here! whatever anyone is trying to hide from me, and Uncle Piri grabs his hat, crumples it and throws it brusquely onto the table like someone playing a trump card, his short salt-and-pepper hair sticks straight up and emphasizes his words, Uncle Piri, who forgets himself, who forgets that we're there—and the coarse talk we associate with him always was a little comical, he won't have any more headaches, Uncle Piri would say when someone died, Nomi and I had laughed when our Uncle Piri said that some stupid person had nothing but dandruff inside his skull—but now we're sitting very quietly around the table, Nomi has kept her eyes lowered for a while now and traces the delicate pattern on the tablecloth with her finger, I'm staring at the plastic fruit piled in a basket next to the enormous radio and I want to wipe this day from my memory before it's even finished, as Uncle Piri calls up every indecency he can think of to execrate his daughter who has taken up with a guy who has no job and therefore no house and no bread on the table, all he's got is a cock and it probably isn't any bigger than a mole's dick! A mole? Aunt Icu asks, but not in her usual witty, flippant way, yes, goddamn it, a mole or a hedgehog if you prefer! And it won't be long before men like Csilla's baboon disappear from the picture, everyone says there'll be war soon and they'll be the first ones drafted into the Yugoslav People's Army, the army'll be happy to have a half-gypsy like him, so let him fight and bite the dust for the Serbs! Aunt Icu, who reaches for the fly-swatter, smacks it down next to Uncle Piri's hand, too bad, Aunt Icu calls out, I missed, there was no fly there, Uncle Piri swears, but your nasty words, can't you see them there on my innocent table? Yoouuuuu, Uncle Piri shouts so loud he makes the table vibrate, you want to tell me that you love your daughter when you let her run off with a good-for-nothing and then feed them both?

And what kind of love is it when you wish death on your daughter's lover?

She could have had a solid man, Uncle Piri says, his gaze lost somewhere between the sink and the Advent calendar, then he grabs his hat and stands up, now she's got one they'll use as cannon fodder, that's the way it is, and Uncle Piri forgets to button up his shirt but puts his hat, his *mici*, on his head, brusquely draws aside the curtain that separates the kitchen from the covered verandah, opens the door to the courtyard, but Csilla, to me Csilla's already dead, he shouts to the dogs, to us, you hear me, you should all know! and to the neighbours he shouts, I once had a daughter . . . Aunt Icu, who makes the sign of the cross, looks at him, and you, she says, you were considered cannon fodder in the last war too, as a Hungarian in the partisans, you weren't even given weapons in your Petöfi regiment, you and your shoulder forgot that part a long time ago, my Piri, but I haven't.

And that night, after all the others had fallen asleep, Nomi says, even the bed has changed—or the night, I answer, and neither of us falls asleep before dawn.

122

WORLDS

We sit in the smoking compartment, we sit down, both of us exhausted from the long Saturday, always a busy day at the Mondial (not as busy as before, under the Tanners, but still) and our train pulls out, heading towards the city, I'm not at all in the mood, I say, why don't we get out at the next stop and go down to the lake? Come on, Nomi says, you know how it is, when you first sit down, you notice how tired you are but that passes quickly, it doesn't last more than half hour at the most. Besides, it's a huge concert, there are bands playing all night, Ildi, we can't miss it, and Mark, he'll be there too, don't you think? Possibly, and I take a can out of my bag, you want one too?

Nomi and I drink beer, looking at our reflections in the train window, it's us even though we look completely different than we usually do in the Mondial, we look like men, like slobs, Father says, getting worked up and launching into one of his endless harangues about his daughters who have the wrong friends, wrong friends with wrong ideas! I'm telling you, if you ever show up in the Mondial looking like that . . . and Mother doesn't say a word when she see us dressed like this, at the most she shakes her head, where we're going, it doesn't matter what you wear, we say, and sometimes we believe what we say and sometimes we know we're lying, when we stand in front of the mirror to see if our dark blue construction-worker pants look as if we just threw them on— so where are you going? Father asks. To a place without laws, where everything is permitted as long as it doesn't hurt anyone, Nomi says or I say, our oversized sweatshirts making us look sexless. In any case, you have no business coming here, we don't actually say it, but almost, when Father tells us he's going to pick us up in the car, he wants to take a look, he'd like to know what kind of place it is—without any laws? don't make me laugh, only war has no laws, and you have no idea what war is like, not the slightest, and, why shouldn't I come get you, are you ashamed of me?

Father didn't ask any questions today, Nomi says, Mother must have lectured him, yesterday I heard her tell him that if he kept at us like that, we'd probably move out soon, I think that really scares him, Nomi says. You think so? Yes, I'm positive.

What was the matter yesterday? Nomi asks, knocking on the reflection of my head in the window, all of a sudden you looked completely different, I don't know Ildi, sometimes I worry about my big sister, and I tap the tip of Nomi's nose in the reflection with my index finger, worry, but why? I feel so unreal sometimes, especially when I'm waiting tables, maybe even fake, then I break into a sweat, everything starts spinning. . . Fake, Nomi asks, I don't get it, in a regular old business, you're neither fake nor real, and Nomi takes a gulp from the can, the customers want something from us and we want something from them, and what's appealing about it is that everything in those surroundings is a bit like fool's gold. Fool's gold, I like that, I answer, but I still think you have to have an authentic core no matter what kind of work you're doing . . . My core is nobody's business in the Mondial, Nomi interrupts, especially not my authentic core Ildi, don't get stuck on things you can't change, putting her arms around me, Nomi says, let's talk about something else, our future, for example, about our future? yes, you know what we'll do when we're old? and Nomi brushes my forehead with the tip of her nose, we'll live together like Mrs Köchli and Mrs Frueler, we'll potter through the afternoons, eat magnificent pastries, we'll read out loud to each other, that is, you'll read and I'll listen. I can't think of anything nicer, I answer.

Wohlgroth is the name of 'our' place, an abandoned factory now occupied by squatters. We head towards the buildings that have towering piles of rubbish bags and overflowing containers plastered with graffiti, bicycles lying on the ground to the left and right. Things have already started, Nomi says. The outside walls have been painted, some say smeared, splashes of colour, lines and figures, tags and messages, and Nomi and I, we hold hands as if we were a couple, people know us, hello you two, Suhansky calls, his eyes already unfocused, what's up, what's down? and you? and a bonfire has been lit in the courtyard, dogs run this way and that around the fire, howling, what's going on here? oh, OK, a pagan spring pyre, and Nomi and I stand for a moment watching the dogs as they become even more frenzied, someone throws another half a chair onto the fire, broken toys, all kinds of refuse, newspapers, more news-papers, a whole pile of them, goddamn liars, those hack journalists! Suhansky yells, shut your trap, someone yells back, trying to calm down his dog. Come on, let's go upstairs, Nomi says, yes, we take the stairs up to our favourite cafe, with a view of the city and the train tracks, where I like to sit and watch the trains pull in and out, where I drank chai tea for the first time in my life, nothing crazy, just spiced tea with milk and honey, but it made me feel bold, important. People know us, they know we're from Yugoslavia, which for them might as well be Moscow—and Nomi and I, we smoke, point out what's changed since our last visit, over the bar a plastic Madonna glitters pink, yellow, light blue and green, a mural spray-painted on the wall keeps growing, countless figures intertwined with one another, humans mutating into animals, look at that monster there, Nomi says and points to a humanoid monstrosity, with a swollen head and a perfectly straight parting in his hair, stuffing coins and bills down his throat, his circulatory system sure is in great shape, I say and we laugh because the red veins are so well drawn with spray paint that you can practically see the blood pulsing in his neck and we imagine how our customers would react if this mural were the first thing they saw when the opened the Mondial's door. It would cover the entire back wall and contrast sharply with the mustard-yellow linen tablecloths, the wall clock, vases and the light-coloured curtains. Excuse me, Miss, did you paint this? is this picture some kind of symbol?

Mark and Dave, who sit down next to us, say, we want to have fun too. Fine, Nomi answers, laughing, then tells us a joke! Where have you two been hiding all week? Mark asks, saying hello first to me then to Nomi. Is that how the joke starts? I ask, and Dave gives Nomi a kiss, a rather long one, it seems to me, you want a kiss too? Mark asks, no, but you could tell me what's the name of the band playing on the speakers. Guts Pie Earshot, Mark says, that's some name and some voice, I say, they're playing today too, and with the tip of his tongue Mark draws a line along his cigarette, opens the paper, crushes the tobacco between his thumb and fore-finger, they're from Germany, Mark says, not looking up while mixing grass into the tobacco, they're really political, they only play in occupied buildings, in political actions, effective, I say. Nomi and Dave are still kissing, Mark hands me the joint, even though I don't want to, I take a drag, a long drag, would you order me another chai? I ask. The guy who's half asleep behind the counter is getting on my nerves, I look at Mark's low-cut jeans, his hoodie sweatshirt that leaves a band of skin uncovered, a chai with rum, I call after Mark, of course! (And for a moment, I'm alone, I see the train tracks, how they intersect, I, who love watching trav-ellers pass by for a few seconds at night, to follow the happi-ness of a relaxed face heading towards some hope, I could sit here for hours and travel all over the world, to places I've never been, to Barcelona on a Talgo train then on to Madrid and Lisbon, I'm no traveller, but someone who leaves without knowing if I'll ever return, and each time before I left, I carefully cleaned my room, washed all the clothes I wasn't taking with me, folded them neatly or hung them in the closet, I covered my mirror so it wouldn't see the room without me, my empty writing desk, alphabetized bookshelves and freshly made bed, I always prepared for a departure with no return on our trips to the Vojvodina, and for a long time that was the only direction in which I travelled.)

I haven't seen you in any lectures lately, Mark says as he sets the chai on the table, we're very busy at the moment, Nomi answers for me, with what? Dave wants to know, we help our parents, I tell him, Mark passes the joint again and asks, your parents? Yes, imagine, we work on the Zürich Gold Coast, in a cafe, it looks a bit different there than it does here, and Nomi and I, we laugh, and Mark says, we're out with two Gold Coast Barbies, who'd have thought, and he laughs too. What are you laughing at? I ask and Nomi, taking a few drags on the joint, says, we should all love one another, and Dave says, we could come by, I'd like to see you two zipping around your Gold Coast cafe, and taking a sip of chai that tastes only of rum, I say, I don't think that's a good idea. Why not? they can come see us, Nomi says. So this cafe belongs to your old man and your old lady? What's the band's name again, what kind of Earshot? I ask and take a drag on the joint, change of topic, you mean, Mark says and I look at him, his small, white face, his long teeth, his thick, rumpled hair, I don't like the expression, 'old man' and 'old lady', I counter, what do your parents do? *So what*? Mark says in English, what have they got to do with me, unlike you two, my parents don't give me any cash. And where'd you get your clothes? I ask (soon it will work out, the pot will kick in, I think, soon I'll see animal heads instead of faces, Mark will turn into a cat and I'll turn into a mouse, or the other way around), night-shift at the post office, Mark says and he looks good when he says it, for how long now, three or four months? I ask. Ildi, come on, kiss me, you're a bitch when you start to think, and everyone laughs, I laugh too and notice Benno standing in front of me, Benno, who's easily overlooked, always in his jeans jacket, his shoulders hunched, haven't seen you in ages! Benno, who sits down with us, never says hello but, what do you all think of the siege of Sarajevo? do you know they're digging a tunnel? they've been working at it day and night for a few weeks, the city needs this tunnel or it's all over, says Benno, who's always on top of what's going on in the war and he really does know things about which we don't have a clue. Can we have a quick drink first? Dave says, or we'll die of thirst! Drugs make you stupid, you know that, yes, Benno, we know, you've already told us, but what about the tunnel? It's not in the media yet, Benno says, unruffled, the tunnel is supposed to pass under the Sarajevo airport, flight traffic is blocked anyway, nothing's going in or out, and you can't cross the runways because of the Serbian snipers, you see? And we pass the joint around again, Benno waves it off and says, we have to consider, fundamentally, what it means when an entire city is under siege, here we're playing for a bit of free space, in Sarajevo, they're fighting just to survive, relax, Dave says, it's Saturday night or are you planning on signing up as a volunteer? Exactly, Benno says, you're either a caveman or you're civilized, we've become so stupid, we even believe that, so don't listen if you're not interested, in any case, I'm mostly talking to the sisters, you two, we're still looking for people to work in our media group, we're gathering uncensored information, money too, so we can support the last independent newspaper in Sarajevo and we really could use you, you speak Serbo-Croatian, that would help, Benno says and looks at us inquiringly. We can't speak a word, I say. I thought you were from Serbia. Yeah, we are, but from a town where most people speak Hungarian and we've been to school here or we'd have been taught Serbian, Nomi says. I see, you're from the Vojvodina, too bad, well, you could still come by, we always meet on Tuesday evenings. Where? Up here! Benno, shrugs and is gone.

With all that intensity, he's got to be compensating for something, Mark says (why don't I contradict him? I'll only come if you ban dogs from your media work group, I think and picture a handful of freaks with their dogs sitting in a circle, discussing the war, their dogs' tails waving like flags), ciao Benno, I call after him and look out the window again

130

but now the trains aren't moving, we are, someone has loaded us onto a giant forklift that is carrying us faster and faster towards the dustcart, who's driving? I ask and say, Mark, watch out, you're losing all your teeth, oh, and Mark laughs, Nomi laughs, Dave laughs, I laugh, you'll have a mouth but no teeth, and I see the Madonna's heart blinking, growing larger and getting closer, we're driving to get to the heart, I say, and Mark snorts, Ildi, you kill me, you're so funny, hey you guys, stop laughing for no reason, Dave says and wipes the tears from his eyes, I am, I'm, I'm, I—you, come on, let's switch, you kiss Nomi and I'll kiss Ildi, the fork-lift has a propeller that's blowing cold air in our faces, Dave? His large face right in front of mine looks like a sad clown's face, get lost Dave, the pile of refuse gets bigger, I have to get ready for what's coming, Nomi, Nomi, where are you? and I apparently burst into tears, hey Ildi, everything's OK, I'm here, right next to you, and I, I say, why are my hands so cold? do you know why we're here? what we're looking for? We're having fun, that wasn't Nomi, it was probably Dave, Dave, why are you always in front of my face, hold on Dave, the speed, can't you feel it, Dave says, Mark claims you kiss like a goddess, that's what I want now, close your eyes—go away—Nomi where are you? let's go, down to the basement, the concert has started, Mark, who holds me up because I have no more legs, no legs? you're tripping, Mark says, yes, I'm legless, let's go, come on, forget your legs, Mark calls— but what are the police doing here? Mark, why are we surrounded and what does it have to do with my legs? Ildi, those aren't cops, there are only people like you and me, Ildi, watch the steps! Nomi, where is she? downstairs in the basement, Mark answers, come on, let's go! the forklift, I say, why are you telling me those aren't policemen, there are dogs everywhere, can't you see them? Mark grabs me and carries me down the stairs, have you got married? Eyes, mouths, filled with blood, why are they all wounded? and Benno flies over us, Sarajevo, he yells, do you understand? Sarajevo! And I bury my head against Mark's arm, I don't want to see the dogs any more, no bloody mouths, and my heart is beating where my legs used to be, can someone's heart beat where their legs should be? Mark tries to throw me into a hole, I scream at him, defend myself with hands and feet, so he won't throw me, it's a sofa Mark says, damn, Ildi, it's just a sofa, I can't carry you any more! And if you throw me into the hole, I'll land in the rubbish bin, I knew it, Mark, I could see it in your eyes! I tear myself free and throw myself onto the ground, Mark why are you trampling me to death with your screaming? It's not me, the band is screaming, Mark says, what? what band? why can't I lie here on the floor, why is the floor rushing into me? you're just feeling the vibrations, Mark says, listen to me, I'm going to get you a bottle of water, you have to drink it, you're having a pretty bad trip, you've got to get it out of your system.

At some point we ended up in the toilet, Nomi pouring water on my head, talking to me, stroking my cheeks, my head, hello, can you focus? focus, Nomi says that rum and grass don't mix, complete beginner, I say and lift my head, I look at myself in the mirror, Nomi, who presses her head against mine, we look alike, she says, our lips, eyes, skin tone, just not our hair colour. Do you remember how Mamika said that every person has more than two faces? How could I forget, Nomi answers.

I'd like to have only one face, I say.

Nomi, who pauses for a long time, looks at me, then says, every person has several faces, you need more than one to survive.

I can't work in the Mondial any more and I can't come here any more, it's—

Ildi, you're in a really bad way today, come on, no big decisions now, let's get cleaned up, put on some make-up, and go dance, my beloved sister, don't be such a drag.

So Nomi and I, we danced with Dave and Mark, we were intertwined, kissed each others' necks, and I let myself go, my mouth planted on Mark's shoulder like a leech, my eyelids heavy with exhaustion and relief, your skin is as soft as snow, Mark whispered in my ear (and as cold?), maybe you can make a decision one day, I thought, you can decide to change, to be different and then, the next day you realize it's a piece of cake, and my shoulder was wet with Mark's kisses, his fingers feeling my breasts to the beat of the music, Mark and I, we're dancing around the chairs in the Mondial, colours are dripping from the pictures, it looks nice here, I whispered in Mark's ear, the yellow, the red, the blue, the drops of colour on the walls, on the upholstered chairs, and the pattern on the carpet shivered, everything trembled lightly, two vases fell in slow motion, the shards are pretty, I said to Mark, the blurred landscape paintings, and we spun around, wrapped tightly in each others' arms, until Nomi called us out of our waking dream, the basement was almost empty, the music now coming only very softly from the speakers.

Mark and Dave, who accompanied us to the train station, waited for the first train, and we hugged, Nomi Dave, me Mark, when will we get together again? Soon, and I remember that the morning seemed cold and I saw myself standing near the tracks with tangled hair, baggy trousers, my T-shirt all sweaty, I saw the tips of my shoes touching Mark's, are you coming to class next week? No, I answered, I don't have any time, and I heard my voice, looked at the man in the newspaper kiosk staring at us with his mouth open, I saw him, me, us, the pigeons on the train tracks, heads bobbing, pecking hastily at the asphalt, the day, already lighter, tinting the sky with red, and I saw us from the kiosk, as if I were standing behind the newspapers, magazines, packs of chewing gum and chocolate bars—I saw us larger than life, and myself like a wildly fluttering pigeon, startled by human steps.

In the summer of 1987, our parents sat in the living room after work, bent over the book on civic education some official had given them, and Nomi and I tested our parents on the Swiss Federal Council, the Parliament, direct democracy, the founding of the Swiss state, Swiss history, our ham sandwiches left grease spots on the pages, it was a set ritual—we buttered pieces of bread, covered them with slices of ham, carried the tray of sandwiches and seltzer water into the living room. Nomi and I didn't have to take the Naturalization examination because we were still minors, *furtheralism*, Father said, and we laughed, our mouths full, what is it you want to further? Father pronounced 'democracy' as if it were the name of a beautiful, elegant woman rather than a system of government, when something is so important, it should sound elegant and beautiful. Nomi and I asked them questions we couldn't even answer, 'half-cantons', what can that be, you've either got cantons or you don't, and we didn't only laugh, we racked our brains because the language kept getting in the way. Names like General Guisan, how can you remember that? Rhaeto-Romanic, not *retromanic*! Nomi, who says, I'm happy I don't have to take the exam. And one rainy day we wished our parents good luck. We weren't surprised when they came home muted, we didn't pass, Mother said, we have to take it again, a few of the questions they didn't understand at all, how can you give an answer if you don't get the question? said Mother, who had explained a particularly complicated strudel recipe in great detail to the examining board because she didn't know that *sudel* is a Swiss word for scrap of paper and the officials had told her she was allowed to take notes on a *sudel* if she found that helpful.

And it's odd that, on this particular evening, we're playing monopoly, I have no idea if any of us ever enjoyed the game, I doubt it, in any case, the board is open on the table, we roll the dice, buy properties, Father goes to jail a few times in a row, when we played a game together, it was usually cards, most often gin rummy, and Mother frequently won and her luck at cards made Father see not only red but the entire colour spectrum, however, on this evening it's not about winning or losing, but about washing the salt from still very raw wounds in the privacy of our own home. Father's condescending jokes about the *cheese-heads*, the Swiss heart specialists in the middle of nowhere in the Alps, their anaemic white cheese has no flavour whatsoever, Father says, it's only good for some hahahaha-housewife to smear on as a facial mask, he says, rolls a six (and buys a house in Freiburg, that's definitely a bad investment, Nomi says), and you know what, now I'm talking to you as a butcher, you know why the Swiss have to chop everything up beyond recognition? For the Swiss, there's nothing worse than a glob of fat, as soon as they see one, they immediately picture a finger pointing at them, think of your *chlesteral*, yes, they do, and the housewives who, at eleven o'clock in the morning, are still sitting around in cafes with their new hairdos, gabbing about the new course they're going to take or where they're going for their next ski vacation (Mother, who has been buying up the waterworks, the electric company and the railroads, would surely also like to sit in a cafe drinking coffee in the morning some time), should we keep playing? I ask, why not, we just started and do you know what all the Swiss put in *cervelat*, their national sausage? they take lots of frozen meat and rind, lots of cheap spices, then chop it all very fine and mash it together, because the Swiss don't want to know they eat animals, so they end up with a light-brown sausage-like thing, a *Wurschtli*, with no trace of truth left (Father buys hotels on his Freiburg and La Chaux properties, those never pay, Nomi says, we'll see, Father answers), but who here wants to hear that? Father asks us, and why doesn't anyone ever invite us over, or if they do, then just for little cocktail sausages and potato salad? Why do their dogs always come first? (Nomi and I, we laugh as Father gives an imaginary dog a swift kick.) Here you can go to pot and they'll still organize a proper burial for you (in the Vojvodina, Father likes to go on and on about how the Swiss keep everything in order, you know where the street ends and the pavement begins, and you don't get trees growing any which way), and Father rolls the dice right across the table, sweeps all the game pieces off the board with his arm, he obviously doesn't feel like finishing the game, but would rather sing the praises of his own culture's high points, our white cheese is superlative, with real texture and flavour, our paprika salami is world-famous, you can be sure! even American film stars eat our *kolbász*, and we Hungarians in the Vojvodina are even more hospitable than Hungarians in Hungary, our language is a puzzle even for scholars; Mother suddenly interrupts Father and says in a gentle voice that it's unpleasant sweating all the time when you speak German and what makes you sweat so much is probably knowing you're making mistakes, no matter how hard you try, and Mother looks at us, one after the other, her eyes open wide as if she's just made a shocking realization. The monopoly board lies before us, the paper money, the tokens, the dice, Mother's words that cut straight to the heart and expose the source of Father's exaggerations, the helplessness in the face of painful experience, of disappointment that lies behind his exclamations (there's so much to say about the hasty conclusion that someone who speaks incorrectly is stupid, for me my parents' mistakes when they speak German have a charm of their own; this would be the time to mention that Father and Mother are transfigured when they speak Hungarian), and as if reading my thoughts, Nomi says, we'll be your simultaneous interpreters next time you take the exam, then you won't have to sweat it out, Mama, instead the examiners will break into a sweat when so many words come flying at them.

Still, we didn't celebrate when Mother and Father passed their Naturalization exam on the second try. Well, that's done, Father said, and Mother put away the documents, the civic-education book, he sat in his chair, she on the sofa and we looked at them expectantly, but Father turned on the television and Mother reached for her knitting.

And? Nomi asked. And what? Father answered, we're not Swiss citizens yet, the Swiss still have to ratify our request by vote. In any event, the officials were very nice, they congratulated us on passing the exam, Mother added.

Do you hear them calling? Dragana asks me, *if you listen close, you hear their voices*, and Dragana's eyes roll about like spilt marbles. Our families call us and what do we do? and she grabs my hands, I have to do something, *you listen to me?* (Dragana works for us on weekdays from seven in the morning until six in the evening and on weekends she and her husband work for a cleaning company.) I can't stand by and watch *how they make my son dead*, will they shoot him or hang him?

The siege of Sarajevo began a year ago on 5 April 1992, the voice on the television announced.

(Father, who stands up suddenly, it's impossible to get your mind around it, he says, it all looks exactly the same there one year later, that's not humanly possible, and Father goes over to the dark brown built-in cabinet, turns the handle, reaches for the bottle, fills his glass with whisky, goes to the kitchen, opens the freezer, and we can hear him knock the ice cubes out of the tray. Someone's making a mistake, Father says when he returns to the living room and sits in his armchair with his glass. Isn't Dragana from Sarajevo? Nomi asks, yes, of course she is, but is she Serbian or Croatian or maybe even Muslim? I don't know, Father answers, I don't even want to know, it's better if we don't get drawn in, and he switches to the Hungarian news. We can't afford to talk politics at work, Mother says, especially now when the situation is getting more and more tense—you know what, we have to show people that we're *endividules* and at some point they won't notice us any more, we'll be like air to them, that's best and if you're ever asked for your opinion, we simply don't have one . . .)

Ildi, can't you hear them calling? and I, I don't know what I'm supposed to say, they all claim that we Serbs are to blame, and Dragana presses her hands to my cheeks, the people on television, *they can tell whatever they want*, they have no idea what's really going on, everyone's to blame, Ildi, the Serbs are shooting from the mountainsides, Izetbegović is sacrificing his men, so that he can say the Muslims are victims and the Serbs are to blame for everything, and the Croats ally themselves with the Serbs when it suits them (right in the middle of Europe, I think, today, not sometime in the past), yes, I can hear them calling, I suddenly say to console Dragana, to comfort her, or at least to finally get her to stop talking, Dragana had waited for a moment when we were alone in the kitchen (Father out on a major shopping trip, Marlis in the cellar, tidying up the supplies), tell me, how do you hear them? what exactly do you hear, *you hear them in the night? Worst is when the moon's so round and stupid-looking*, then they all spit in my ear, my sister, my son, my aunt, they spit in my ear and call to me, Dragi, Dragi, have you forgotten us? *Ildi, you know how old my son is? He's nine*, she says, *nine years*

old and he not allowed come to Swiss (and Dragana raises her
hands in the air as if she'd just been arrested), she will have
to wait almost four more months, because of the law! that's
longer than a human life now, when hundreds die every day,
and I flinch when Dragana holds a picture out towards me,
I have to look at him, her son! And only reluctantly do I look
at him, the boy with a shy expression and eyes that are as
beautiful as only eyes can be, a child in his grandparents'
arms and behind them a house, half of a house, I think.

(My Mamika, whose murmuring I always heard when I
lay in bed, unable to sleep, the faint rattle of her rosary beads
as Mamika turned them and turned them again and then,
after she'd finished her prayers, her voice, high and clear,
singing, 'From my mother I have the heart of a dove, from
my father my joyful, musical nature. Dearest, with your soul
so white, my parents taught me to treasure all that is beautiful
and good, love and passionate kisses . . .'

Last night, as I lay sleepless in bed, I thought of
Mamika's rosary, Mamika's belief that prayer and song can
take the edge off the sharpest reality and this continuous,
silent prayer carried her through the worst periods of her life,
she followed these words blindly into a future that wouldn't
have been possible without them.)

I knew you could hear them too, Dragana says, kissing
the picture and tucking it back into her blouse, and even if
the Swiss were to allow her son into the country, he couldn't
come because he is trapped in Sarajevo. And I'm alarmed

by the feverish, hopeless look in Dragana's eyes, by the way she looks at me and tells me that she can hear her son's high-pitched, piercing whistle (the truth is horrifying and uncertain for everyone), and suddenly, right at that moment, Janka appears, probably because Dragana won't stop talking about the voices she hears, the voice of her shoemaker whom she hasn't seen for years, even the creaking of his old bicycle echoes in her ears, and he had often scolded her, telling her she shouldn't walk so crookedly through the world, shouldn't lean to one side or the other. My aunts, uncles and cousins were always very present to me—but Janka?

Dragana turns away, grabs the vegetable peeler and starts preparing the potatoes and carrots, I think the simplest chores are no longer just tasks but proof that we aren't doing anything here, she says, and suddenly I can picture very clearly the two worlds that face each other but can't be united, those of us here in Switzerland and our families in Yugoslavia, in the former Yugoslavia, as they say now. Here are my enemies, Dragana says, pointing at the potato peels, and wipes her eyes with the back of her hand. Yes, we live here, like the Swiss, with front-row seats, I think, that much is true.

Dragana's entire family—what's your son's name? Danilo!—lives in Sarajevo, and with the tip of her paring knife Dragana carves the eyes out of the potatoes. (The 1984 Winter Olympics, back then when television was still gospel, the results which I recorded in forms I'd specially prepared for them—who set new world records? Ingemar Stenmark? Or Bojan Križaj? I have a clear memory of Mother, deeply moved at the sight of Jane Torvill and Christopher Dean— that a couple could glide across the ice like that—the jury unanimously awarded them perfect scores for artistic expression, how is that possible? Mother asked, her eyes filled with tears—where is Sarajevo? we asked Mother back then because we wanted to know where this marvel of love was possible, and Mother opened our school atlas and we probably found Sarajevo in the section 'Countries of the Balkan'.

Now, in 1993, the Olympic stadium is destroyed and the dead are being buried right in front of the ruins. Who'd have thought, people say, who could have imagined this was possible, people write, and I remember how Jens Weissflog prepared for his ski jump, how he took a deep breath before pushing off hard, crouching low before taking flight, Jens Weissflog, soaring over the roofs of Sarajevo for eternity.)

I got a letter from my *sestra*, Dragana says, should I tell you what she wrote? No, I'd rather not, I think, I don't want to know what Dragana's sister has written. You know, Ildi, there are almost no trees left, they're burning everything for heat, my *sestra* says, the city looks like a plucked chicken, none of the parks or avenues have any trees, but that's not the worst, they have no water to drink, no water left to flush away their shit, they don't even have heat in the hospitals. . . maybe later, I interrupt Dragana, tell me about it later! Dragana spins around to face me, she fixes me with her wild eyes, you're afraid, she says, naturally, we're all afraid, have you heard anything from your family? Can you still call them? And Dragana points the paring knife at me as if I were a large potato with several eyes she needed to carve out. But maybe I'm the one who wants to get rid of her, in any case, it occurs to me that there might be one less problem in the world if the two of us, a Bosnian Serb and a Hungarian from the Vojvodina province in Serbia were lying dead on the linoleum floor in the kitchen. No, the phone lines are dead, I answer (and all of them, except for Janka, had gathered until now on Beogradska Street at Uncle Móric and Aunt Manci's because they were the only ones who had a telephone, they all, even the oldest, drank sweet Turkish coffee, no one ever sat down at the table without first washing their hands, they all sat together on the sofa, their shirts heavily starched, their blouses freshly ironed, their hair neatly parted and smoothed down with saliva, because you never know what technology can do these days, you can almost see with the telephone, in fact, can't we already see our relatives in Switzerland, our brother? And oh, the children! when you hear their voices fluttering through the connection? And it might be hours before the first one gets up from the sofa and leaves the circle of relatives parsing every word that was said after the receiver was hung up. Each international call was an event that filled an entire afternoon.)

Ildi, do you need anything other than an egg? Dragana asks, dumping the peels into the compost and wiping her forehead with the back of her hand. Yes, a grilled ham-and-cheese and an asparagus canapé (and I'll call international information to get Janka's telephone number, maybe Janka has a telephone that still works and, international information, that in itself sounds promising). How long has it been since you were last able to call? I ask Dragana. Since those godless soldiers—my Serbs!—started shooting from the mountains around Sarajevo. I swear to you, they do whatever they want with us, they tell us we've always hated each other, Serbs and Croats and Muslims, I could certainly believe that, but no one who has a heart really believes it, we're all Bosnians, *you believe me?* Dragana tells me that all her relatives, who had always felt like Bosnians, were now classified as Bosnian Serbs, their beloved city, under siege by the Serbs, was being shot at by Serbs and Croats and Muslims (once you've got a crazy idea in your head, it spins faster and faster, such madness sets it spinning faster than anything else), and Dragana feels for the stalks of asparagus in the can, and I'd like to know why they landed on the moon, Ildikó, *the politicians should all be stuffed into a rocket and shooted to the moon*, and if they've got enough fuel, they can keep going so they finally find the right god and leave the rest of us in peace, and Dragana starts speaking more and more rapidly in her mix of German and Swiss German, her Serbo-Croatian sing-song fading, Dragana's consonants start to waltz, Sarajevo will soon be wiped out, you'll see, and she spreads mustard on a piece of bread, covers it with slices of ham and cheese, the egg meanwhile hops in the hot water, *why does everyone in the world think we Serbs are cannibals*, Ildi? and Dragana presses the sandwich in the toaster, Dragana and I, two animals staring into each others' eyes, we, who are meant to be mortal enemies because Dragana is a Bosnian Serb (or is she a Serbian Bosnian?) and I am from the Hungarian minority in Serbia (the insanity that spins in my head, in everyone's head), and it's absurd and entirely possible that one of my cousins could desert because he, as a Hungarian, doesn't want to fight in the Yugoslav People's Army and then be shot by one of Dragana's cousins who is serving in the Yugoslav People's Army and they shoot deserters, but it's also possible that one of Dragana's cousins could desert because he considers himself a Bosnian and, as a Bosnian Serb, doesn't want to fight in the Yugoslav People's Army, then Dragana's cousin could be shot by my cousin because my cousin didn't desert from the Yugoslav People's Army, perhaps to save his own life; but it's also possible that both are shot by a Muslim or a Croat or blown to bits by an unexploded shell or a mine somewhere, in some unknown place, some no-man's-land, while the two of us are here in the kitchen making sandwiches.

(And our guests, are they Swiss Germans or German Swiss?)

Dragana, who puts the egg in an eggcup, presses the white plate with the canapé into my hand, you have to come back for the sandwich, she says, and me, I finally start moving towards the dining room.

The thought of Janka haunts me that entire April day and I try to calculate how many years it has been since we last saw each other; I pour beans into the appropriate receptacle, fill the filter with freshly ground coffee, it must be nine years now, I think as I press on the brown powder without paying attention to the amount of pressure I use, whether I only press lightly or I push down too hard, I believe it's been nine years and of course I hear Janka's voice even though I've only ever spoken to her once, ears have a surprisingly good memory and I place the filter in the holder, I have to ask Nomi, who's waiting tables today, if her order was for light or dark coffee, if she ordered an orange juice or this or that, Dragana, who calls from the kitchen, the sandwich! and it's only natural that Nomi asks me what planet I happen to be on at the moment, and I should answer that I was wondering that too. I should change the subject completely, tell her that the two of us should at least sit down and figure out what we could do, maybe we could talk to Benno, to go to one of his media group's meeting, I'd like to ask Nomi if she's considered the fact that our family might not survive this war, that our Great-Uncle Pista won't be able to have his operation since there's no medicine left because of the embargo, that they might all be dead tomorrow, Uncle Piri and Aunt Icu, Csilla, because she lives in one of the poorest communities, Janka, who could easily have been Nomi or me and about whom I only know that she interrupted her studies in economics, left the capital and got a job as an announcer on the radio in Novi Sad, our entire family now belongs to the past, is beyond reach, the Berlin Wall and the Iron Curtain are both gone but we're still cut off from one another, as if there had never been a connecting road, a train you could board according to a schedule, rails that were laid down, for what? I'd like to ask Nomi, how we could find Janka, if she thinks we could ask Father about Janka, how best to hire her (Nomi, who a few days after my twentieth birthday told me that we should scrap our plan for the future, that it would never work, we can't go back, it's just a childish dream, we opened up our hearts and a hollow dream wormed its way in, everyone knows the usual fate of the emigrant, you save up for the future, only to end up unhappy in your old homeland. No! I then asked Nomi if she was happy here, in Switzerland, Nomi, who laughed and said we're hybrid creatures and they tend to be happier because they're comfortable in several worlds, they can feel at home just about everywhere but don't have to feel at home anywhere in particular), and Nomi, who wears many hats, who works in the kitchen or at the counter, waits tables, deals with the suppliers and whom everyone likes, reminds me that our timing wasn't optimal, we took over the cafe at a difficult time, but we're doing just fine, aren't we? and if there weren't people who do like us, we wouldn't know what others are saying about us behind our backs! and Nomi empties the ashtray full of butts into the refuse. Besides, who cares if the Schärers are still going around telling everyone we bribed the Tanners with fifty thousand francs!—which, by the way, Mrs Freuler confided to her just the other day—our answer is no! it was one hundred thousand—who's calling us cheap? (and what's with the men's toilet, always drenched in piss, I want to ask Nomi, and who put pictures of a sun with a false smile up on our door?), Nomi points out that it's already past eleven o'clock and I take the portafilters from the Cimbali, empty the grounds from each one in turn and replace it, then I let the machine run empty, clean all the grooves with a thick bristled brush—regularly cleaning the machine is indispensable for good coffee—wipe down the handles with a damp cloth, clearing any last grounds from the grooves, the Cimbali, which I'm getting pretty familiar with, my hands, which I now know even better in relation to the Cimbali (Nomi and I can now work with our hands just like Aunt Icu, that much I'm convinced). Have you thought about the fact that the situation in the Vojvodina could escalate just like it has in Bosnia? I whisper to Nomi over the Cimbali, and the word 'escalate' gives my tongue an unpleasant feeling, just as 'Balkan War' or 'embargo' do. Yes, Nomi answers, still knocking the ashtray against the side of the rubbish can, and we look at each other, and I see my beloved sister, now, at this moment, looking just as helpless as I feel.

JULI

We drive off in our silver-grey Mercedes in April 1989,
Father and I, that is Father drives and I sit beside him, ready
to hand him the map to keep us from getting lost, I, who
have always loathed car trips, try to concentrate and not distract the driver with unnecessary chatter. We'll go via
Munich, he says weakly, turn on the radio so we can hear
what they have to say about the traffic.

There's no particular news about the traffic but there is
about the weather—a storm is coming and it may bring
snow. You hear that, my father says, snow! That's all we need.
At the right moment, I hand him a bottle of water, the usual
April weather, I say. He takes a sip and answers that April
could spare us its shit weather. Yes, that's true, I think (we
could have flown to Belgrade and then taken a bus, but
Father starts ranting whenever the topic of flying comes up,
did we come into this world with legs or wings? and it makes
no difference if you tell him that wheels aren't exactly one
of our evolutionary traits either).

We drive, drive without speaking. A few kilometres past
Munich we stop briefly in some backwater for a cup of coffee
and a smoke. I search for a word that could start a conversation, I, who've always detested these backwater dives, leaf
through the menu, read the names of a few dishes I don't

recognize and Father asks if I'd like anything to eat. No, I answer, I'm not hungry. What I really want is to talk to Father about the menu, about something we're both familiar with, but he takes a drag on his cigarette, looks past me, and I notice that something new has opened up behind the lenses of his glasses, something completely unfamiliar which I'm certain he doesn't want to share with me. Don't forget to use the toilet first, he says and taking off his glasses, rubs his eyes, I don't want to have to stop again before Salzburg. Fine, I answer, stub out my cigarette to stop the smoke, and for a moment I look into my Father's defenceless eyes, I wish I could console him, I'd gladly give him my heart as consolation, now, when he's such a helpless child, I'm a helpless child too, his as a matter of fact, I'd like to tell him that if nothing else, but I stand up and head off towards the toilets.

It really starts to snow, the flakes swirl against the windscreen before the wipers quickly but briefly clear the view again with rapid strokes. If only those dogs were lying, my father says, Ildi, turn the radio back on so we can find out if we're going to get snowed in (and I wonder how it would be if the two of us, my father and I were stuck here, unable to go any further, yes, it wouldn't surprise me given the way life goes, it could very well be that we don't get any further, that fate forces us to sit in the car, knowing that our family is waiting for us in vain), and we hear the announcer describe the conditions as difficult, drivers should be cautious, he says, stuff it in your craw, my father swears, you'd have to be an idiot not to drive carefully. Why don't you tell us instead when the sky's going to leave us in peace? I hand my father the bottle of water, he waves it away, who's thirsty in this kind of snow? And I, I picture Mamika, laid out in her best dress, the snowflakes blanketing her face softly, gently. I wonder if she will be laid out tomorrow if the weather stays bad, I wonder if there are daffodils at the market yet, probably not, but I can surely find grape hyacinths, which Mamika loved. My father drives even more slowly as the snowfall thickens, we'll never get there at this rate, and he grabs a cigarette, clamps it between his teeth and his movement indicates he has nothing more urgent to do at the moment than smoke a Marlboro, so he won't lose his cool, the bluish smoke swirls helplessly against the windscreen, what should I do? Father suddenly asks, and I am so surprised I can barely think of an answer, I say, wait.

Wait? for who? for what? Father swears after a moment's pause. He has to give his swearing free rein, the words—earthy, coarse—flow out of his mouth like nimble fish, and I've never told him that there's nothing I'd rather listen to than his oaths and curses; at these moments, especially, when Father gets so worked up his tongue bounces from one word to the next and its bravura sends communists and other criminals of world history off running but quick! then I know there are sides to him I do understand and I wish I could reproduce Father's oaths, translate them into the other language so that they really shine—Stalin, what's this Siberian greeting from your ice-cold arse, you want to spoil the mood before we even get there, like Adam and Eve, still innocent and without a pot to piss in, running around butt-naked in your socialist paradise?—but even if I could never pull it off, I'm confident that Father would go down guns blazing to make sure his mother tongue doesn't fade, as long as his cursing flows, his beloved words won't die off, will they? (And if it were possible to translate his phrases into the other language, into German, then I could show him that I understand how he communicates through silence or profanity. If a single word has no equivalent, then how can you tell the story of half a life in a new language? Then, only silence or the condensed, strong language of cursing can convey what happened, how it was, how it might have been; that's what I'd tell Father and he would probably be amazed that I spend any time at all thinking about him or his language.)

The rest stop where Father finally parks the car is almost full, so we'll have to wait after all, until God smiles again, he says and turns off the motor, his hands rest motionless on the steering wheel, his fingers are remarkably short and strong. I ask him if he'd like a sandwich, there's ham or salami, and Father answers that this is a strange gathering and gestures with his head towards the dozens of parked cars, their hoods already blanketed with an inch of snow, he'd prefer ham, and as Father unwraps his sandwich, his tears flow.

It was a spring night without stars and I remember that when I opened the door to my room, I noticed for the first time the round, functional ugliness of the street lamp that illuminated the narrow footpath lined with hornbeams, because the blinds on the hall window had not been pulled down as they usually were; as I lay on my bed reading, I was momentarily stunned by the thought that it might be Father I heard weeping—I, who until then had only heard my father swearing, scolding, snoring, laughing or humming—I stood for a moment on the doorstep, thinking that the ugly street lamp seemed a little lost since there was no one whose way needed lighting.

Mother sat across from Father at the small round table in the hallway, trying to get him to talk, to take the telephone receiver from his hand. But Father seemed to be clinging to the receiver as his sobs fell into the mouthpiece.

It took a long time until Father could get a word out and in this eternity, as his head trembled helplessly, grotesquely, as his body was racked with sobs, I'd wanted to creep back into my room, I'd wanted to crawl under the bed as children do, I'd have rather done anything at all than face reality. But I stood in the doorway without moving and let my thoughts turn the street lamp into a moon with a horrible grin, I didn't stop my beloved trees from freezing into shadows. And I even imagined that the moon could speak. Or was it from Father's mouth that the sentence finally emerged—Mamika is dead.

A good priest is one who finds the right words and then remains silent, Mamika once said when, as a child, I'd asked her why she always spoke of 'our dear priest', I remember this now, as I watch with my hands folded as two men lower Mamika's coffin with thick ropes into the shovelled-out ground and as those encircling the grave, those left behind, are shaken with stronger and stronger emotions, the lower the coffin descends (and 1989 will be entered into my personal history, later, when I think of 1989, I will surely remember the fall of the Berlin Wall, how surprised I was that Swiss students were driven by their euphoria, their craving for Berlin, to travel there and experience the fall of the Wall, to celebrate the fact that they could witness a historical moment; certainly I'll remember many things that happened in 1989, but in my personal history, it will be remembered as the year Mamika died. It will be my last visit to my homeland for more than a decade and I'll see my father as I never saw him before), but I'm reluctant to be sad once I've read the dedications on the banner adorning the wreath, Rest in Peace from Your Loving Sons, our beloved Anna, you've left us, one of Mamika's friends sobs. Your loving granddaughters, I think, and withdraw into myself a bit, wait for the right moment to throw the tiny blue flowers onto her coffin, the surprisingly hollow impact of the flowers that I can still hear today, and in my mind I sing one of Mamika's favourite songs—'*If I were a stream, I'd be safe from sorrow, the mountains' valleys I'd follow, the grass on my banks to life I'd wake and the birds' thirst I'd slake . . .*'

Once everyone had thrown a handful of dirt onto Mamika, some able, in hushed voices, to say a few fitting words about her difficult life and others, like my father, repeatedly overcome with fits of weeping, we finally set off on that bitterly cold April day in 1989; the glowing white chestnut trees, whose timid spring had been interrupted by the sudden onslaught of winter, were fortunately not weighed down by our funeral procession.

My little girl, Mamika said, water is gold.

I, who've learnt how to fetch water from the well, learnt not to dawdle, not to let myself be distracted by the roses or the Dame's Rocket that grow next to the well, by the cat that winds itself, spindle-thin and with its tail raised, around and between my legs, and Mamika constantly scolds him as a good-for-nothing freeloader, I carry the enamel jug with both hands, my feet padding forward slowly but evenly so as not to spill any water, not a single drop, liquid gold, Mamika says, as she washes herself after me in the clouded, soapy water, in her bathroom which is also her kitchen, my eyes don't want to watch but glance furtively at her now and again, curious and ashamed, to steal a bit of gold from Mamika's skin. Why don't you take off your slip? I ask and my grandmother who has undone her braid, whose grey hair reaches down to her hips, says, go out in the garden, love, and play a nice game, go on! And I push my mustard-yellow stool up against the wall of the house, climb up on it and at first I stay crouched, then slowly straighten up, pull aside the flowered curtain in the kitchen window, Mamika, who bends over the enamel bowl, and I can see her bare back and her enormous pink underwear, like Cossack pants that bag unattractively over the elastic band below her knees. And I immediately wish I'd never seen those underpants, embarrassingly large and droopy on my delicate Mamika, and I can't for the life of me understand why she would wear such a sack with more than enough room for two pairs of chickens. She wouldn't even be allowed to sleep in those underpants in Switzerland, I thought then and this thought seemed mean to me, mean but logical.

Why does that particular memory resurface now? and I raise my head to look at the sky in its perplexity, my father, who has linked his arm with mine, doesn't turn away but looks at me with his tear-filled eyes and we slowly move away from Mamika's grave, cousins, close relatives and distant ones, Great-Uncle Pista, Mamika's last living brother, Uncle Móric, who lays his hand on his brother's—my father's— shoulder, and later I can't remember if it is our family's unvaried, almost silent procession, this collective movement of a group who, having lost a beloved member, can only feel the difficult side of life, that made me burst into tears as if I had never cried before in my life; or if perhaps it was Juli— the childlike idiot!—who, clutching tight to the rusty metal fence at the entrance to the cemetery, calls for my grand-mother in an eerie voice—*kedves Panni néni, Panni néni, kedves Panni néni* (dearest Madame Anna—Mamika, who often admonished us not to make fun of Juli, God sometimes chooses to speak to us through very peculiar creatures, she said), Juli's calling was interrupted by whimpers as clear as glass, as if life now only knew the language of sorrow, and I, I can't stop crying, maybe because Juli's bare feet are so exposed to the cold, her toes sticking out over the tip of her worn-out sandals, and I would give a lot to have Juli look at me again with her eyes, untouched by time, and ask me for a *sweetie*, but her wailing stretches the laws of moderation that ensure your own survival at times like these—because losing a loved one shouldn't be more than you can bear— and I can't stop crying because Juli reminds me relentlessly that a new life, my life without Mamika, has begun.

Can you change lives overnight, enter from one day to the next into a new life? That's what I'm wondering, but back then the question was an indefinable sense of agitation. We're going to Switzerland, *svájcha*, that's what you told us, Mamika, when Uncle Móric sat down in your kitchen one afternoon and laid on the table the papers, *a papírokat*, that he'd got from the embassy in Belgrade. Did everything go well? you asked him, yes, he answered and I can still see how the dirty white envelope lay on your table next to the bottle and the schnapps glass that Uncle Móric had emptied in one gulp. *A papírok*, the papers, they were different from every- thing around them—the wobbly kitchen table, the blue-and- white enamelled basin, the tin cups, the blessing embroidered in brightly coloured letters, the credenza in which you kept all your valuables—and now they lay on the table, the papers, so light and without any sign that they meant something special. And that evening, when the envelope lay on the table, just as on all the other evenings, we ate bread and cheese, drew the curtains, Nomi and I lay down next to each other in bed and God winked at us as we said our prayers, you caressed our cheeks with your warm hand and maybe we stayed awake, the three of us, maybe we fell right asleep.

Svájcha, you said sometimes, Father and Mother are in Switzerland, in a better world. And do you know how I pictured this better world? For me 'better' simply meant 'more'. More of all the good things I knew. Father and Mother lived in a country where there were more pigs, more chickens, more geese, where there must be an unbelievable amount of wheat, corn, sunflowers and poppies growing everywhere. In the pantries there were more sausages than you can count, huge, fragrant hams, jars of preserves tower on the shelves, in Switzerland you surely ate pancakes every day, not just Fridays; but it still meant nothing to me when you said that Mother and Father would soon come for Nomi and me. I would rush out of the house into the garden to forget that sentence as quickly as possible.

Mother and Father did not come for us. Instead, Uncle Móric drove us to Belgrade, us and our suitcases, and he talked a lot on that November drive and the poplars and the linden, the acacia trees and the grey air between them, the empty fields, the houses with smoking chimneys and I, who wanted to bring along Cicu, the spindle-thin cat, I cried because I wasn't allowed to bring Cicu, what do you want with such a mangy cat in Switzerland, Uncle Móric probably said and laughed and we said goodbye to everyone before getting into our uncle's red Moskvitch. It wasn't the way one imagines a farewell; we desperately had to go to the toilet again even though we'd just been and the pigsty was on the way to the toilet, our toes, which had looked directly into the little pigs' eyes several times each day when we stuck them between the two boards of the wooden fence, the grunting, constantly moving snouts sniffed at our toes and tickled them and because the piglets knew us, we gave them names— black-spotted piglet, crumpled-ear piglet, limping piglet— because each pig was different, we hid in the kitchen when Uncle Móric or a local butcher came to drive them out of the stall and onto a small truck, they were slaughtered in Uncle Móric's courtyard or in the butcher's and you, Mamika, were always very busy on those days, you were upset too, because you could hear the piglets squeal, so high and piercing and drawn out as only pigs can squeal; they know what's coming, you told us once, and one of the essential things we learnt from you was surely that we can feel compassion for animals, we can have sincere feelings for them—this we learnt from you even though you saw so much human suffering in your life and suffered so much yourself.

The geese, Nomi loved most of all because of their beautiful necks and glittering eyes and because their bottoms are so soft. What? Why? You became furious when Nomi refused to eat goose and refused to tell you why she wouldn't and the next time there was roast goose for Sunday dinner, you looked at Nomi, and? and when Nomi shook her head decisively even though she wasn't even four years old, you said it was probably because she felt as close to the geese as you did to horses and that's why you would never eat horse-meat, and although we were impressed that you didn't get angry again, we thought it was strange, even worrying that you talked about certain spiritual affinities between humans and animals and only later, when you told us about our grandfather, did we understand you.

When we were all sitting in the car, with you between us in the back and a suitcase next to Uncle Móric in the pas-senger seat, and we pressed against one another because it was so cold, then Uncle Móric tried in vain to start the Moskvitch and I remember that his big jug ears turned red and Uncle Móric who never swore but whose ears always turned red when he was angry, yelled, everybody out! no, no, we won't miss the train, he said when you looked at your watch, I already figured time in for this and Uncle Móric steered the car with the door open to a place in the courtyard where he could fit under it more easily and you, Mamika, went into the kitchen to make another coffee so that Móric could strengthen himself afterwards and we said we'd go to the toilet one more time, again? and while Uncle Móric lay under the Moskvitch, Nomi and I lay on the ground to peek under the wire silo, we lay down on the cold November ground because at some point we'd begun building our own world under the corn silo—empty cans, broken toys, scraps of paper, feathers, grains of corn that we arranged according to certain patterns and each time we lay down we were anxious to see if everything was still exactly as we'd left it and if it wasn't, we'd come up with explanations for what had happened in the meantime—a mouse, a cat, some kind of creature had mixed up the order of our things.

I can't remember how much time went by before we were sitting in the car again and Uncle Móric grabbed the wheel with dirty hands, Mamika, he said, pray that this lemon doesn't conk out halfway there, and Uncle Móric had to get out again to shut the gate behind us and Nomi and I, we already wanted a pretzel stick even though we hadn't even left yet and with a dawning hint of anger you reached into your purse and stuck a pretzel stick in your own mouth as well and the Moskvitch dipped when Uncle Móric sat down and said, three mice are nibbling at my ear, and he laughed because Nomi flicked his earlobe, we drove off, at least an hour late, maybe more, and when the Moskvitch jolted along Hajduk Stankova, we automatically turned our heads towards the corner, the one we called 'Juli's corner', because Juli stood there almost every day, on the corner of Hajduk Stankova and Beogradska Street, she must still be at the market, you said, when Nomi and I looked at you questioningly, as if our departure depended on Juli, depended on saying goodbye to her, in other words, we couldn't drive away without having said goodbye and Uncle Móric grew more and more impatient because Mamika told him he should pull over to the side, he could leave the engine running, that's what you told him when he said that he probably couldn't get the car started again if he turned it off now. So we sat there and waited for Juli, which seemed logical to all of us except Uncle Móric, of course, and Juli came too, after a while, during which Uncle Móric had almost started swearing, not only did his ears pulse red but even his nose, when Juli turned the corner from Lucia utca Nomi and I climbed right out, my mouth would like a pretzel too, she said and we gave her some sweets and pretzel sticks; November pulls out everyone's hair, and Juli was wearing a chequered kerchief and a patched knee-length coat, we're going to Switzerland, Nomi said, *Schaiz*, Juli replied, that's across the river, and even farther, I added, yes, you told me you were going to *Schaiz*, will you be back tomorrow? and Juli stuck three, four pretzel sticks into her mouth. I nudged Nomi's arm, come on, we have to go, and you rolled down the window and called out, goodbye my Julika, *Panni néni*, your girls haven't told me when they're coming back, soon! and we patted Juli's arm, got back into the car and Uncle Móric stepped on the acclerator so hard that we were pushed back into the seat, if the train leaves without you, it will be your own fault!

I have no idea what all Uncle Móric said, I, in any case, had never heard him talk so much and the car smelt of coal, of petrol, it's time for a rest now, you told Uncle Móric, but he misunderstood and just kept talking, he said that he couldn't stop to rest now because every minute was precious. I'm trying to remember all that Uncle Móric said but it escapes me. Maybe I lost myself in that window as the bare trees flashed by, the colourful houses that in winter looked like they wanted to sink into the earth because they were so ashamed of their bright colours in this grey November during which it's only natural to light candles for the dead and lay flowers on the cold and no doubt already frozen earth.

I had certainly lost myself in that window, in signs, the barred sign indicating the city limit for ZENTA, CEHTA, SENTA. It meant nothing to me at the time that our town's name was written three times—in Serbo-Croatian, in Cyrillic letters and in Hungarian.

DALIBOR

He stands at the counter, asks, do you have any work? I answer with yes, of course, you can see I do. He keeps standing there, obviously hasn't understood my awkward joke and I say that he should sit at the staff table and point at table number one, directly behind the counter and he, he turns away from me, looks at the table I've pointed at and sits at it so that he can see me. Would you like something to drink? I ask him over the counter and he shrugs, doesn't seem to understand much, I think and bring him a coffee. *Thanks*, he says without smiling and I try to make him understand with hand motions that I'm going to get the boss. *Do you speak English?* he asks, *yes*! (and I'm inwardly embarrassed, because English is not a language I'd have expected from him), *wait a moment*, I say, *why not*, he answers (and I'm still embarrassed inside because he doesn't know where to look but my legs start moving automatically).

I knock on the office door, tell my mother that someone's here looking for work, my mother, in the middle of ironing the mustard-yellow tablecloths, is giving the linen her full attention (and I will probably never forget how this mixture of steam, linen and effort smells), Mother, someone's here who would like to speak to you, I say; the boss, who slowly raises her head, as if returning from a long journey, says, we don't need anyone, you know that. Yes, I do know, I think. Tell her she should leave her telephone number, we'll be in touch should things change. Him, I say, it's a he. The boss, who looks at me in surprise for a moment, the steam billows in front of her, then you can save yourself the trouble, what on earth do you want with a man? and she winks at me, we don't want to upset our rooster now, do we? But it would be good to have a bouncer, don't you think? and the boss is so astonished that she has to laugh, and me, I want to take the bull by the horns, who is it you'd want to throw out? I quickly ask, Mr Pfister or Mr Tognoni? the Schärers, absolutely, what do you think? but her laughter has already dried up, the boss's face looks tired again, Ildi, we should be happy that no one has thrown us out, happy? happy! and the boss picks up the iron, fills it with water, all those refugees, the ones who have already come and the ones who will come later aren't making us any more popular. So you admit they don't like us, that they want to get rid of us? (My voice tries to win.) Admit? you misunderstood me, so many Yugos are coming now, the Swiss are less open, just as we would be in their position, you see? (what kind of position, awkward position, false position, pole position? my head spins), when masses of people stream in, you can't expect sympathy for individual fates, and I, speechless, wonder why these mustard-yellow tablecloths, which we took over from the Tanners, fit in so well in the Mondial's decor, but nothing occurs to me. Do you know how many have come so far? I ask. Very many, certainly several thousand, in any case, so many that the Swiss are debating it and are afraid, the boss says as she folds the tablecloth in thirds and then folds it again. And back then? when you came here? did you have as much time for the fears of the Swiss then? No, I didn't understand at the time, Mother says and lays the freshly ironed and folded tablecloth on the pile, we have to keep our self-control, that's how it is, and we have to come to terms with it. Can you live like that? I ask Mother. Yes, of course. And I, holding tight to the door handle, I look Mother in the eye, I don't believe you, I say softly, probably too softly for Mother to hear since she's already leaning over the ironing board, reaching for a new tablecloth.

Write down your telephone number, I tell him in English, we don't need anyone at the moment, but that could change soon, *your phone number and your name please*! and before he writes, he asks if it's true that only Yugoslavians work here, said his cousin, who's lived in the village for a long time, his cousin, who likes to make up stories, which is entertaining but can lead to unpleasant situations. And I ask him if knowing that was true, that we were all *Yugoslavians*, would change anything. Possibly, he answers, smiles, takes the pen, Dalibor Bastic, do you like my name? And I don't want him to see that my head, which once again I can't control, is uncomfortably warm and I turn away, straighten my dress and feel the urge to barricade myself behind the counter, but I stand there—Glorija, who nervously squeezes by me to fill the coffee orders herself, murmurs, have you gone deaf? as she passes—I, look back at him who is clearly amused, I say that I haven't introduced myself, and I, the one who should be in control of the situation, I say, your name is unusual, *strange*, but have to admit it's got something to it. Your dress, on the other hand, doesn't suit you at all, he answers, you look like you work in a dentist's office, I do, as a matter of fact, but only people with the sharpest eyes, with *professional eyes*, notice; Glorija politely asks me to get back to work, *sorry*, he says, I didn't mean to keep you!

And when I'm back behind the Cimbali, he takes a deep breath, lights a cigarette, watches me openly as he blows curls of smoke in my direction and, naturally, I'm annoyed that all my movements are conscious of him, even though only my eyes and the tip of my nose are visible behind the Cimbali, I wish it protected me more from this Dalibor. That he looks at me as boldly as only children do, impresses and irritates me and because it irritates me, I get even more annoyed; I knock the coffee grounds from the portafilters, knock them again to distract myself, turn on the grinder to hear its loud frenetic noise and the next time I raise my head, he's standing in front of me, the Cimbali between us, he reaches over the pre-heated cups, holding out a note for me, and because I'm in no hurry to take it from him, he waits and looking down, I search frantically in my head for the right thing to say and the situation is not exactly romantic if you consider that a note with a name and telephone number is being held over the heating plate of a Cimbali, filled cups covered with two dishtowels to keep them as warm as possible (so that they'll keep the coffee nice and hot). That a young woman can't think of anything better to do than make unnecessary noise, doing what she usually tries to avoid, obviously trying to chase away the one looking at her calmly by taking out all the filters, knocking out the grounds and drawing another coffee even though Glorija hasn't handed in any new orders, in fact, she even bends down to turn on the radio; *thanks for your help, thanks for your time*, he says and she, still ostentatiously busy, starts wiping down the Cimbali's stainless-steel front and when he finally lifts one of the dish towels and sticks the note between two upside-down cups, she finally has to return his look, at which he gives her a brief charming smile and she can't tear her eyes away from his lips, not because of his smile, but because he has bad teeth (as does she), and then, then suddenly he's gone.

Your boyfriend? Glorija asks, fluttering her blue-shadowed eyelids. You don't really expect me to tell you, do you? I put the scrap of paper in my pocket and can hardly wait to call him. I imagine how he'll answer on the end of the line, I, who try to remember all day long what he looks like, what colour his eyes are—dark or light, if he has a high forehead, a thin or a wide nose, but I can't remember anything about him.

Bastic, he says once, then repeats it several times because I don't answer, hello, hello, and I wonder how many days it will take before I will finally say something, but it doesn't take long, it's me, the girl from the cafe, I say after a moment and my voice sounds surprisingly detached, probably because the stench in the telephone booth has sobered me. Would you like to see me? he immediately asks.

My country is a deathbed, he says, and I'm a *refuger, a refugee,* I say and he laughs when I correct him, showing his crooked teeth.

The benches here aren't covered with bullet holes and they even have backrests. Should we sit?

So we sit on a bench by the lake, connected by the tattered dictionary between us, and we imagine ourselves far away from the opposite shore, we picture a distant horizon, *the sea,* which Dalibor misses so much he wakes in the middle of the night with the taste of salty air on his tongue (the word for sea in his language is beautiful—*more*). He tells me about the sea at Dubrovnik and I tell him about my river, I've never told anyone here about my river, I say, and he brushes his particularly graceful fingers over my forehead and the small grooves on your forehead are like the tiny rills on a river, he says, his fingers move slowly, as white as they are, I still can't see your veins, I say, and we should go swimming, he says, even if *my fantastic body* has an aversion to fresh water (and I'll tell Nomi about Dalibor, I'll tell her everything in minute detail, that when he talks about his *fantastic body*, his smile is so childlike that his proud arrogance softens into an engaging naivety, Dalibor, whose hair is as thick as Uncle Piri's, whose eyes are so clear-sighted, I'd like to look into them for ever, a kind of look I haven't seen for a very long time), he can't possible have hair on his legs and certainly not on his back when his skin is so white! and I, I wait for him to get undressed, to casually unbutton his shirt while taking a drag on his unfiltered cigarette, wait for him to say, come on, don't be shy, get undressed, I even believe he could bewitch the swans with his eyes and make them swim here with the two of us, watching us, and I also believe he could conjure the twilight to darken the sky and bathe our bodies in a gorgeous sunset and Dalibor stands, rolls up his trouser legs, takes a few steps towards the lake and I watch him, the *refuger*, as he bends over towards the ground, hanging his head as he searches for flat stones, straightens and pauses a moment like an athlete waiting for the starting gun, then lets the stones fly, horizontally, so that they touch the water's surface for just a fraction of a second and convert that power in such a way that they immediately shoot up into the air again and I wonder how you could describe the noise of stones skipping over the water (you can hear the air, the speed in the air, and the light, thin sound of the stone hitting the water, a feathery sound you might say, the energy between the elements, water, air and matter, but I didn't know the slightest thing about physics), Dalibor, who turns back to me with his trousers rolled up and a stone in his hand, look at this stone, is it valuable, *precious*? would anything be different if it didn't exist?

why are you asking me? I answer. Never mind, he says and throws the stone high in the air, tell me something about you, about your family in the Vojvodina, you know, I once visited a friend in Novi Sad and fell in love with the city right away. The stone falls back down, hitting the other stones with a hollow sound. I don't know Novi Sad, I answer, my family lives in a village about an hour from there, but my sister lives in Novi Sad, she works at a radio station, I don't know any more than that, I hardly know her, she's my half-sister, I say. *Half*? and Dalibor sits next to me, very close, I can smell his sweat and say, yes, she's my father's daughter from his first marriage. Yeah, Dalibor says, either she's your sister or she's not, that's up to you to decide. I feel naive next to you, I say. That's not my problem, Dalibor answers, and we turn to face each other, he strokes my cheek and murmurs something in his language.

I don't know much about my family, I say and show him just how little with my thumb and forefinger. *Who knows much*, Dalibor says, tell me what you do know.

Three weeks ago my mother's sister, my Aunt Icu, wrote us a letter—and apparently it came, Dalibor says. She wrote that she has to stand in line for hours to collect her pension and, in February, when it was finally her turn, her pension was only enough to buy an apple. Luckily, she still has her own apples in her pantry, she wrote that only so we understand what money is worth now, nothing, in other words, you can't even use it to wipe your ass because the paper is too rough. And there's not enough room for all the zeros on the bills any more. There are people who earn money or, rather, food by standing in line. They queue up and then, when it's their turn, they give up their place to the highest bidder for three eggs, a loaf of bread, whatever and those who can collect their money a few hours earlier this way, spend it as fast as they can, they'll buy anything, even something they don't need, twenty pounds of bouillon, buttons, facecloths, some fabric, whatever, as long as they can unload their cash. There's hardly any money anyway, they have to organize a system that can practically work without it, they've still got enough to eat, but no petrol, the fields are ploughed with horses, no oil, no coal for heat and this year it's so cold they have to gather wood from the forest near the river's edge, which is against the law, but who cares about those regulations these days.

The worst is the fear that the men will be conscripted, Béla already got his orders, so did Csaba (my cousin and my cousin Csilla's husband, I explain), Béla has gone into hiding with a friend and Csaba, he fled across the border to Hungary, and Csilla is suffering the fate many women share in these unfortunate times, she has to take care of her twins with absolutely nothing and her mother can't help her much because Piri is as fierce as a guard dog and as unforgiving as a bad father (and I tell Dalibor Csilla's story). What else is there to write about? they say that milk costs more and so bread costs more too. Yes, good diversionary tactics, Dalibor

173

says. Lots of parents aren't able to send their children to school because they can't afford the bus ticket any more. The schools are half empty and we're becoming stupid, Aunt Icu wrote, if we aren't already.

It's always the wrong ones who suffer, Dalibor says tracing the small hollow at the base of my neck with his finger, in ten years we'll know more, but then it wil be too late, what we know won't do any good.

What do you mean? I ask.

For all the dead, anything we learn will be too late . . . but you should be happy that your town isn't divided like so many others, *it is evident*, Dalibor says, that you can't divide cities, or a whole country, on ethnicity. If you do, you get the naked insanity of war. And the western European democratic politicians who stand by when these divisions are drawn are sitting at the same table as the war-mongering nationalists. Tell me, why don't they work with the opposition who are trying to establish democratic values, *tell me, why not?*

We bring Dalibor to Wohlgroth in mid-May, hoping to find him a job in our favourite cafe where he'd only earn a little or next to nothing, but at least he'd have work and we try to explain to him that the building is occupied, several builidings are, a former factory, that several hundred people live there, we tell him about the concerts, the communal kitchen. It's an attempt to take charge of things, we explain with gestures of our hands and feet, with English and a Serbo-

Croatian dictionary, Nomi and I, we feel we have a duty to explain a political programme, we beat the drums for Wohlgroth, I do especially, as if I had to convince some conservative local politician of its importance, and in doing so I act like most politicians, I whitewash it (but I've only realized just now, in retrospect, that every time I was in Wohlgroth, I felt completely defenceless, my entire body vulnerable, I was afraid that something could happen at any moment, a dog could attack, two dogs could trap me in a corner, a man could fix his hungry eyes on me—you don't look like us, what are you doing here? but I also felt an irresistible desire to find a place that would define me), and when we get off the train at the main station, Dalibor stands still on the platform, he looks right through us in the direction we've come from, then turns and looks in the opposite direction, I don't like trains stations that take you prisoner, he says to the pigeons, to the platform, in any case he's not talking to us, and Dalibor looks up at the roofing over the station, at the benches, the trolleys you have to feed with coins, he turns to look at the small loudspeakers strewn along the platform at regular intervals that I've never noticed before, *it's better than sightseeing,* Dalibor says with a laugh, links his arms with ours, *and now, let's try to get a job!*

A few hours later, we're shouting in the cellar, it's impossible, Dalibor shouts, and I remember that a green light was flashing on his face, I can't work in a place like this. Why didn't you tell me that upstairs in the cafe? I shout back, hold my right ear towards Dalibor, and look at the stage on which some guy with multicoloured hair is dancing with his microphone stand, he forces his voice until the veins on his neck stand out, because I couldn't believe you two were convinced I could work here, Dalibor explains. So you'd rather work in the Mondial, I scream. A hundred times more, he screams back, almost as loud as the singer, and I grab Dalibor's hand, pull him towards the exit, the concert's not over yet, he says, for us it is, I answer and pull him up the stairs, I need to talk to you.

Listen, why did you sit there at the table and let them explain everything to you and say that you'd already waited tables and worked the counter, you even asked what days you could work, you asked and smiled and looked around, so I assumed that you liked it, you introduced yourself to the bartender, you looked at the tracks outside, it's a nice view from up here, you said, you agreed with the bartender that you'd work a few days next week on a trial basis and now? (and I swear in Hungarian). I don't understand you at all any more, I say, throwing my hands up. We're sitting on a sofa in the courtyard, no bonfire today, I think, and I see Mark with his hands in his pockets standing with a group of people and watching me, Dalibor, who lights a cigarette, who's that guy over there? Dalibor asks and takes a drag on his cigarette, *is he your hero?* and he points at the group with his cigarette, at Mark, I don't have any heroes, I answer and I get angry with myself for having answered at all, but you're changing the subject, I say (it was the first warm evening in May, and for a moment I consider telling Dalibor that I love the acacia trees and the sweet, heavy scent of their tiny blossoms, that my favourite honey is acacia blossom honey with its light colour and thin consistency, but I don't tell him, or that the first taste of sweetness I can remember is acacia blossom honey on a thick piece of bread that Mamika sliced for me), Dalibor, who leans back on the sofa, blows his cigarette smoke up towards the sky, this place isn't good for me, he says, I can't take the people here seriously, that's not good, neither for them nor for me and I don't know how to explain that to you but thanks for your help. Dalibor, who looks at me, asks, where's your sister? she's disappeared with her boyfriend, I answer. So you two come here often? Dalibor asks, handing me his cigarette, pretty often, often enough to know that there are a few nice people here who want to change things in society.

I'm not sure what you're angry about, Dalibor says. It's probably because you said working at the Mondial would be better, is my answer.

Better because I want to work, that's all. I don't want to think about possible social constructs as I watch the dogs shit all over the place, I don't want to know if there could be a better society because I don't believe it's possible, *but look, your hero is coming*! Mark, who really is heading towards us, hey, Ildi, how're you doing, he says, don't you want to introduce me to your companion? I haven't seen him here before. You won't see him here again either, I answer, he's here for the first and last time. *Squat?* a foreigner? Mark asks. Yes, and I introduce the two of them. We were just about to leave, I say, I just want to show him a bit more of the city. What, the charming little streets in the old city? or the beautiful windows in the cathedral? No, Sihlfield, where they used to chop off the criminals' heads. Mark can't help but laugh and I watch as Dalibor stands up, turns away with an absent look and heads towards the exit, only when Mark says, your companion's going solo, do I realize that Dalibor is gone.

You can't tell me there's nothing going on, Mark says, looks at me directly, he forgets to put on his mask, stretches out his hand, you're mine . . . Mark's mouth says. Mark, I say and brush his outstretched hand with my fingertips, it's not going to work, I feel—nothing, are you telling me, Mark interrupts, not enough, I say. And I stand up, say that we might see each other again some time, that I'm sorry. I should have told him sooner, I think, I should have told you sooner, I say, the concert's over, and Mark nods at the people streaming out of the cellar, their faces covered with sweat, Mark drops onto the sofa and me, I'm still standing there in front of him, Mark closes his eyes, in the next moment his face is wet, you should never have started with me, he says softly, you already knew back then, the first time (at Mark's place, in his two-room flat on the busiest street in the city where trucks and cars thundered past from six in the morning until midnight), you got up, sat in the kitchen and cried,

I watched you, Mark says, his eyes shut, the courtyard is getting more and more crowded, a couple throw themselves on the sofa, necking, I'm going now, maybe we'll see each other some time at the university, I say and Mark, who finally opens his eyes, yeah, he says, go already, I have no idea why you're still here!

And then, then I walked for hours, I felt light, warm, warmer than the air around me, probably because I was walking fast and the station clocks showed me how late it was—after two, and I was struck by the spots on the pavement, all the trampled chewing gum, a taxi driver, dozing over his steering wheel, not much going on today, said another, leaning against the driver's side door, smoking, it's too warm today, and I nodded. I was sure I could catch up with Dalibor, I walked, faster and faster, maybe even ran now and then, I asked myself what in this city did I love—a few places, an avenue with giant plane trees, a statue of a naked woman in the middle of a small meadow, a few bargain stores I often shop in with Nomi, the public transportation that will get you anywhere and on time, and I realized not long ago that for me, cities don't exist as a whole, but just in the small, run-down areas that I like, and I looked down at the tips of my shoes, worn-out red Converse that carry me through the night, and I want to keep walking blindly through the city until I find Dalibor and I'll run into his arms, I'm sure of it, and if we don't see each other today, we'll never see each other again, I think, and I have to chase that thought away quickly, I have to focus on him, on his soft skin, on the way he holds his cigarette between his thumb and forefinger, his lips that always tremble slightly when he tells a story, it's impossible to lose sight of someone if you constantly think only of him, Dalibor's ears that look like small, vulnerable beings, like *Schmuckstücke*, I told him and tried to explain this German word for ornaments to him in English. My ears are more valuable than diamonds, he answered, laughed, the dark spots on his teeth, his teeth's uneven rhythm, it's called a piano-keyboard mouth, but the image doesn't fit, I think, why does my love for him start with his teeth? I ask myself, eyes, sure, but teeth? and my pace speeds up even more, my Converse are driving me on, you haven't fallen in love since Matteo, they tell me, and it sounds like mockery or a sarcastic truth, Matteo was a long, long time ago, Matteo and Dalibor, if I imagine the two together, they resemble each other so much they could be interchangeable, I like the fact they're similar in my imagination, Matteo, of whom I know nothing, only that he's been living in Italy again for years now and I walk along the river, reach my right hand out to the railing, leave it there as I walk, the iron is cold, colder than the water? Matteo, who was suddenly gone one day, people said the de Rosa family never settled in, Matteo, whom I met on the edge of the forest, by the lake, in the underpass and we kissed in Hungarian or Italian, that is we taught each other the most important words, Nomi and I, we were playing table tennis at the public swimming pool when Matteo's school friend told us they'd moved away,

Matteo and his family, and I, with the table-tennis racket in one hand and the little white ball in the other, Matteo hadn't told me they were leaving, hadn't said a word, and Nomi took the racket out of my hand, crooked her finger around my thumb, they'll surely come back, she said, and I was absolutely convinced that something fundamental would happen to me, something that could never be hidden, the little creature that beat against my ribcage would burst out of me and I'd have a wound I could show but I didn't shed one tear. I listened to the children's happy screeching from the swings or the monkey bars, I saw the small, brightly coloured tools they used to built sandcastles and dig holes. Come on, let's get some ice cream, Nomi said and pulled my little finger and I felt my first love was over for good—I was thirteen years old at the time.

I take my hand off the railing and pick up my pace. I don't want to think of Matteo any more, just of Dalibor, I turn around and put my thumb out, turn again as a car drives past and walk a while longer until a couple picks me up in their white Beetle.

Dalibor is sitting by the lake as I'd hoped he'd be, where we'd met most often, he's sitting on the stones with his legs drawn up, smoking, singing softly to himself. I stand behind him and all the sentences I'd planned to say have vanished, Dalibor, whom I'd never heard sing before, chanting something about the spring breeze and the lake's dark water in his language (we should be able to understand all the songs in every language, I think, God should have restricted the Babylonian division of languages to the spoken word; Dalibor's song is so beautiful and his singing so free, it touches me so deeply that I can't bear to not understand the words). When he is silent again for a long while, only a few lights still burn on the opposite shore, I ask Dalibor, what did you sing? Dalibor turns—and I'm sure that the soft notes he has sung have altered his looks—my favourite song, he says, it's about the sea, how deep it is, vast and terrible, and he reaches for me, we embrace and whisper a few words in each other's ears, we kiss, for the first time, it's so nice that you're here, we kiss in several languages, I've fallen in love with you, in Hungarian, German, Serbo-Croatian and English.

US

In July we celebrate Mother's fiftieth birthday. We sit in the
car, drive along the lake, past houses, villas, docks, bathing
areas that block our view of the lake and Father puts a cassette in the tape player, real Hungarian gypsy music, Father
says, one hand on the steering wheel, the other beating time
to the music and caressing Mother's knee now and then.
Nomi, who points at a shack we'd just passed, do you remember? of course, the neighbouring village's discotheque where
on Saturday nights our heads would spin from the mirrored
ball and boys who already drove mopeds, Father, who always
picked us up at the same time, at eleven (we tried to make
him understand that he could at least wait for us on the other
side of the street and shouldn't get out of the car), look at
that, Mother says to us and to Father, please drive a bit
slower! that's where we lived when we first came to Switzerland and Mother points to a decrepit little three-storey house
near the lake. Really, Nomi asks, why didn't you ever tell us?
we've driven past it so often. We're never sure if you're interested, Father says with a laugh, and you know we lived with
Sándor and Irén, on the same floor, we shared a kitchen and
a bath, Father turned around to face us, back then, at twenty,
we were really modern. Mother has to remind Father we're
on the road, Father, who had treated himself to an aperitif

at home in honour of Mother's birthday (even though, strictly speaking, it's not true, Mother's birthday was actually on Friday but we couldn't celebrate on Friday, so we delayed the party until Sunday and Father always has an aperitif on Sunday).

How long did you live like that, in your WG? I ask (and WG, short for the German word *Wohngemeinschaft*, or commune, was another one of those terms we had to explain to our parents; what? you choose to live with strangers? what if you have to share a bath towel?) *wasn't a weegee*, Father says (because there's no word for it in Hungarian!) but a necessity. You said you were modern back then, I answer; it was a joke, Ildi, didn't you notice? I think we lived like that, with Sándor and Irén, for about two years or so, right? Father, who holds his hand with his wedding ring out to Mother, two years and four months, Mother says and takes Father's hand. Nomi looks at me, probably for the same reason I look at her (the memory of one New Year's Eve when they'd dressed up, Father had dyed Mother's hair that afternoon, very carefully, strand by strand, Mother had trimmed Father's moustache with nail scissors, and Nomi and I, we sat next to each other on the sofa and felt warmth spreading inside us all the way to the tips of our fingers because our parents stood before us in the hallway that evening looking so elegant, Mother in her long, black-and-silver gown, Father in his dinner jacket, we were excited because Father had put his arm incredibly gently around Mother's hips and her hand rested tenderly on his thigh. We're leaving, they said, and whenever anyone speaks of a happy childhood, I think of my time with Mamika and of the moments when my sister and I saw how happy our parents could be).

For her fiftieth birthday, Mother wanted fish, dinner in a seafood restaurant, and for a surprise, Father invited the couples they'd been friends with for a long time, Zoltán and Birgit, Sándor and Irén with their children, and, of course, the two sisters, Mrs Köchli and Mrs Freuler. As Father parks the car in front of the restaurant that only serves seafood, he tells us to cover Mother's eyes. What, a blindfold? yes, let's go, make it quick! and Father hands us a silk scarf, a real surprise only works if you see everthing all at once, and even though we think Father's idea is childish, we go along, Mother is obviously delighted that Father has come up with something special for her birthday. And we lead Mother blindfolded into the restaurant, Nomi leads her by one hand, I lead her by the other, and Father pulls us over, guides us as if our eyes were also bound.

For the surprise, a long table is set with a white tablecloth and a large vase of the red roses Mother is so fond of, a few presents beautifully arranged on the table wait for Mother's hands to unwrap them, the guests are sitting silently in their chairs, the violinist and bassist of a four-man band who start playing a processional as we enter, and only with a second glance do I notice something else that's part of the surprise, a place set at the foot of the table, it has been set even though it will remain empty, filled only by a framed photograph of Aunt Icu. Do you think that's a good idea? I whisper to Father while Mother's eyes are still covered and Nomi looks at me with her eyebrows raised, why not? Father asks, I had the picture blown up specially and her favourite sister should be here too, for her fiftieth birthday!

How could we object? Mother, now allowed to take off the blindfold, claps her hands as she takes it all in—the familiar faces, the flowers, the music the band is playing for her, a soaring, upbeat melody, and Mother falls into Sándor's and Irén's arms, and those of their children and Zoltán and his wife Birgit, she greets the sisters with a hug, and immediately starts dancing with Father. She's wearing my favourite of her dresses, a bronze-coloured dress, its neckline accentuates how gracefully her neck rises from her shoulders and looks unimaginably elegant when she dances, and the other couples stand up, snap their fingers, the two sisters, who had remained seated for a moment, help each other stand and join in the dance shyly but happily.

Nomi and I sit with Attila and Aranka, Irén and Sándor's children, a little older than we are, with whom we have a special intimacy that's difficult to describe, we never need time to get comfortable with one another, but pick up exactly where we left off the last time, even if it's been months since we last saw one another, and we speak German, switching to Hungarian now and then, in a rapid tempo we tell each how things are at work, life in general, about problems with our parents, and I often think we should see one another more often, not just when our parents get together, but we probably all know that it wouldn't work outside of this cosmos.

Are you in love? Attila asks me straight out, you look completely infatuated, his name is Dalibor, I answer, *szerelmes*, yes head over heels, Nomi says, *szerelmet, füstöt, köhögést nem lehet eltitkolni*, love, smoke and cough, none can be hidden, Aranka says and we laugh at this Hungarian proverb, and I have to tell them about my new love, also because Dalibor is from Yugoslavia, I tell them how we met, that I don't actually know very much about him, the first few weeks he was in Chiasso, then in Kreuzlingen. A refugee, Aranka asks, yes, a documented refugee, but still unemployed, and I tell them how hard it has been for Dalibor to find work—our parents wave at us, urge us to dance, maybe later, we say, we're not in the mood yet—and your parents? have you introduced him? too soon still, I answer quickly, we've only known each other a couple of weeks. Serbian? Aranka asks. Yes, a Serb who lived in Croatia, in Dubrovnik. Difficult for your father then, difficult or impossible, I answer (and we'd often joked about how hard it would be to find the ideal man our father would wish for his daughters, a needle in a haystack, but the last thing he'd want is a Serb, no Russians either, or a Swiss, the ideal man would be Hungarian, best of all a *vojdasági magyar*, a Hungarian from the Vojvodina, someone you wouldn't have to explain history to, who knows what it means to be part of a minority and because he knows has emigrated to Switzerland, a Hungarian from the Vojvodina who is successful here in Switzerland in a proper profession, so nothing to do with words, painting or music; he'd also have to have hair on his upper lip, to wear his hair cut short and always be the first to pull his wallet out, discreetly, he would never let a woman pay for him and prefer heavy, manly food—the opposite of those pale men who eat as much salad and vegetables as cows eat grass—his clothes would always be neat, especially his shoes, he'd have served in the military and would certainly never join a protest in a democratic country, above all not on 1 May!). Maybe we don't give our fathers enough credit, Nomi suggests, we always think we know how they'll react, not without reason, Attila counters and asks me to dance, your father can't object if you dance with me, he says and we stand, the violinist takes a few steps towards us and asks as he plays if we know what the birthday girl would most like to hear and I answer right away 'If ever I'm rich, I'll board a plane,' Mother, who stops short when she hears the musicians play the first few bars, takes Father's hand and bursts into tears after the first verse, and Mother's crying is contagious, we all have tears in our eyes (there should be a word for these infectious tears, I think), Mrs Köchli and Mrs Freuler reach for their handkerchiefs too, even though they don't understand the words and the song has a catchy rhythm, Father takes Mother by the hips again and calls out to the rhythm of the song: To my Rósza, on her fiftieth birthday! To my beautiful, beloved Rósza and to many more years

together! Attila and I are dancing next to the sisters, I translate Father's toast for them and the musicians play a flourish,
Father, who calls to the waiter to bring some champagne,
shakes the bottle, we need foam, he says, and a few splashes
on the ground bring good luck! we clink our glasses, toast
Mother and want to lead her to the table so she can unwrap
the gifts but she resists, it's still too early for presents, she
wants to say a few words first, so we gather in a half-circle
around Mother, who lays her right hand on her heart and
says in both languages that she is very happy that we've all
come to celebrate with her and Mother takes her time,
reflects, wipes her hand across her forehead (Nomi, standing
next to me, hooks her arm in mine), I'm now fifty years old,
Mother says, and at fifty I can still remember exactly the first
time my mother gave me a dress she had sewn herself for
my first communion and I don't want to bore you by telling
you how it looked, but I wore that dress until I was fifteen,
my mother had sewn it so that each time she let the hem
down a little, a new pattern would emerge and when there
was no seam left, she sewed on a bit of lace (Mother, illus-
trating her words with hand gestures, asks me to translate
lace and seam into German), and when I really couldn't fit
in the dress any more, she made pillow slips from it and just
today, I can't say why, I took the pillows out of the cases, I
brushed my hand over the material and only today noticed
that my mother had embroidered something on the fabric,
something so fine that you can only see it if you hold the

cloth up to the light, for my beloved daughter, that's what I read today on my fiftieth birthday—and Mother says that her heart is still so much *in movement* because of this, that she had to tell us about it (and I can feel from Nomi's arm in mine, that she is moved by Mother's words too, and I know that Nomi is thinking of the pillows that have always been set out in our parents' room, the only thing we knew about them is that they meant something special to Mother). Mother's mother, who now stands among us in in a light pleated skirt in the fashion of the 1920s, an embroidered blouse, with a wreath of flowers and a small veil crowning her head, and my eyes slip down towards her feet, are caught by her right ankle and a bit of bandage that her black shoe can't hide, my mother's mother's eyes, large, beautiful, knowing, eyes that look back and forth, into a future with a husband, eight years older than she, neither happy nor unhappy, but inevitable, the union with a man almost two heads taller, wearing a crew-cut and trousers tucked into his boots, a pair of pale gloves in his hand.

You loved your mother very much, didn't you? Mrs Köchli says to Mother softly, as we sit down at the table, Mother, who has opened the presents and thanked everyone and asked the waiters to bring in the first course; Mother, who taks Mrs Köchli's hand, yes, she says, I still love her just as much and look, here is my sister Icu, my husband had her photograph blown up so she could be here with us, I miss her as much as I miss my mother; Mother, who tells Mrs

Köchli about Aunt Icu, that her sister is seventeen years older than she is, that's why she grew up alone, without her sisters, yes, there's another sister, a year younger than Icu, but she has nothing to do with her, a terrible argument, Mother says, and everyone around me is talking excitedly, spooning up their soup, sipping from their wine glasses, toasting Mother now and then, Father, who is talking politics with Zoltán; but I listen to Mother's voice, because she is telling Mrs Köchli what she really should be telling me, I listen to her and at the same time wonder why it is she apparently can easily tell Mrs Köchli stories about which I don't know a thing and I wonder if Mother hopes I'm listening in as she tells her story, I, in any case, pretend I'm concentrating on my dinner. (And every once in a while I look at Nomi, on my right, who's talking to Aranka, telling her something about the squatter scene, about punks and concerts, that she thinks it's fun to check it out occasionally and I nod sometimes, maybe even say something, but I'm somewhere else entirely, I only hear Mother's voice.)

The story of a woman who is over thirty when she has her third child and because the others have already moved out, she gets remarried when the late-born daughter is still young, raises her as an only child, spoils her rotten, according to her father who works as a truck driver and is often away from home, and as the child grows, her father sometimes stares at her fixedly for a long time, a stare the girl only knows from the soldiers, a look full of meaning, what that meaning is, she learns when she is seven years old and her parents are fighting one night, her father beats her mother, has she noticed that the child doesn't look anything like him, the father yells, her mother lets the man yell and shout, doesn't answer, it's not his child, he's already heard how she got around all those nights he wasn't home, she was out collecting a stranger's seed, he can see it in the girl, you can see the neighbour's face in hers, she's made him a laughingstock, he's going to throw her out, chase her out of his respectable house, and the girl's mother still doesn't defend herself, the father keeps beating, he's calculated exactly when the child would have been conceived, they weren't even sharing the bed, besides she always got a gleam in her eye when Józsi was here. And the father hits so hard that the child opens the door, crying, and takes her mother in her arms, caressing her, and her mother finally speaks. You claim the girl looks exactly like Józsi, is that so? I'm telling you that our daughter has nothing at all from Józsi, your jealousy is not only making you blind but forgetful too—don't you remember our child was born prematurely, have you figured that into your strange calculations? If you really are convinced of what you say, then *you* pack my things and put us on the street, right now, this instant! Grandmother, who apparently had never spoken like that in her life, so certain, almost combative, her husband disappears for a few days and when he returns, he opens the door, sits at the table and as Grandmother kneels down to pull off his boots, says make me something to eat, I'm hungry.

The main dish was brought out, various kinds of freshwater fish, grilled and served with parsleyed potatoes and spinach, accompanied by a light dry white wine, the kind Mother likes, I turned off the lights and Nomi brought in a multi-layered birthday cake, Mother blew out the candles to our applause, the small candles were removed from the icing, the cake cut, the pieces served out, and after dessert, Mrs Köchli and Mrs Freuler said goodbye, the band struck up again, everyone danced, just like back home! Father shouted exuberantly and the men started drinking beer with chasers and the women were resolute, tonight we're driving home, said Irén, said Birgit, said Mother, and after the musicians had packed up their instruments, the men's heads started smoking because they had to talk politics again, the mothers, sitting at the other end of the table talked inaudibly amongst themselves; Nomi, Aranka and I were standing at the window, looking out at the lake and the lights glowing on the opposite shore and as I turned back towards the room, Zoltán's head seemed swollen, it reminded me of an enormous peony, and it sounded as if he and Father were going to argue like madmen, but each was only trying to drown out the other, they should finally just take away power from all the shit communists everywhere (the waiter juggling the schnapps glasses between the men's waving arms), they're responsible for the war! exactly, the Reds were always about blood . . . I heard the phrases the men flung into the air, Father and Zoltán most of all, pronouncements that hung there for a while, lost and strange, and I was less surprised than usual that the men were so blind in the right eye, they never spoke of the nationalists, definitely not of the sinister alliances between the communists and the nationalists now inciting hatred in the former Yugoslavia; and when Nomi told me I seemed absent, I had the impression that everyone had taken a stand, the men drunk and arguing politics at the head of the table, the mothers whispering secretively at the other end, and the three of us, the daughters, here at the window, could watch it all, part of the scene but outside too. Yes, neither fish nor fowl, Aranka said, or maybe both, Nomi added; and we waved at our parents, went outside for a breath of fresh air, by the lake, the dark water repeated Mother's story, the story of my grandmother, whom I never knew, and the gentle waves asked me a question—why did Mother and Father come to Switzerland, what was the real reason?

Maybe it wasn't Uncle Móric who drove us, but Nándor, that was more likely since Nándor, unlike Uncle Móric, liked to talk and when he talked, his ears always turned red, his ears, which were just as big as his father's ears, in fact, it was very likely Nándor who drove us because I can't think of any plausible reason why Uncle Móric would talk so much precisely on that day, Uncle Móric could very suddenly start talking loudly and decisively, so much so, that you'd think he's never going to stop, but then he does stop just as suddenly as he started and if I think about it more carefully, Nándor's the one who usually drove the Moskvitch and not Uncle Móric, even though it belonged to Uncle Móric, who always said that he preferred to drive his tractor, he liked driving his tractor most of all, Uncle Móric, who sometimes took Nomi and me with him when he drove out to the fields and I can hear Uncle Móric say, this land used to belong to us, and then the question why land can belong to someone and then later not belong to them was one of those unasked questions, I think now, Uncle Móric, who, as I said, never talked much, often repeated the same old things, maybe I'll live to see the day when this land is returned to us, and the tiny blue veins on Uncle Móric's nose told another unknown story.

Nomi and I, we saw the fields, the black dirt of the plain, we learnt what weeds were, we saw hares zigzag across them, we looked for molehills and the scarecrows grinned at us in their flashy outfits, we learnt to tell the different wildflowers apart and when Uncle Móric raised his head to the heavens to declare that the day was heading towards rain, *esöre áll az idö*, we did the same to understand what our uncle meant by it and when it started to rain, we talked about what kind of shower it was—a sprinkling, a gushing rain, whether it dumped or poured, hail as big as pigeon eggs, we'd say; but why a broad stretch of land on this plain once belonged to

us and now didn't any more, that's something we only understood much later when they finally told us the story.

It was most certainly Nándor who came to pick us up
from Hajduk Stankova in the red Moskvitch and drove us to
the bus station, but first, because it was as cold as Siberia's
ass, he had to crawl under the car, swearing the whole time,
and figure out what the problem was, why the damn car
wouldn't start, that's why we missed the bus that we'd wanted
to take, but because you, Mamika, would much rather have
got to Belgrade much too early rather than too late, there
was still no reason to get upset and Nomi and I, we still had
a bit of time, we climbed up the stairs to the roof, fed the
pigeons, looked through the cracks in the roof at the cold
grey November sky, climbed back down the ladder to visit
our animals, the manure pile, and we told the outhouse a
story because your outhouse was a little white shed with a
heart-shaped opening in the door, Nomi watched her
favourite goose from a distance and said, I'm going to send
you a drawing, and we looked for Cicu for a long time, we
made our Cicu sounds, which Cicu usually reacted to, and I
no longer know if my favourite skinny little cat came or not,
in any case Nomi wanted to bring the birch-broom you once
gave her as a present, but you said you would bring it the
next time you came to visit us in Switzerland; and because
Nándor was still busy with the car, you disappeared into the
house to make another coffee and Nomi and I pushed down
the door handle, stuck our heads out, waved at the neighbour

across the way who let his little pigs graze in front of his house on warm evenings, I've often racked my brains trying to remember what this man's name was, he always struck me as benevolent when I watched him from across the way as he let his animals graze, but I can only remember Mr Szalma whose house was to the right of yours and when Nomi and I took a few steps towards 'Juli's corner' and saw no sign of Juli, we turned around and walked past your house, that is, our house, and we called Juli, Puli, Julipuli, Juuulipuuuli, as we'd often done when we were in a teasing mood and Juli seemed the perfect target for our indefinable agitation, we walked straight towards Juli's house where she lived with her mother, Juli's mother, whose name we never knew. Good afternoon, is Juli there? we asked and I remember how happy Juli's mother looked when we asked for her daughter, Juli's not here, she's doing errands, but come in! Not for anything in the world did we want to set foot in the house where Juli lived, no, no, we're leaving right away on a trip, we told Juli's mother, we don't have time. Ah yes, you're the girls going to *Schaiz*, Juli's mother said softly, that's a long trip, and we couldn't stop her from going to get us a few apples and a bag of cookies, thank you! and we were happy we could turn back, go back to our house, we pushed down the door handle and saw your anxious face, where have you been? I've been looking everywhere for you.

We got into the car, you sat between us, put your hands in your lap and Nándor looked back at us, all right then, let's

go, and we backed out of the gate and Nándor left the motor
running when he got out to close it behind us and as we
jolted along Hajduk Stankova Nomi said to me, up that way,
there she is, and because you knew that we wanted to say
goodbye to Juli, you asked Nándor to stop, just for a second,
you said when Nándor shook his head, what do the girls want
with that lunatic? and we got out of the car, we stood in front
of Juli and she just looked at us, she didn't even ask us for
sweets, we're leaving now, I said or maybe Nomi did and we
patted Juli on the arm, got back in the car and looked out
the back window at Juli until the Moskvitch turned the corner and on the paved main road, Nándor stepped on the gas.

Nándor bought our tickets at the bus station, helped the
driver load our bags and helped you into the bus, Nándor
gave us big, sloppy kisses and told us to come back soon in
his loud voice and we waved goodbye as the bus pulled away,
you pulled out a packet from your purse and we nibbled on
pretzel sticks, just like little mice, you said, and you checked
one more time to make sure you had all the papers, my sweet
girls, you said, Nomi, who sat in front of me, in the window
seat, and I remember there was no sun that day, it smelt of
coal and ground meat, sausage, garlic, apples, of bread,
because someone was always eating something and you had
packed us some bacon, roast chicken, *lecsó* vegetable stew and
the pancakes that Nomi and I also liked to eat cold, and I'm
certain that when there were no more pretzel sticks we ate
the sour-cream pancakes, every time Nomi took a bite, she

would hold her pancake up and ask, what's this? a lazy dog, Aunt Manci snoring, a peeing cow, last night's moon; we played all sorts of games to pass the time, through the smudged windows we counted bicycles, stray dogs, smoking chimneys, this bus trip that differed from other bus trips in that it was much longer, the driver, who parked the bus several times, left the engine running and shouted, laughing, time for a break-to-pee-to-get-some-air-to-stretch-your-legs-or-pray.

For the entire length of the drive, as far as I can remember, we only spoke a few words with one another, you were constantly humming a song, and because the bus engine was so loud, the driver had turned the radio up and sang or whistled to the tunes, I had to lean my head on your shoulder to hear you, Nomi peeked at us through the gap in the chairs then fell asleep and when, late that night, we dove into an ocean of lights, all the heads in the bus were glued to the windows because we had finally arrived in Belgrade, you said to me, look at that, the city was waiting for us, waiting for our dusty old bus from the provinces.

REAL BIG

As the sun shines through the windows in the Mondial one morning, an ordinary summer morning, I'm constantly looking out of the window between orders, outside, at the leaves of the chestnut tree, dark green and trembling slightly in the sun, and there is much more going on than usual this morning, so much that I don't have time to look anywhere in particular, Glorija, whose beautifully polished nails are constantly tapping on the counter because her hands and feet are faster than I am, where are you? here, I call back; as the sun draws pools of light on the carpet, on its brown-and-beige pattern, I keep having to ask Glorija what she just ordered, a morning on which I keep losing the thread, can't work smoothly, am easily distracted because I can see the air, how it's filled with tiny beings, dust motes, and Glorija says she needs a cheese sandwich and a four-minute egg but she'd rather hand her order in to the kitchen herself, thanks anyway! and as I turn on the grinder, I picture to myself how the dust motes settle everywhere, on the croissants, how they make themselves comfortable in people's hairdos, I know it's all Dalibor's fault, he's responsible for my slowness, for my attraction to the light, I can see Dalibor, how he looks at me, I see how his lips laugh when he touches my hips with his fingers, when we lean against the chestnut tree, you're beautiful, I say to him, to the chestnut tree, and the moon spins through the leaves, we lie down, we're lying on the ground and our hands search for each other, and I hear his voice in my back, I'm excited, he says, I say it too and my hair brushes his stomach, and I love the way his breath makes his navel rise and fall, in the slight, excited trembling against my lips and right after I've pulled three espressos, I hear the language that is completely banned here—Serbo-Croatian (Mother and Father had forbidden Glorija and Dragana to speak to each other in their native language several months ago), Glorija's voice is unusually loud, but resounding even louder are Dragana's consonants and vowels, I listen to the two voices interlock for a moment and realize how unpleasant it is to hear two voices, very loud, and not have any idea why they're raised, only a few words flash, *zena* (woman), *dom* (house), *rat* (war), *ti* (you), and over the Cimbali I see that heads have turned towards the kitchen, I wonder if I should serve them, if I should act as if nothing was happening, Tuđman! I hear, Milošević! I wipe my hands on my apron and walk briskly to the kitchen to find out what is going on.

Father, who waves at me to shut the door, Dragana, who is holding on to the washing machine, trying to pull herself up, Marlis, who tries to help but Dragana ignores the proffered hand and continues speaking at the top of her voice, Glorija, still on the floor, her stockings torn, her words lost in a high-pitched whimper, what's going on? I ask, kneel down next to Glorija and try to calm her, Marlis, leaning on the counter where we stack the dirty dishes, starts to cry and Father, smacking his hand on his forehead, starts cursing in our language, any mutt on the street has better things do than what I'm forced to watch here, *mi történt*, what happened? I ask Father, you can understand what they're saying, I tell him and help Glorija up, nothing but a flea fart, he shouts in Hungarian, nothing at all, one bumped into the other, accidentally, and they went after each as if one of them had tried to assassinate the other even though they were soulmates until now; Glorija, her knee cut open, keeps whimpering, and the customers, Father swears, who's serving the customers? I'm going, I say and Dragana, now silent, stands at the draining board, her back towards me, looking out the window (Dragana probably knows at this point that she won't be working for us much longer, her blouses, hanging on wire hangers in the employee closet a few weeks later, a pair of shoes with the heels unevenly worn down, waiting in vain for the right feet, Dragana, who never even tells me she's not coming back), you could at least give Glorija a bandage, I say as I'm walking out the door, am I supposed to console them all, too? Father shouts after me angrily, I have to ask Mother to help, Mother, in the office working on the books, and I try to explain what happened in a few words, Mother doesn't ask a single question but gets up immediately and stands behind the counter and I wait on the tables, a few of the guests are craning their necks, what on earth's the matter with the waitress? and the screams, who was that? Nomi, who has got a day off, whispers to me what I should say. Screams of joy, I say, nothing more, our line cook and our waitress just realized they have a mutual friend, yes, it's true, exuberance can sound like anger!

Today *the real big men* have moved into the Mondial, I think once I'm back behind the counter and Glorija is back waiting on the tables after she got new stockings from Mother and tidied herself up, I'm not Tuđman! Glorija says to me in a strained voice between orders, listen to me, if someone told you you were as evil as Tuđman, what would you say? (I think of 'Little Big Man', I think that I've never seen Dustin Hoffman act better than in that movie), Ildi, you have to admit I was right, Milošević and Tuđman, they're like black and white (I can hardly remember anything more than Dustin Hoffman's face, how impressed I was with his earnestness), do you know Tuđman? I ask and try to keep a straight face, try not to laugh. Yes, of course I know him, have you noticed also that Tuđman has big beautiful eyes? and I shake my head, knock the coffee grounds out of the filter, Milošević isn't the Bosnian head of state, I say, but he governs all of Serbia, Glorija answers quickly, everyone knows that and she sets the cups on the saucers. Dragana says she's Bosnian, I reply, and you rang up one coffee too few. Ildi, Bosnian, that's just a memory, a memory of a lie, and Glorija looks me in the eye, if we Croats didn't believe we're Croatian then we'd still be Yugoslavian. The losers, you mean, and Glorija sets a spoon next to each coffee cup, Dragana is a Serb whether she likes it or not, but if she insults my country, well then, and Gloria pulls the tray onto her right palm, then it's over with us, says Glorija, who sets off, her hair whipping behind her.

Today Franjo Tuđman is wearing a white blouse with puffy sleeves, I think he's got red fingernail polish and his newly bleached hair is still thick for his age, usually the president of Croatia is in a good mood and hums English pop songs softly to himself, he sways his hips almost imperceptibly which suits his understated make-up and his discreetly plucked eyebrows and to make his cheekbones more noticeable, he's not wearing glasses today but contact lenses, maybe even coloured lenses, I think, Franjo Tuđman, whose speciality is dashing through the Mondial, busy and elegant, and tapping on the cash register buttons with verve, was just now lying with a bloodied knee on the linoleum floor in the kitchen next to the freezer filled with bread, croissants and ten-litre tubs of ice cream; Tuđman crashed into a woman, a woman who claims to be Bosnian, one thinks all the heads of state in the former Yugoslavia are possessed (and suddenly every politician is religious, of all things! Dragana says to me, not so long ago they were all communists, Ildi, all they knew was their red heaven, and now? Now each one has his own idea of heaven, *they all think they're biggest, what you think, if everyone get divorced because they're not the same religion?* she, in any case, is married to a Muslim who even eats pork now and then, if she makes it taste good).

204

Mother, who joins me behind the counter, says I should go to the office and write out the day's menu board, and Ildi, please, don't speak about what happened, yes, of course, I say and hand Mother my apron, take a coffee along to drink in the office, I sit at the brown desk, light a cigarette, glance at the calendar on the wall, I always look at the calendar's logo first, a gift from a sales rep, I think and reach for a piece of white chalk, *Dalibor*, I write on the board, *Dalibor Dalibor Dalibor*, until it's completely full and I lean back, I look at his name and think about the fact that I flinched as soon as I thought of Father when Dalibor told me he was Serbian, a Serb from Croatia of all places, I spit on the sponge and wipe the black slate.

'Home-made lasagne with green salad,' is what Mother had told me to write on the board, 'vegetable plate with fried egg' (I thought of Father because I pictured how he would react when I introduced him to Dalibor, a Serb, he would say, of all things, a Serb!), this evening I'm going to talk to Father, I write the sentence on the board so that I won't forget, light another cigarette, I'll ask Father if he knows any nice Serbs (and I know that the nice exception is a weak argument and only proves the detestable rule), Mother, who pokes her head in the doorway, asks, what's taking so long? and I cover the board so that Mother can't see my resolution.

We're alone at the table, Mother and I, Father is in his chair in front of the television, changing channels with the remote when Mother says, please come finally, Father changes the channel, not hungry, he grumbles, gets up, opens the cabinet, grabs the bottle, Mother and I eat in silence, Nomi's place is set, I'm sure she'll be here soon, Mother says, Father doesn't answer, disappears into the kitchen, Mother looks at me, her eyebrows raised, do you know where she is? she asks in a whisper while Father swears at the icetray, probably in Wohlgroth, I answer, or with Dave, but she's never stayed away a day and a night before. That's true, I say loud enough for Father to hear, one time is the first time and we're old enough, aren't we? Mother turns very pale, in her beautiful eyes I can read several stories that all have the same message—no fights tonight! Be quiet, he can hear us! I can't stand it when he raises his voice. A fight is like a bad meal, it ruins your stomach! And I hear Father come out of the kitchen and I lean forward a bit, reach for a piece of bread, and Father passes by me, behind me, the ice cubes clink lightly as he sits back down in his armchair and turns up the television; Mother and I, we eat a few more bites before we give up and sit still as if the table and chairs needed us, we sit and can't think of anything to say because we're only there to register what Father does—smokes one cigarette after another, opens the drinks cabinet door, fills his glass, goes to the kitchen for ice, slams the ice tray, returns to his armchair—and Father's silence is deafening, some people are so loud when they're silent, I think, and I'd like to get up and clear the table, pack up the cheese, the ham, but I can't move, I think of Nomi, that she's really the older of us two, that she does things I wouldn't dare (Nomi, who doesn't refuse to conform out of principle, but on a whim, spontaneously and without any thought, even in elementary school, she had the guts to wear purple overalls even though a clique of four girls in her school, who set the tone, all of them filthy rich, decided what was in and neither purple nor overalls made the grade. When Nomi wore them, the queen bees didn't like her, of course, but at the same time she became popular, even idolized, because her stubborn unselfconsciousness and easy-going way of doing what she wanted made her irresistible, Nomi, who laughed in the four girls' faces when they called her boy-crazy).

It's after ten when Father starts talking, he rails about the two hens and says that you've got to ask yourself what's going on when chickens try to play at politics, as if they had any idea, they have as much of an idea of politics as freshwater fish do of the sea, not the slightest, that is! and I finally catch on that Father is talking about Dragana and Glorija, getting himself worked up again that they had the audacity to argue so loudly, there's nothing worse than two hens pecking at each other, Father rants and Mother takes a deep breath because she thinks Father will be distracted for at least a few minutes from waiting for Nomi, and of course the customers notice when two hens say disgraceful things to each other in Serbian, Father, who toasts the television announcer, by the way, Meili from the municipal council asked me if we were all Yugos this afternoon and I had to explain to him that we're Hungarian, how is it Meili doesn't know that? couldn't all of you out front explain to the guests the difference between Slavs and Hungarians? that Hungarian and Serbian have as about as much in common as a hen and hen of the woods, it must be obvious! Mother, who takes another deep breath, steels herself, gets up, takes the butter, cheese and ham into the kitchen, the way a professional waitress would and I think to myself that it's probably not the ideal time to tell them about Dalibor, Mother returns to the living room with quick steps, stacks the plates noisily, you don't have to disturb me on top of it all, Father shouts, can't you leave the damn plates where they are? what do you mean by clearing the table now? Father gets up again, fills his glass, without ice this time, and I, still in my chair, have started to think Nomi won't come back, that she's moved out without telling anyone, I'd like to go to her room and see if she's taken her clothing, her favourite books, but I sit there, glued to my chair under the living-room lamp, my face frozen in the porch window, we must have done something wrong, Father says, speaking as loud as the television, why else would I be sitting here, waiting for my daughter? (and me, I'd suspected the hens were just a warm up, I hear Mother making more noise than usual as she washes up, the sharp stream from the faucet, the clatter of dishes), and what are you waiting for, Miklós? Father continues, that one of your daughters turns out the way you'd hoped she would? hope isn't worth

208

dirt, and Father slams his glass down on the living-room table, a bad star, and Father's voice rises, ooohhh suuure, next she'll be bringing her men under my roof so that I can be pals with my daughter's boyfriends, we can call each other by our first names, glad to meet ya! Father says and waves a hand in the air (and I remember how, on a class trip not long after I'd arrived in Switzerland, the first sausage I ever tried to roast fell in the fire, your stick was too thin, the teacher said when I started to cry), and life, do they know what life is worth when it's all rules and regulations, when you can't even choose your own goddamn job? Some random communist comes and tells you what training programme you can do, how your name will be written, when and how you can fart and that you're farting against the system (and me, I picture myself sitting outside, in a chair on the grass, the canes of the rose bushes tied, the pansies in the flower beds next to me, purple and yellow, which I'd never liked), and your daughters, their heads all muddled, the one with no interest in school does have something upstairs but she uses it for everything but school, and the other one, what does she do? she studies history, I answer, Father, who doesn't hear me, gets up, opens the cabinet, takes out the bottle, is about to pour himself another drink but sets his glass back on the bar, takes a swig from the bottle, takes it back to his chair, she can't decide because she's got all the possibilities in the world. Miklós, this is enough to make me crazy or to make me laugh—Mother closes the kitchen door behind her and lays her hand on my shoulder, go to bed, she says, and I don't know if she's talking to me or to Father. What would they do in a war, if there were nothing, nothing, nothing, absolutely nothing left? Father's voice gets louder with each 'nothing' and drowns out the television, Mother, standing behind me, her hand warming my shoulder, go to bed, she repeats and now it's obvious that she's talking to me; me, I don't answer, I stay where I am and Mother sits down across from me in my line of sight. Well, Rósza, we wanted our children to have better lives, that is what we wanted, isn't it? yes, their lives are better, as good as the well-fed animals in the zoo, that's right, and like the monkeys they're swinging over our heads, they think we're idiots (I've never considered the two of you idiots, I want to say), well, Rósza, would we be doing what we do if we'd had the same opportunities as our daughters? Stop it, Mother says, you're drunk. I am drunk, I'm plastered, I'm a drunk and I'll always be a drunk and I don't want to be anything but a stinking drunk, you hear me? (Maybe we should have been more open with our parents, Nomi and I, about our boyfriends; for a long time Nomi and I believed we should spare our parents on that front, so that we could do what everyone else did here, we translated the 'hot topic' into Hungarian in a way that made it sound acceptable, a *Fez*? that's a birthday party where we blow out candles and play some games . . . we knew our parents didn't entirely believe us and they didn't want to admit they knew what it was like to feel that heat in their own and in other bodies even though they'd grown up in a different culture. I want to get up and go out into the night, the stars are so beautiful because they're telling us, we don't understand you, you're too far away, the reason stars are so inconceivably beautiful, Dalibor had said, is because they leave us in peace.)

By the time Nomi comes home, the whisky bottle is empty, the television has been switched off, Mother and I are still sitting at the table, and Nomi, who peeks around the corner, beams at us, blows a kiss, Father snores, asleep on the sofa, what's the matter? Nomi asks with a laugh and joins us at the table, where were you? Mother asks. I went to an amazing concert and stayed over at my boyfriend's, I was drunk, I slept almost the whole day and had breakfast with Dave in the afternoon, now I'm here and I'm glad to see you. Nomi is beautiful, I think, her face like freshly risen dough and her dark eyebrows' neat arch, you could at least have called, Mother answered in a weary voice, yes, true, Nomi says, I completely forgot, but I don't want to have to call always, Nomi says, you knew I'd come home, right? Father sits up, reaches for a cigarette, coughs his cough, stands up with the lit cigarette, comes towards us, his hand outstretched, he wraps Nomi in his arms, I take the cigarette from between his fingers, Father buries his face in Nomi's shoulder.

None of us expected the phone to ring so early in the morning. It's five-thirty, Father has just left when it rings twice and falls silent. Nomi, Mother and I, all meet in the hallway and wait next to the table on which the telephone sits, maybe Dragana is calling in sick or Glorija, Mother says, but we all know it's something else. A few minutes later it rings again, hello, hello? It's you, Mother says in our language and holds the receiver in both hands and soon says that she's very sorry to hear the news. Oh, my dear, she says, I hope everything will be fine, what? the connection is so bad I can hardly hear you, yes, I'm also glad that I could at least hear your voice, Mother, still holding the receiver, looks at us, her eyes evasive, they've conscripted Béla into the Yugoslav People's Army, not right now, two months ago already, he's fighting in Bosnia, in Banja Luka.

And I know that I'm not allowed to ask questions, that I have to stay quiet, that we have to get dressed, that there's nothing we can do. Mother turns and disappears into the bedroom, closes the door behind her and she—the person I am—stands there in the hallway and my eyes are caught by the framed jigsaw puzzle Nomi and I assembled and glued together years ago, a seven-hundred-and-fifty-piece landscape picture of mountains, meadows, flowers and, the toughest of all, a crystal clear sky. Nomi looks at me briefly then sets up the ironing board, fills the steam iron with water to press one of the timelessly hideous blouses and I withdraw into the bathroom to do on that morning what I do every morning—wash my face, neck, underarms, brush my teeth, put on mascara and discreet lipstick, so that I can make a pleasant appearance soon. And inside we'll gnaw on the bad news and hope that the next few days will leave us in peace, will be faceless and mundane as they pass and I have no idea what I should do, what now? I should I should I should . . . and instead of coming up with a plan of action, the only thing that occurs to me is how Uncle Piri could use the community room to give a lecture on the *kusok*, as he calls politicians, his term always struck me as a fitting twist on the Hungarian word for politician, *politikusok*, because in Hungarian *s* is pronounced as *sch*, so Uncle Piri's term sounds like 'cushy'—and Aunt Icu's proud, impassive expression would spur him on—those paper bandits, those paper-chewers, they look like a calf has just licked their faces, but it wasn't an innocent animal's pink tongue, oh no, it was the devil's forked tongue that licked every single one of those *kusok* faces! Just look at them, he'd say whenever we tuned into some political debate on television, one *kusok* is just like another—once he's got where he wants to be, he's got a face that's been licked like all the others and it looks more than a little like an arse smeared with grease, how is that possible? And as soon as she heard the word 'animal', Aunt Icu would launch into a tirade about Béla's pigeons, those creatures are making me crazy, they do nothing but coo and crap from morning to night (Béla's pigeon-breeding had turned the entire attic into a ghostly sea of bobbing grey-white-green heads, Father, when he saw the pigeons for the first time, apparently said, look at that, I haven't seen so many pretty communists in one place for a long time), Béla, who didn't take his pigeons with him when he got married and moved into a house painted moss-green across the street because he was worried his goddamn creatures were too sensitive to survive the ridiculously short move, as Aunt Icu would rail, those creatures with eyes as ugly as slugs, they fly everywhere, do you really think they care if they live here or if Béla pampers them a stone's throw away? Aunt Icu, who always complains about the pigeons but otherwise never lets anyone say the slightest thing against her son, Aunt Icu's gold earrings would tremble with delight when her son called her *anya*, mother, with an intonation perfectly pitched to get him exactly what he wanted.

On Saturdays I have to be in the Mondial by seven, my face ready, Good Morning! and I definitely won't turn the radio on at work today even if everyone asks, Miss, why is it so quiet today? (after several long weeks, when we finally get a sign of life from our family, it's a sign that what each of us here, deep down inside, feared might happen is happening, that the family still back there, in the East, has not been spared, that the war does have a face, a face that commands—Pack your things, let's go, on the double! Arms, legs and deadly speed that kills anyone who resists it), today I'll be deaf, I think, I, who have, in fact, not wanted to hear anything for a long time and certainly haven't wanted to see anything, no radio, no TV (what's actually going on in the world?), no newspaper? I've so often resolved not to let anything reach me, for days at a time I didn't listen to the radio or read any papers, I withdrew into my room, even covered my ears when Father watched the news for hours; I cut myself off for days when stunned by headlines like 'Is There a Way Out of the Balkan Horror Show?' only to look feverishly in all the daily papers for articles about the Balkan War (Balkan War, that sounds like some local speciality, like Vaudois sausage or *Wienerschnitzel*, Nomi joked, exactly, Balkan War is a regional speciality, a home-made concoction that comes from their warlike character; we're occasionally able to make fun of terms like 'Balkan Horror Show', because we want to give our pain wings and I know that after today it will be different, I know that from now on I won't be able to read a single line about the Balkan War without thinking of Béla).

I swing my wardrobe door open quickly to feel the air on my face, dazed, I stand facing the Mondial outfits it holds (your clothes must be attractive but discreet, colourful but not loud, I choose and combine according to average taste, which means never too dark on top, under no circumstances a black blouse, in general, lighter colours on top than below, a black skirt is OK, a black shirt, never), for a while now I've been giving my Mondial outfits names. The Daisy Duck blouse I mentioned, but there are others, the army drab dress, for example, with a pointless piece of cloth, about as wide as my hand, that hangs from shoulder to hip, those shirts of the Timelessly Hideous brand (light grey or light beige, thick material, unobjectionable cut), and the so-called two-piece outfits, which I call my Pfister dresses because every time I wear one Mr Pfister pays me a compliment and since I can't decide what to wear, I pull open the drawer and grab a packet of Lady Luxury, I scrunch up the stockings inch by inch with two hands, stick my feet into the reinforced toes, pull the stockings above my knee, too quickly, I get annoyed at the runs, pull the stockings back off, Nomi, who knocks on my door, says, we have to leave soon, yes! I answer, standing in front of the wardrobe again, I imagine myself squeezing into a blouse, fastening up the buttons covered in the same cloth as the blouse, and as I picture how I'll soon be standing in the Mondial in a blouse buttoned up to my neck and a skirt, I see Béla, see him crouching in my wardrobe. His face is pale, a young man scared to death, he makes an unmistake-able gesture, I should close the wardrobe, he even moved his lips, I say to Mother, who is standing in my room next to Nomi, I shut the wardrobe because Béla asked me to, I tell them; Mother says the news was a shock, naturally, and she opens the wardrobe to show me that it was just an illusion, my imagination playing a trick on me, Nomi, who takes a dress out of the wardrobe so that I don't have to choose, and me, I say that it must mean something that Béla appeared to me in my wardrobe, I'm sure it does, Nomi says and helps me into the dress, we have to hurry, she says, Mother, standing next to us, looks out the window, it could just be that tomorrow it will all be over. What do you mean, it will all be over? I ask. The war, Mother answers. There's always one day when a war ends, why shouldn't that day be tomorrow?

Tito held Yugoslavia together with an iron fist, announces Mr Berger, who raises his eyes from his well-respected daily newspaper, leans back a bit in his chair because it's a Saturday, Tito was a charismatic leader, you have to admit, Mr Berger is in a discussion with Mr Tognoni (an immigrant who made it, he owns several construction firms) and Saturdays are hardest for me, if it weren't for work, Saturdays would be golden days, with surprises possible at any hour, a day to spend under the chestnut trees right in front of the Mondial, Saturday, the day when all the individual orders become one giant desire, on Saturday every mistake weighs twice as heavy, we know this, Nomi and I, waiting tables, the requests are accompanied by a friendly look, friendly and pitiless, I think (the exceptions, like Mr Schlosser, who sits in his quiet corner, perfectly content with his *café crème* and his magazine, the *Neue Revue*, or the two sisters, Mrs Köchli and Mrs Freuler, who shake our hands before they sit and their handshakes are so prodigal in their warmth and openness that I'm always surprised by the sincerity of their greeting), all the Saturday kings and queens whose slightest command we follow, and I've never told anyone that I meet everyone on Saturdays except myself.

Tito had Yugoslavia well in hand, you must admit, Mr Berger repeated, did you know his real name was Josip Broz?

and smoke rises from Mr Berger's pipe as I stand at their table, waiting for his and Mr Tognoni's order (never rush a guest, especially not on Saturday). The Balkans are one giant crisis, Mr Tognoni orders a full breakfast with no jam but with a soft-boiled egg, the Balkans are not one entity, Mr Berger, whose smoke rises to my nose and tickles my wide nostrils (you've almost got an African nose, someone said, a customer, your nose would fit in a black face. Really, you think so, you really think so?), ah yes, Mr Berger says to my blouse, a *café crème* for me and a very light *café au lait* with sweetener for my wife, my wife isn't here yet, but you can bring it now because my wife will be here soon. Gladly, I say. And the Balkans are a multinational state with an interesting history and Josip Broz was an intelligent man, he defied Nikita Krushchev, he, Tito, tried to find the Third Way, which was, of course, doomed from the start and, have you ever been to Yugoslavia? Oh really? And Mr Tognoni was in Yugoslavia once, in Ljubljana, not far from Italy at all, he says as I set the table, placemat, napkin, knife and spoon, don't dismiss Ljubljana, it's got a lot to offer, Slovenia isn't comparable to the rest of the Balkans, Austro-Hungary had a decisive influence there, don't forget. And I put the basket with a croissant, a roll and slice of bread on the table.

Yes, Slovenia doesn't really have anything to do with the Balkans, I'm convinced of that, Mr Berger's pipe says, Miss, it seems my wife is not coming after all, naturally I take the *café au lait* with sweetener back and instead of a roll he'd like a milk bun, white or whole wheat? Mr Tognoni is an immigrant who has not only made it professionally but is active in the municipal council and supports the conservative Swiss People's Party and further, as he recounted, he and his wife did a Japanese algae treatment last week, whole wheat, Mr Tognoni says without the trace of an accent. The Balkans won't spare us or anyone else, he says (he must have arrived in the 70s, when the Swiss complained about the influx of *Tschinggen*, or wops—at the time Italians were Enemy Number One), soon we'll have a kebab stand right in the middle of our community! and I serve Mr Tognoni his soft-boiled egg, and it's not the Slovenians who are coming (the construction workers whose taciturnity I miss on Saturday mornings), and Mr Tognoni's aftershave is discreet, I think as I serve him the orange juice that comes with his full breakfast, I wouldn't mind a few Slovenian workers in my business, and Mr Tognoni thanks me.

Where are you from originally, by the way? My parents were from northern Italy, from Piedmont, Mr Tognoni reports and I set down the double espresso he ordered with his full breakfast and Mr Berger motions with his pipe that I can bring the *café au lait* with sweetener, gladly, I say and, Miss, bring me another croissant. White or whole wheat? I ask. Doesn't matter, Mr Berger replies, Miss, may I ask you a question, you two are sisters, right? and Mr Berger's pipe points to Nomi (Nomi, who would probably have come up with a pert answer to his question—how nice that you and

219

your wife and Mr Tognoni are out on an educational field trip on a Saturday), yes, we're sisters, I answer. My wife and I often wondered if you were sisters, look at their mouths, I told my wife, but their hair, my wife said! Even a child knows that hair can distract you from seeing a resemblance, a hairstyle can make a big difference, isn't that right?

(And I'd like to pull a comb from my blouse pocket and fix Mr Berger's and Mr Tognoni's hair, to fluff up their thin hair, not in a mean way, just because I'd like to send their hair on a roller-coaster ride, to see the joy of speed light up their faces for a second, to see it conjure youthfulness back into their faces, I'd like to see their excited fingers pulling at candyfloss), the Schärer brothers, who now sit down at table seven next to Berger and Tognoni, shake hands, how are you? they've just come from a bike ride, the slender Schärer says, one hundred and twenty kilometres, every Saturday! Berger, Tognoni, who nod at each other knowingly, Miss, the thin Schärer says, two coffees, black! (the slender Schärer and the thin one, because you can hardly tell the two apart).

Tell us about the situation in your country, Mr Berger says when I bring the two coffees for the Schärers, Mr Berger, who reaches for his pipe which needs to be filled. You must be aware our waitress comes from the Hungarian region of the Balkans, you know, where it's about to explode, the Vojvodina, that's what it's called, that region, an autonomous province until recently, wasn't it? (the Bergers, who'd politely asked last week what part of the Balkans we came from.

From the northern part of Yugoslavia, south of Hungary, I anwered and Hungary is always the key, everyone knows a Hungarian dentist and the memory of the 1956 Uprising is still fresh because right after people showed their sympathy for the insurgents by finally getting rid of tons of worn-out clothing, and for a good cause too; everyone knows the *puszta*, the Great Hungarian Plain, Béla Bartók, ah, the fiery music that is such a treasure! Your mother tongue is Hungarian, then, not Serbo-Croatian, Mrs Berger deduced, yes, I confirmed. So you're not from the Balkans at all, then? Not really, I answered, but still somehow we are, I thought. Mr Berger suddenly wrinkled his brow, lectured his wife Annelis, you see, I told you, people from the Balkans have a different shape to the backs of their heads), and I put the light *café au lait* with sweetener back on the table for Mrs Berger, who is now sitting at the table. Oh really? and Mr Tognoni (who should be sent on a much longer roller-coaster ride than Mr Berger) is suddenly interested in her, the person I am, I had no idea, Mr Tognoni says with a faint glow in his eyes, I thought you were from Russia, now who could have told me that? Your imagination, Mauro, it led you by the nose, Mr Berger laughs (and what I wanted to explain about my country would probably not have interested Mr Tognoni, Mr and Mrs Berger or the Schärers, they most likely would have looked at me with pity and some embar-rassment—we were thinking of something else, Miss, we wanted to hear about the culture, the history, the language, the problems there, not about the air between majestic poplars and acacia trees, the tiny flowers that bloom between the paving stones, the dust, the mud, about Béla . . .). I'm sorry but I don't have time, because of my . . . of course, Miss, we see can see you're busy, but please bring us another round of fresh orange juice, and I smile, turn away (maybe next time I'll ask them a question, I think, about the Wars of Religion, the Battle of Sempach, the Swiss Mercenaries or the legends of the devil, that's what she, the waitress I am, would ask tables six and seven and Mrs Berger would forget to lick the milk-foam moustache discreetly from the corners of her mouth, shocked that a waitress could ask questions about Swiss history or Swiss culture. I come from the Balkans and study history, I'd say, Modern History and Swiss History, how ridiculous of me to want to prove myself to people about whom I would feel completely indifferently if they weren't regulars at the Mondial); and I, my attention suddenly diverted to the Schärers, I realize only now that the two brothers never say anything, they join the conversation simply with an occasional 'ah yes' or 'I see'.

It's nagging at me, Mr Tognoni says as I put the glasses of juice on the table, I could have sworn that someone told me you were from Russia, and Mr Tognoni is worried because his memory might be worse that it used to be, it certainly wasn't me, Mr Pfister says and sits down next to the Schärers, if you want to know anything about our waitress, just ask me, I know everything about her, Mr Pfister gives me a charming wink; and when I bring his light *café au lait* and orange juice, he, Mr Tognoni and the Bergers have already moved on to the advantages of Tai Ginseng and Gingko tablets.

At eleven thirty, Nomi and I sit at the staff table, eating veal stew and puréed potatoes with buttered carrots, I can't stand the chatter any more, I say, Nomi, who looks at me, mixes the gravy into her potatoes, their yakking about Yugoslavia, Nomi, who still looks at me as she opens her mouth, takes a bite, chews, swallows, what do you expect, Nomi says, and I, who have stopped eating, I light a cigarette, I'd like to pro-voke them, I say, *them* who? Nomi asks and spears a piece of meat with her fork, you know who I mean. Then do it, and Nomi's fork hangs in the air, the tines pointed at me, just as people want to chew, they want to chatter, there's nothing inherently wrong with that and it's not meant for you, says Nomi, who lays the fork on the rim of her plate. If not me, for whom then? and I look past Nomi, at the Mondial, now almost empty as it always is at this time of day. For the day, the boring morning, for the air, imagine what it would be like if the air were always bad. Maybe it is and we just don't see it, I answer.

Ildi, Nomi says, no one can help it that our family lives in Yugoslavia.

We can't help it either, I answer, put out my cigarette, stand up irritated, take our plates into the kitchen, and when

I see Marlis, eyes glowing, harmlessly mumbling something to herself, I suddenly realize how harmless the constant chatter is compared to the Schärer brothers' quiet lurking, constantly watching and waiting for the precise moment when, out of envy, they can make a deeply cutting remark.

•

MAMIKA AND PAPUCI

We only have a few days to visit our relatives in the Vojvodina in the summer of 1988 when our parents were running their first cafe, feeling oddly rushed, we sat in living rooms we'd known for years and which hadn't changed in all that time since they were only used for celebrations, for special occasions—furniture that still smells of the factory even though it has sat in the same spot for ages, floor to ceiling built-in cabinets, upholstered furniture, side tables decorated with embroidered tablecloths; the wall coverings in these showrooms are always in perfect condition, the crystal glasses look unreal, these rooms' indescribable atmosphere of cool emptiness, and Nomi and I agree that we don't care for these rooms, even though we don't want anything in our homeland to change, these rooms in which not even the slightest detail is ever altered strike us as horrible, frightening, and when Aunt Manci invites us into her 'good room' with the life-size doll that stares at us with its stony, glinting eyes, still there! then Nomi says, then I say, Aunt Manci, couldn't we sit in the kitchen instead? (Luckily, Mamika and Aunt Icu don't have special rooms for company.)

It's raining, not constantly but often, in fits, Nomi says, the weather is sympathizing with us, and we race through our family visits, as if a wasp had stung you in the arse, Uncle

Piri jokes and we laugh as we cry and say goodbye just hours after our tear-filled reunion, and we're already seated in the next kitchen or in one of the showrooms, having another drink of Traubi Soda or tonic or schnapps and we have to decline politely because we already had a piece of cake after lunch, we decline and say, maybe later, so as not to offend anyone, after we've told them a bit about life in Switzerland, about our cafe (and someone asks if the Swiss have time for a coffee, and how! Father answers, some of our customers spend the entire morning in our cafe, and naturally they're all impressed, so much time spent sitting in cafes and still so wealthy! well, of course, kids, the Swiss let their money work for them, and everyone laughs because they can't imagine exactly how you can have your money work for you), after we've heard what our relatives have to tell us, that life is still hard, oh, oh, the corn and the beautful sunflowers, if it keeps raining like this, it will be a terrible harvest (and I remember that Uncle Móric said he wished he were my American uncle when I told him that I'd been to the United States after my graduation! Uncle Móric nodded, where the great machines are invented, the wheatfields are endless and everyone is born lucky, I never understood why you didn't emigrate to America back then? he asked Father, I would definitely not have stayed in Europe, Father, stroking his moustache, answers, well, Big Brother, if you had visited us even once in all these years, you'd know we made the right decision, Aunt Manci, who quickly reaches for the plate of cold cuts, salami, ham, bacon, encircled by tomatoes, yellow peppers, pickles and red onion, and words gush from Aunt Manci's mouth, we're going to start raising Mangalitsa pigs, they're very much in demand, a heirloom breed with denser, more flavourful meat), and we get up to leave sooner than usual, reaching for our bags and packets during the first pause in conversation—with time we've developed a highly refined system of gift-giving, Nomi places the coffee, chocolate and soap on the table, I describe the various bags of clothing we've brought, Mother and Father offer the special presents—sugar-free chocolate for our Mamika, pigeon feed for Béla, hair dye for Béla's wife who is a hairdresser, flesh-coloured bandages for Aunt Icu whose work at the factory is giving her varicose veins, asthma spray for Uncle Móric whose airways are constricted because he's not only a farmer but worked for years in the mill, a blender for Nándor and Valéria, who now have two children—and when we sit exhausted in the evening in Mamika's kitchen, Nomi says that she can't remember who said what, that it's all mixed up, Father reminds us that we're still invited to Great-Uncle Pista's, that he'd promised him we'd visit today, then Nomi and I rebel, we just can't do it any more, Mamika, who convinces Father to visit Pista with Mother and on the day before we leave Pista can come for coffee, that way you can at least give your great-uncle a goodbye kiss, Mamika says with a laugh.

It was on that evening, when Nomi and I were alone with Mamika, after we'd run across the courtyard to help Mamika feed the animals, we sat at her kitchen table and watched the rain beat against the window for a while, that Mamika said, I'd like to tell you something about your grandfather, this crazy rain is telling me I should. Has your father ever told you anything about your grandfather? We know that Papuci was in a labour camp, Nomi tells her, and that what he wanted for a present on May 1st was a kilo of lice powder (a few months earlier Father had told us about Grandfather in a raw, penetrating whisper that brooked no contradiction when we were discussing whether or not we should close on May 1st. Close? on International Workers' Day? Father interrupted us when Nomi and I voiced a slight protest, listen to me, we will offer a very special menu on International Red Shitters' Day, a nice, spicy goulash or some Swiss speciality, like veal tenderloin with roast potatoes, and I suggest we offer our guests a coffee on the house—and you know why? I'll tell you why, you silly girls who are looking sad because all you want is a day off. On May 1st we were allowed to send an extra kilo to your grandfather in the labour camp, the monthly allowance was doubled on May 1st and you know what we sent to Požarevac? No? You'll never guess! Lice powder is what Mamika, Uncle Móric and I sent him, the strongest lice powder we could find! That's what Papuci, your grandfather, asked for on May 1st to get some relief for his bleeding, bitten skull. When he returned from the camp, we didn't recognize him. His head was covered with scars, the lice had eaten away his black curls and left just sparse white hair. My dear daughters, for me May 1st will always be a kilo of lice powder, a supplementary kilo the Reds granted him on their holiday, a day on which *I* will always work and I'll cook a special dinner for Papuci, I swear to you! But you, you want to demonstrate?, wave a red flag? or shout 'Brezhnev, Brezhnev'? or 'Stalin'? or 'Lenin'? or 'Long live communism?' or maybe 'Long live expropriation'? so are you with the Reds or the Greens? I'd like to know which of your Swiss friends has been shitting in your heads or did you manage to shit in your own?), it's true, Mamika said, I forgot about the lice powder, but I remember now, we sent an entire kilo to your Papuci, and Mamika stood up, said that we should sit in the other room, that she had a picture of Papuci on the credenza, the only picture of him she had, and she wanted to show it to us.

Listen to me, Mamika began, your grandfather was killed and many others with him. I'm telling you what I know about it so that you'll never forget as long as you live that anything can happen, even the most horrible things, and there are signs when people want to exterminate one another—and the signs look very bad at the moment, my dear girls (and only later, when we were back in Switzerland, did I realize that Mamika was the only one that entire summer who said there might be a war).

You're wondering how I know that? A wrinkled old woman like me?

I don't know for sure, but I have a heavy sense of foreboding, and Mamika looked at us with her blue-grey eyes, she paused and seemed to gather more than just her thoughts.

Your Papuci and I always lived with our animals, which is what farmers do. But do you understand what it means to 'live with animals'? We considered our horses, cows, pigs, geese, ducks and all the rest of them as part of our soul. We also learnt to listen to the animals in every imaginable way.

On our farm we had four dogs and we knew from their barking if a stranger was near, we knew that Vigéc was always the first to bark and the others would start in soon after, softer and more restrained. In 1942, the first time the Fascists showed up at our farm, the sun had just risen and we were all at table, Papuci, your father, Uncle Móric and I. Vigéc started barking and we stopped chewing, not because he'd started barking, but because after a few barks he was suddenly quiet again. Papuci stood up, looked at each of us, one after the other, told us not to move and quickly washed his hands before he went outside.

I obviously couldn't just sit there on my behind. I snuck out the back door into the garden and saw and heard what happened from there. Three men in uniform, whom I'd never seen before and who must have come on foot or on bicycles, were leaning against the well with their arms crossed. Vigéc sat very still next to them, his ears pricked as if he were waiting for a signal, and that in itself was very unusual. When Papuci whistled softly through his teeth, Vigéc returned to his regular spot. One of the men came forward, said without any greeting, without introduction: Kocsis, we need men like you. We've heard you're smart and have good instincts. Your horses are the best in the region, and the man praised your grandfather but his voice had no warmth, instead it cut through the air, his voice was used to executing orders and to giving them.

I could only see Papuci's back and I've never forgotten how he let his arms hang. That he didn't stick his heavy hands anywhere, neither in his pockets nor behind his back, I thought was remarkable. Still, his back looked proud and straight precisely because he refused any kind of cover.

I don't know you, Papuci said after a pause that seemed unbelievably long to me, so I can't make much of what you say. But maybe you can tell me, a simple farmer, where you got your fancy, shiny boots?

I expected them to beat Papuci, at least to insult him, and I put my hands together and murmured a prayer. Nothing happened. The man who had spoken first said nothing and Papuci stood there without moving or saying a word and the only thing the men did for a long time was to take each other's measure with their eyes. Then the leader gave a curt order and the three of them left.

And what happened next, my dears?

We received visits almost once a week. The men were always different but they wore the same boots and their hair was cut short, so that not even the wind could play with it, Papuci said. Each time they asked him if he had considered their offer and each time Papuci goaded them with a sharp remark, see here, I don't have any room for other people's ideas, I'm happy with what I've got, what's wrong with that? Without a word, the men would take a horse, a few pigs or load some of our corn or wheat harvest into a truck. Móric and Miklós were disappointed and furious that Papuci let them steal our possessions, especially our animals, without a word. One day Papuci caught Móric who had just turned twelve pointing the shotgun at one of the uniformed men. Papuci slapped him so hard he bled: You're no hero when you put all our lives in jeopardy!

Uncle Lajos, one of Papuci's many uncles, had fallen in with Fascists of the highest rank, that's something you should know. He never showed his face here, but he probably kept the 'bare necks', as we called them, from killing Papuci. Your grandfather was conscripted, he was meant to go fight for the Fascists somewhere in Russia, but it never came to that because circumstances suddenly changed after Stalingrad.

I don't remember any more if it was in 1945 or '46 that Lajos and quite a few others who had collaborated with the Fascists were shot on the riverbank. The water ran red for weeks and the fish, which we had no desire to eat, multiplied and got fat. For years after that I didn't make my fish stew, which I'd always served on Fridays and which everyone loved so much. Even the worst criminals should get a trial, Papuci said after we'd search for Lajos' body in vain.

After Stalingrad, then, it was the Partisans who showed up at our farm and ravaged it in their own way. War had fanaticized them too. They searched for Fascists everywhere, even in the smallest farms, they raped our washerwoman, tormented our animals, if they felt like it, they ate and drank so much they had to vomit. Believe me, my dears, there are many more horrible things I could tell you, but what's the point. The fact is that each year brought new terrors that prevented us and many others from living our quiet lives. And we had to explain things to our children for which we ourselves had no explanation.

Well, you know, we're living in a new country! That's how we tried to make light of the fact that our farm, still exactly where it had always been, was once again supposed to belong to a new nation, the Socialist Federal Republic of Yugoslavia. No need to go anywhere, all different forms of government come to us as if we had summoned them. Monarchy! Fascism! And now the Reds, who also have something on their minds, what that is, we'll find out soon enough, Papuci said. At this point all we know is that our head of state has a short name and we know why—have you ever heard of a brand of chocolate or detergent with a long, complicated name? Everything we don't necessarily need has to be lodged into our heads with a short, stupid name. But who said we need politics anyway? Isn't the simple life enough?

Mamika said with a wink, that's how your Papuci talked, once he got going.

The expropriations started in 1946. Again, some individuals showed up on our farm, but this time, they were people we knew. Bourgeois Kocsis, you should become a comrade while you still can, you should give up your wrongfully acquired land, a new time has come. The man who said that had worked with us until very recently. Géza, Papuci said and nothing more. What should we do? I asked when Géza and his men once again had left our farm blind-drunk and with their bags full. Nothing, Papuci answered.

In those days I dreamt of our horses, they'd look at me with their big eyes, they seemed to be speaking to me and each of their stories ended with death. I can remember one dream especially vividly because afterwards I was convinced something terrible would happen. I dreamt I was torn from a deep sleep because it was raining like the great flood. There was no one in the house aside from me, neither Papuci nor the children. When I looked out the kitchen window, I saw our best horse was tied to the acacia tree. It didn't move even though the water had risen to its fetlocks. I was desperate and yanked open the window and screamed into the courtyard, I wanted to encourage the horse to break free. But the horse seemed resigned to waiting for death and I couldn't set it free because I didn't see any way of getting through the water. I couldn't even have opened my door. In the next moment, I was holding a large brush and I was brushing the horse's bare bones, which is all I managed to save. I wept and wept, brushed, hoped, begged heaven to help me resuscitate my beloved horse with my brushing.

I didn't tell Papuci about my dream but as the communists' 'visits' became more and more frequent, I saw the insatiable greed of our former friends, who now belonged to the only true Party, the impertinent way their eyes gleamed when they looked into every drawer, every corner, then I asked Papuci to go into hiding. My dove, he said, they don't even know where they should stick their noses, they'll calm down.

A few days later, little Feri, the boy from the neighbouring farm, ran into our kitchen and told us breathlessly that they'd arrested his father. They're taking everything, the child said, his eyes frantic. The horses had panicked and started kicking, the geese wouldn't stop hissing, the dog, usually so calm, bit one of them in the leg and was shot immediately, and the boy waved his arms wildly. I stroked his forehead and tried to calm him down but Feri hopped from one leg to the other, cried and looked in the direction of his parents' farm. Where is your mother? I finally asked. In town, at the market. She's selling her apples and pears, and the boy's nose was running.

Papuci stood up and went into the storeroom, he came back after a short while with a bag bursting at the seams, very calmly told me to take the children into town to my sister's.

He stroked Miklós' and Móric's cheeks, kissed them on the forehead and I'll never forget how our two boys looked at that moment, their faces were pale, terrified, as if they'd guessed what was coming. And take Feri with you, Papuci called to me after he hugged me and disappeared through the kitchen door.

Mamika paused for a long time, blew her nose, asked me to peel her an apple. And when I sat back down next to Mamika, she took small bites of the apple and pointed to the picture of the Virgin Mary that hung above her head, just look at her! A Madonna wearing necklaces, rings, bracelets and a diadem, lightly bowing her head, smiling but not smiling and in her breast was stuck a saber handle adorned with rubies and emeralds, whose point, and this is what I remember most clearly, is hidden behind Mary's hands. She can bear the pain, Mamika said, because she is the mother of us all, she is our hope in the darkest of times. And neither Nomi nor I dared contradict her, we realized how paltry our doubt was compared to what Mamika had lived through.

They took Papuci to the labour camp in Požarevac after he had hidden for weeks in the corn and wheat fields. An acquaintance, one we were fond of I have to admit, denounced Papuci, he had whispered into the officials' ears—that's what we called denunciation back then—that Papuci showed up at the Sáváris' usually between eleven and twelve to wash and to get something to eat. Two days later, they told me that Papuci had been hauled away in a car with four other men and Bori, the village beauty, screamed at them at the top of her voice, she called them exploiters, kulaks! and tore out the hair of the moustaches. There's a reason the years between 1946 and 1952 were called the Time of Torn Beards.

Before taking Papuci first to Požarevac and then to the coal mine in Kostolac, they interrogated and beat him for days in the cellar of the building where Miklós went to school. Miklós could hear Papuci, imagine, and the teacher had all the trouble in the world keeping him from rushing down to the basement which would have got him killed. That's exactly what they want, the teacher shouted, they want you to run into their open blade! He couldn't excuse Miklós from lessons because the 'enforcer' checked every day to see that all the students were present. My poor Miklós, Mamika said, he was only eleven years old.

Papuci refused to give up our land and join the party, Landowner! Fascist! Goddamn Hungarian! that's what he was called by the enforcers, those who executed orders others had given them. He was a simple farmer, that's how everyone knew him around here, Papuci apparently told them, and he never wanted anything more. If they were going to kill him, they'd kill him as a human being and nothing else.

I didn't see Papuci again for more than a year and when he finally returned home, I didn't recognize him. An emaciated, beggarly, white-haired man knocked on the door of my sister's house, where I'd been living since Papuci's arrest. You should have seen your Papuci when he was a young man, his proud, but not arrogant bearing, his thick, dark hair that looked more like fur than human hair, his gaze that was never rushed but always took everything in calmly before he acted. And now? What did they do to your hair? your father Miklós asked, Miklós who had begun seeing beyond the world of children long before. I'm not the only one who was put to work, the lice were too, Papuci said and tried to smile.

One night he told me what he had lived through in the camp and then never again. At some point I asked him a question, I think it was about what they'd been given to eat. No questions, he answered, I told you about those times once, that's enough.

My beloved Papuci never recovered. The more he learnt about the conditions we'd lived in, that everything, absolutely everything had been taken from us, that others had 'inherited' and were living on our farm, so-called comrades worked our land, that we were allowed, if we wanted, to buy back a small section of our fields, that Papuci's horses had been sold at auction, Red László had bought most of our pigs, fat Jenci from Ada had hauled off our poultry, that I hadn't even been able to save our provisions, not even our preserves, our canned apples, sour cherries, apricots, peaches, the sun-dried, pickled cucumbers; I begged the 'enforcers' at least to let me take the kitchen utensils but they preferred to let it all rust. The 'inheritors' had moved in only a month before Papuci's return, and I told him that the farmyard had been cordoned off and guarded by some Reds or other, I knew because Miklós had once ventured as far into our farm as the well and even managed to recover our small, mustard-yellow stool that had been left in the apple orchard.

Imagine what would have happened if they'd caught him stealing his own stool, Papuci said. I'd rather not, I replied.

That's the end of the story, Mamika said and took off her glasses so she could wipe her eyes with the back of her hand. We buried Papuci that same year, he was only fifty-one! It was a wretched, desolate funeral because we knew he could have lived much longer. After Papuci died, Miklós and Móric fought more frequently, they both became more stubbornly irreconcilable, the only explanation I can find is their father's early death.

When Mamika finished her story, she stood up and slowly went over to the credenza, pushed a few placemats aside and returned to us, sat on her bed with a photograph in her hand and she placed it between Nomi and me, we looked at her questioningly because there were about thirty men in the picture, all of them with coats, hats, moustaches and grim faces. It was very cold on the day this photograph was taken, Mamika said, and the men, all of them farmers in this area, had met to share information, one winter a year or two before the outbreak of the Second World War.

Let's guess, Nomi said, I said, and we looked closely at the faces for a long time, the longer you look, the more different they become, Nomi said. Yes, Mamika replied, and? Nomi and I, we touched the same face with our fingers—and it was Papuci.

LOVE. THE SEA. THE RIVER.

My cousin's been conscripted, I tell Dalibor as we stretch out on the stones, close together, and look up into the leaves of the chestnut and linden trees. They look like giant hands, the leaves of the chestnut, Dalibor says, mighty trees with giant hands. Yes, I reply, did you not hear me? Dalibor, who sits up, pulls his knees to his chest, *the lake is very quiet today*, a day or rather a moment that could make you believe there was nothing terrible in this world, and when I prop myself up on my elbows and clear my throat, Dalibor stands up, rolls up his trouser legs, takes a few steps towards the lake, he takes off his shirt even though the weather is rather cool, he tosses it aside, stretches, leans backwards slightly before he curls his slender body inward and pauses a moment before rushing forward over the stones, still bent forwards, gathering the stones up quickly with his outstretched arms and I straighten up suddenly, laugh, you have energy to burn or what, I call to him, Dalibor, who doesn't react, keeps running along the shore, the soft, clear sound of the stones crunched against each other by Dalibor's feet, his hands, now full, knock the stones together, an unpleasant noise that grates on my ears, do you hear me? I call to him, Dalibor, who stands up straight only once his shoulder blades are shiny with sweat, and I hear him breathing, almost panting, as he stands with his back towards me, waits a moment, then lets the stones fly.

This game is no longer a game, Dalibor yells, in fact he's wondering if there ever will be any *games* for him again and he punctuates his comments with a clattering noise, trrrrr, t-t-t-t, trrrrrr, and he lets the stones fly faster and harder over the water, he bends down for new ammunition, no longer looking for the flat skipping stones but for projectiles that will hurt, the lake is suddenly witness to an expected scene, and the swans that Dalibor had just referred to as *our elegant guests* flap their wings excitedly, the ducks, now frenzied, start quacking wildly. Stop, I yell to Dalibor, what's that for? *leave those creatures in peace*! I leap up and run towards him, and when I'm only a few steps from him, he turns, stares at me with a look I've never seen before, stay right where you are, he shouts, or you're next—do you know what it's like when even nature looks monstrous? do you know what it's like when you have to shoot because if you don't, you'll be shot? No, I have no idea, I answer. Do you know what it's like when you shoot your best friend in the head without feeling a thing? And then you beat his face in, your best friend's face in a dream, because it's haunting you with his calm, his peacefulness, not only that, he forgives you, you have to kill him again because he's making you crazy with his redeemed face, calm down, she says, the person I am, and I stretch out my right hand—it's a helpless, pleading gesture—but we both love the water, I say, some day you'll show me your sea, I say, trying to breathe calmly, and I'd like to show you my river, with sandy banks you usually only find at the seaside, I'd like to do so many things with you, I say, the time will come when we can go there . . .

Dalibor, who now looks at me, his gaze releases something, forgive me, he says, I forgot myself for a moment, and I can hear my heart beating in my fingers, were you afraid of me? he asks. No, I reply. Are you sure? and Dalibor wipes the sweat from his forehead, dries his eyes, I have to know for certain, he says. I'm sure, I reply without hesitation and Dalibor, who extends his hand, touches me with his fingertips, I'm sorry about your cousin, he says, where is he? In Banja Luka. Family? Dalibor asks. Yes, a wife and two children. Tell me about him, Dalibor says. Are you sure? Yes.

His father, my Uncle Piri, had to stand by helplessly and watch the men in uniform take his son (and not Csaba), Uncle Piri, who shoves his *mici*, his cap, backwards, forwards, backwards and then spits repeatedly at the trunk of the olive tree when he sees Béla, caught in lock-step between two soldiers. Aunt Icu, who sits on her stool in the garden, staring at the wilted lilies of the valley and, under the influence of the apricot-coloured roses, plunges into an intense inner murmuring in the belief that she can pray to the month of love, of spring, of flowers, to return her only son healthy, in one piece, viable, and after calling her in vain several times,

Uncle Piri stands in the garden and listens to his wife hum an old, almost forgotten song he'd learnt during his military service—*My name is Fabian Pista, a soldier I must be. They want to cut off my hair, for that is how one serves the emperor. My name is Fabian Pista, a soldier I must be. They want to cut off my hair, I will not serve the emperor.*

Béla, who had been hidden by friends for several months, only ventured out at night to meet his wife and children in a remote spot by the river, Béla's stomach started to consume itself, this is no life, his wife said, your own stomach acid and your black thoughts are killing you, a few days later Béla returned home in broad daylight. He deloused the dogs, repaired the roof gutters, weeded the garden and went up to his parents' roof to feed and care for his pigeons. They came for him at dawn on the following day, two soldiers, armed—they usually come for men at night, Aunt Icu had told us, they come on foot or on bicycle, the soft footsteps that mean no good, the too careful pushing on the pedals— take me with you, you dogs, you pigs, Béla swore in Serbo-Croatian, but first tell me which country I'm being sent to die for. For Serbia! Greater Serbia! one of the soldiers shouted, who else, you hick pigeon fancier!

Dalibor takes my hand, let's go to the boathouse, and we get up, we look into each others' eyes once we're standing, do you know your eyes are a colour that's impossible to define? he says, I rarely look into my own eyes, I answer, strange you've never noticed, Dalibor tells me, I'd like to sink into your eyes, into that sea of many colours, and suddenly alert I ask why, don't think too much about it, Dalibor answers stroking my palm with his thumb, and we leave, the pebbles crunch under our feet, and as we pass, I greet a few familiar faces, we pass the well, two children play with the stream of water, squint at us as they spray us, Dalibor falls as if wounded by the shooting water, the two children giggle, spray again until Dalibor gets up, waves at them, and we pass a large field that is covered with beach towels in summer but now lies quiet and empty, what can anyone do? I ask when we sit down in the boathouse where we won't be disturbed and with a beautiful view of the lake, you mean for your cousin? Dalibor asks, for my cousin, my family. I don't think I understand you, Dalibor says, because I'm a fatalist (and it takes me a while to figure out what he's saying because I don't know the English word for 'fatalist'), you can support Doctors Without Borders, Amnesty International, organizations that defend independent media, do that, Dalibor says, and do it for yourself, which is perfectly fine, *it's OK*, you can't help anyone directly, that's your fate, and Dalibor, who lights us a cigarette, yes, you're a fatalist, I say and lay my left hand on his back. Did I ever claim the opposite? Dalibor asks after a pause, what do you expect from me? Why do you think I expect anything from you? and I take my shoes off because I want to freeze, I want to feel my toes grow cold on the wooden floor and then warm them against Dalibor's feet, I want him to feel himself warm me. I think you expect something, and Dalibor doesn't look at me but at the rotting boathouse floor, the lake water quivering in the gaps between the boards, dark green, almost black, if nothing else, you believe I've got insight into the war, but all I know is that this war, like any other, should be ended as soon as possible, but instead all we get is an endless debate about what kind of war the Balkan War is. If politicians weren't constantly talking about how complicated the situation in the Balkans is, then we could avoid the wars—Ildi, why did you take off your shoes? and Dalibor looks at me with those eyes into which my eyes would like to sink and me, I let my toes disappear up under his trouser leg, they want to be as close to you as possible, my feet, they want to belong to you. Maybe we really should listen with our feet instead of our ears, Dalibor says, laughing, takes my hand, kisses it, palm and fingertips, and he breathes into my hands a few times before saying, feet that listen would probably come to different conclusions, we would certainly hear differently and today I'd be able to fly, I'd be an acrobat, which is what I always wanted to be, it was my dream job, an artist of the air, Ildi, that's what I would be instead of some *refuger*, who will forever have to pray in vain because he was forced to kill.

We met for almost exactly half a year, Dalibor and Í, mostly at the lake, in the abandoned boathouse, we undressed, sometimes hurriedly so there wouldn't be enough time for shame, we didn't often kiss because that's the most intimate touch, as he said, as I said, and I stole glances at his body, his hips, so impossibly slender, his thin but muscular arms that sent another message than the usual—We will carry you over the threshold. And I, who felt his rushed, panting breath, its rhythm disrupted sometime in the recent past and never recovered. It's not working, he said, it's not going to work! and despair's face was his, I met you only to understand that it won't work. What won't work? I asked and knew the question was pointless, it takes time, I said, maybe things won't change overnight, but some day it will be easier, believe me.

And he, the *refuger*, held me tight, hid his eyes behind closed lids, disappeared with his mouth on my shoulder, sobbed, his naked body, overcome with the desire to be close to mine, a desire that suddenly turned hostile and Dalibor looked at me with empty eyes, as if we had nothing more to say to each other, as if he had never caressed my neck in a way that reminded me of the softest, most gentle spring breeze, a breeze that made me feel even the finest hairs on my skin; didn't you say you'd fallen . . . and Dalibor looked at me with those eyes, recited in his language a poem a friend had written for him, he translated it into English and said, yes, I fell in love with you for exactly that reason.

And I, standing in the telephone booth at the train station, tried to call Dalibor, I dialled the number, I hung up when a strange voice answered, Dalibor's cousin, the voice that said at one point, without my having asked, Dalibor has gone to Dubrovnik, he says hello and that he'll come back for sure.

Our train travelled through the night, we surely dozed off now and again, sometimes you covered us with a cardigan, Mamika, caressed us with your soft hand and I believe you hardly slept, in any case I can't remember ever being awake and seeing you asleep. We dozed, slept, ate and sat perfectly still when the border guards examined us and our papers and when they said something in a language we didn't under-stand, you spread your hands and shrugged your shoulders and I assume we looked very convincing in our fear and inse-curity, the border guards gave us back our papers with seri-ous faces, but occasionally with a smile, they gave us permission to continue our journey and when the train rolled on, I kept watch for the ceremonial red ribbon that marked borders in my imagination as a child, but saw only a starkly lit train platform, a few men in uniform walking here and there, I remember an enormous station clock, a closed snack bar, we travelled on into the night, to a new country, we've already reached Austria, you said, the night received us into its darkness without any questions (later, I'll always remem-ber my first, naive idea of a border; every time we drive to the Vojvodina or back to Switzerland, I search for something that fits with this image of a red ribbon, but never see any-thing except watch towers, patrolling guards who wear their weapons as naturally as a pair of shoes, guard dogs straining at their leashes, usually flags flutter or hang slack from poles set close to each other, the stones, the shrubbery, the grass and the few trees all appear colourless to me, unnatural, and the question remains, why is a border nothing but a complicated, austere threat?).

A man pulled open the sliding door, stowed his backpack and sat down in our compartment and Nomi and I, we looked him over, we were so curious about this man who must have been Austrian that we didn't take our eyes off him when he took a sandwich and a thermos from his pack, can't you plant your eyes somewhere else? you said and tugged at our sleeves because we kept staring at him, he looks a little like Nándor, Nomi whispered to me, don't you think? but it can't be Nándor if he's Austrian, I answered laughing and the man offered us sweets, us and you, we looked at you to see if we were allowed, then shyly reached for the cookies, the man said something, we nodded, thanked him in our language and he answered in Hungarian, we were shocked, of course, until we noticed the man could only speak a smattering of Hungarian. After the cookies, you offered him some of our roast chicken legs and the grease on our mouths gleamed in the compartment's dim, yellow light and for once we were allowed to eat everything together, the important thing was to make the time pass a little faster, you said, and suddenly the man stuffed his things into his pack, yanked open the sliding door and a moment later was knocking on our window, smiling and waving goodbye.

In any case, it was daylight when we arrived, whether it was still morning or already noon or even later, I don't know. Mother and Father were waiting for us at the station, on the platform, Mother waved when she saw me get off the train. I helped you off, Nomi, you and I, we stood there with our suitcases as Mother and Father opened their arms and said nothing for a long time or maybe just, you're finally here! and I remember their arms around me, I could feel my parents' joy, their relief, but I remember I didn't want to let go of your hand, I don't know if I wanted anything more than to stay near you, Mother, with tears in her eys, Father, who threw Nomi into the air; I don't know if I'm imagining it or if it's true that even then, on the day we arrived, I had the sense that between my parents and me there would be years we could never recover, it wouldn't be as bad for Nomi, probably because she's two years younger.

Father picked up our suitcases, Mother put her arms around our shoulders, you must be tired, she surely said, we'll eat something delicious at home and then you can rest.

Mamika, I'm trying to remember how it was, arriving in a new home, the new apartment, the new bed, the new toys, to have a toilet in the apartment, a television, a telephone, how it felt to open the door and walk into a completely unfamiliar world, an apartment whose rent was more than Mother earned in a month, what went on inside me, inside Nomi when we saw the asphalt-covered courtyard, the decorative plants in the windows, on the balconies, and the playground behind the building. No matter how hard I try to remember our first day, our first days in Switzerland, my memory goes blank after the train station, after Mother and Father met us on the platform.

I remember very clearly, however, during that time, after a few days or weeks? that we got lost, you and I, we went for a walk by the lake, we admired the swans with their long necks, we were stunned to see people feeding bread to the swans and ducks, we stopped at every rubbish can and looked into each one for a long time, they seemed so clean and well-maintained, and because it had snowed that day or the day before, I drew snow pictures on every bench we passed and you had to guess what I'd drawn, we were so caught up in our game and in everything we saw that we lost track of where we were and night had just fallen, we should ask someone, you said, but what? what should we ask and how? we only knew the name of the street where we lived and you said 'Excuse me' in Hungarian, stretched out your hand when a woman with two shopping bags approached, you said, Todistrass, and shrugged your shoulders, the woman shook her head, said something and kept walking. This went on for a long time, no one seemed to know where Todistrass was. Our fingers were stiff with cold and I remember your small nose was all red, your eyes glittered with anxiety when you asked an elderly gentleman one more time for Todistrass; the man, who wore a strangely flat cap, smiled, pointed his finger into the night, said Tödistrasse and when he realized that his fingerpointing wasn't any help to us, he led us through the streets, past streetlights and up a hill until we stood outside our building, Father, who was already waiting for us in front of the garage, smoking a cigarette, began scolding us once he had thanked the man for his help.

You and I, we discussed the tiny difference between o and ö every day after that, surprised and shocked that no one figured it out except that one man and we practised: Tödistrasse, Tödistrasse. It takes so very little to get completely lost in this world, you said.

Mother and Father worked all day, Nomi and I cooked with you, did the laundry, went to the playground behind the building—one slide, two swings, a covered sandbox, we put snow on the swings, made snow eggs, set them on the steps to the slide, where are the chickens? Nomi asked, why aren't any roosters crowing? why don't we ever see anyone? Astonishing that it was so quiet, so quiet and beautiful as if by some secret agreement, the things around us were there only so we could admire them in their beauty. And we kept playing on the playground but never dared climb on the fence that enclosed the playground, probably because we were still newcomers and didn't want to do anything wrong, because we weren't sure if the fence belonged to us or not, it's best to act as if we're guests, you said, and we only played with the snowshovel leaning against the wall by the back door, when we realized, after several days, that it belonged to the building's caretaker and that it was actually Mother and Father who had taken on the position to supplement their minimal earnings.

Evenings we sat together at the kitchen table and ate what Nomi, you and I had cooked, the same dishes we'd always cooked together; it's so nice to come home to a warm kitchen, Mother said and wanted to hug me but I held on tight to Mamika's apron and turned my face away, into the dark, warm cloth of her dress, away from Mother's desire to be close to me, I now think my brutal directness was to show Mother that she wasn't my mother, but you, Mamika, were and when Father said, you're old enough to let go of Mamika's apron, I looked him in the eye, I really didn't care what Mother and Father said and you, you only said, leave the girl in peace, she needs time.

I'm going home, I have to, to my animals, my garden, you said, and our priest surely misses having me in his church, and I looked at you as if I didn't understand and you packed your bags, you packed your black dresses in your suitcase, the cardigans, I think you asked me to make you a drawing but I didn't draw anything and if you did, in fact, ask me to, then you only did so once and not again, you took me in your arms on the night before you left—I don't remember if Nomi was there too—you sang a song, I felt your voice in my body and everything in me refused to let you go, only when the train pulled away did I realize that this was the real farewell, not the one in the Vojvodina when all our relatives came to visit us or we visited them, when they all gave us something for the trip, hugged us and kissed us with moist eyes, even on the day we left, the farewell shone only briefly when Nomi cried about the birch-broom she wasn't allowed to take with her and I cried about my favourite cat, Cicu; when you left on the train, it was as if the only world I'd known was leaving me—your house, your garden, the beloved animals, the dust and dirt, the pale priest in his dark church, the hum of voices at the market, the sweet, heavy scent of fresh doughnuts, pancakes, Uncle Piri's eyes, the most beautiful eyes in the world, Nomi and I thought, Aunt Icu, who spoilt us with sweets on the weekends we spent with her and Uncle Piri so that you could go to early and late Mass; I suddenly missed it all, people who spoke in loud voices and showed their teeth, the dusty streets and the poplars, the poplar leaves that were so gentle in the breeze—I lost everything I loved with your departure, but when Nomi asked me that evening, do you miss her? are you sad? I didn't say a word.

Later, in the few moments when it might have been possible to talk about this sudden break in our lives, it was always immediately clear that Mother's and Father's feelings about our homeland were deeper, more painful; what was going on inside Nomi and me back then had little or no weight.

HANDS IN THE AIR

A tall, inconspicuously dressed man stands at the counter, clears his throat, Miss, he says in a voice that wants to slip back down his throat, Miss, may I tell you something? It takes me a moment to realize that the man was talking to me, but instead of looking at him, I look at his shirt collar, at his dark red V-neck sweater, a music teacher, maybe, a shy man, I think, yes, may I help you? and I finally look at his face, the man clears his throat again, turns and glances back as if he needs to check what's going on behind him and he leans forward over the counter, towards me, waves me over and speaks so softly that I have to ask him to repeat himself, I beg your pardon? and he smiles when he says, Miss, you should take a look at your toilets, and his smile is so obviously meant to be charming that I want to speak with this shy teacher, an unusual reaction for me, it's not my toilet, I say with just as much charm and in a low voice as if I were telling him a secret. Miss, I, the man says, how should I put it. . . his strange shyness distracts me from my dismal mood, just say it, I interrupt, I can't, he says and I have to laugh, I beg your pardon, but your manner is making me laugh, his face scarlet, the man immediately returns to his seat in the front of the dining room, near the entrance, and I notice only now that toilets aren't necessarily an appropriate topic for a light-hearted conversation.

What did he want? Nomi asks me, apparently there's something wrong with the toilets, I reply, Nomi, who tells me she'll take a look, I'll do it, I say, can you manage without me for a bit or should I call Mother? no, it's fine, go ahead, Nomi answers, and I put my apron on the chair, go to the kitchen (and when I step into the kitchen, I remember right away how Dragana stood at the sink, crying into the lettuce leaves, softly, almost inaudibly, her back betraying her suffering, her fear for her child's life, for her family, I can't stay here and wait until they shoot my son, Dragana said, although there is hope, because if her son were wounded he might be able to get evacuated from Sarajevo—wounded children are the first to get help—and I, unable to bring myself to speak of something that could become a source of hope, Dragana, who hasn't come to work for a week, can't be found), can I tell you a quick story? Marlis asks me as I put on the stained kitchen apron, later, I say, promise? promise! and I take the pail, the mop, rags from the cleaning closet, rubber gloves, the yellow ones, and I wait for a moment when I can slip unseen into the men's toilet armed with the mop, pail, rags and rubber gloves (everyone doesn't need to know when we clean the toilets), I push open the heavy door with my shoulder and the first thing I see is her face in the mirror, I stop short, hear the door swing quietly shut behind me, see the mop handle next to my head, I see myself, my hair drawn into a bun, and a word comes to mind, 'sap', probably because of the soap I'll need, and in the mirror I see not only my own reflection but what had been left for the waitress.

A toilet seat covered in shit, a pair of men's underwear on the floor next to the toilet bowl, the speckled wall that is no longer white, but smeared with shit (the mirror telescopes it all together)—I look, I wait, something will happen soon, my heart will start racing, so fast that I'll feel its pulsing beat in my temples, a certain spot between my shoulder blades will rage with a piercing pain that takes my breath away, I wait and have a sudden image of Rumplestiltskin's crazy dance, of how the jelly filling squirts out when you bite into a doughnut, but aside from this, nothing happens. I bend down for the pail, lift it into the sink, turn the tap and while the water fills the pail, I pull on the gloves, my hands now have only a muffled feel of the water, and when the pail is half-full my fingers, packed in yellow, twist in the wrong direction, the water shoots into the pail in a sharp stream, over my skin, into my eyes, and I wait again for a long moment, turn off the tap, I watch her as drops of water trickle down her face, and now the inescapable thought—we have become one heart and one soul, the waitress and I; and I grab the bucket, the mop, I go to the window and open it, not because the smell of shit is nauseating, but because I'm hoping that the fresh air, the view outside will move something inside me, will spark some feeling, I put down the bucket, lift the window handle and it's my fingers that sweat in the yellow rubber; it's a day with fog you can't take seriously, in other words, the sun will soon cut through the layer of cloud, and as my glance falls on a peaceful, fenced-in vegetable garden, I picture my mother bending down for the rags and the pail, taking the mop from the cleaning closet, pulling on her gloves as if this was nothing out of the ordinary, it's all part of the job, Mother says, no one almost ever goes next to the toilet on purpose, it's bad enough when you can't hold your water; certainly true, I think, shut the window, turn and rapidly cover the few steps to the toilet bowl, I look at it all closely—if I can't feel anything, at least I'll use my head to think this scene through to the end—yes, I can imagine that someone had an accident, that he didn't make it in time to crap in the toilet which is why the seat is smeared with shit and because he got some on his underwear as well, this someone had to take them off; and you can't very well carry around a pair of stinking underwear, which is why they're now lying next to the toilet bowl, maybe we should also put hygienic disposal bags in the men's toilet? But how can you explain away a smeared wall that actually doesn't look so bad? I, who look at the wall, the brown traces, letters? no, there's no message to decipher (I should go thank the shy teacher, tell him I understand why he was tongue-tied); I can't think of any way the smears on the wall could be explained away as an accident and because no excuse occurs to me, I take off the gloves and drop them on the floor; it's obvious that someone smeared the wall on purpose, that's why I don't want to have a layer of rubber between my hands and the shit; I take a rag in my bare hands, wet it, rub it over the wall and the water quickens the almost dry shit to a new life, as I mentioned, the smell of faeces doesn't irritate my nose and the shit turns into a brown smear, a village, a small town, really, with almost ten thousand inhabitants, with a yellow flower on its crest, with villas on the lakeshore that almost touch the water, with doctors' offices here and there, lawyers' offices here and there, with a nature preserve that crayfish, red ones, are taking over, naturally also with cooperative housing, I forget what year it was built, with shops for every little need, with a public swimming pool, a playing field and an ice rink—the fees to have a roof built over it have already been advanced—with a shooting range, fortress ruins and an erratic boulder called the Alexander Stone, a small town that differs from hundreds of others only in that it is wealthier and has a lower tax rate than most, we, who have never been physically assaulted, insulted, yes, *Schissusländer!* shit foreigners! the most common verbal attack—and I force myself to think this scene through to the bitter end—no one has ever called us *Schissusländer* in the Mondial, our guests are generally neatly dressed, wear clean, well-made shoes and have accessories, jewellery, bags and dogs that match their outfits; and I never thought much about what is truly menacing in this decorum that orders coffee with good posture and a quiet voice (perhaps even a second coffee on Saturdays), but

now, when I feel no emotion but think as I clean, I understand that this friendly, respectable, controlled politeness is a
mask and an impenetrable one at that; it has the unsurpass-
able advantage that you can't reproach someone for wearing
a mask (if I did, if I became aggressive, swore that I sure as
hell didn't buy their pleasant front any more! they would
calmly wait until I finished then say, Miss, I don't understand
. . . did something rub you the wrong way?), it wasn't some
crazy, abnormal, unpredictable freak who picked up his own
shit and smeared it on our wall but a cultivated person (as I
write the word 'shit', I can't imagine that word passing the
lips of any local citizens, but maybe it does, maybe they whisper 'shit' to themselves, Yugo and shit go together, the citizens who, in their cultivated lives urinate and have bowel
movements, the fact that shit is stuck on the wall proves that
we, *they*, are dirty), who's going to miss a pair of shit-stained
underwear? the local paper, that presumably wouldn't pub-
lish my announcement, the same paper that ran a feature on
our family six years ago, the community, that was allowed to
vote democratically for us or against us, clean hands that
observe their right to vote, and I, who raise my hand, look
at the faces of this community, and ask, who smeared shit
all over our toilet? the village stream plashes into sudden
silence . . .

Out of the blue it starts to rain, so that a number of local
citizens, already on their way to the village hall, return home

to get an umbrella or put on a raincoat, and so more than a few arrive late, place their umbrellas in the stands, small and some larger puddles form, grow, spread into a waterscape. I watch the men and women hang up their coats and jackets on hooks with a demure silver sheen, the kind you usually see in government offices, a few hands wipe wet faces, there's a heavy, damp smell, I hear sighs of oh, this rain! and a few men tug their sweaters down over their bellies, as they always do after they take off their jackets, a few women straighten their husbands' collars, they sympathetically scold the collar tips that have snuck inside the sweaters during the workday. People greet each other, have a quick chat, the general mood gradually lifts and the seats in the room are filled.

The attendant closes the long, wrinkle-free synthetic fabric curtains a little later than planned and the voices immediately become softer because the drawn curtains are an unmistakeable sign that the mayor will soon come on stage, the voices also become increasingly muffled because the curtains absorb noise surprisingly well.

Dear fellow citizens, I bid you a very heartfelt welcome in the name of our community! the mayor, a friendly looking man in his mid-sixties in a plain suit (whose hand I shook at the Young Citizens' Day celebration), briefly explains the day's business and the attendant turns off the lights, turns on the slide projector, we'll now show you a few pictures, the mayor says, so that those who don't know the Kocsis family can form an image of them and to refresh the memories of those who have already met them, here we have the two children, Ildikó Kocsis, who will be eighteen in a few months, and her sister Nomi, almost exactly two years younger, the children have never been cause for complaint, the mayor says, they speak perfect German, the older daughter has in fact distinguished herself through outstanding academic results, and the mayor probably cleared his throat at this point, the parents, Rózsa and Miklós Kocsis, have an excellent reputation, except for a few minor traffic infractions, their conduct has been irreproachable; the community listens attentively, the projector's rhythmic hum, here is the family at the public swimming pool (Nomi and I with gaps in our teeth and ice lollies in our hands), and here we see them in front of their laundry (on this evening, when a vote will decide our fate, we are sitting around a pot of hot oil with Irén, Sándor, Aranka and Attila, who can't believe we've never had *fondue bourguignonne* and have to explain to us how we have to leave the meat in the oil to cook, and then are supposed to dip the pieces of meat in various sauces, not bad, we decide, it even tastes pretty good, Father, who makes us laugh because in fact he's bored sitting around a pot for hours and taking for ever to eat), we now come to the actual vote, the mayor says once the lights in the room have been turned on again, the slide projector turned off and a young woman dressed as Helvetia stands next to the mayor at the podium in order to help him count the votes. Those in favour of granting the family Kocsis citizenship, raise your hands!

A sea of hands rises. Thank you, and those against granting the family Kocsis citizenship, raise your hands! A few hands are raised, a restrained murmur fills the room; Mrs Köchli, who, as usual, has not put her umbrella in the stand, but dried it in the ladies' room and put it under her chair before taking a seat, Mrs Köchli, who bends down, reaches for her umbrella, waves it in the air before pointing at various faces, then begins swearing in an unusually forceful voice. Mr Rampazzi, who works as attendant in the village hall (who occasionally helped us in the laundry with deliveries and whose son goes to school with Nomi), told us that he'd been looking forward to the end of his workday when Mrs Köchli, whom, quite frankly, he'd always found a bit odd, shot up like *a rocket*, she scolded those who'd voted against the Kocsis family, asking if they even knew the Kocsis', she waved her umbrella in circles, ranted, what she said he couldn't exactly remember, but her face was bright red and she fulminated against the Schwarzenbach Initiative, of that much he was certain because he had lived through that himself, since then things haven't changed, not by a mosquito fart, Mrs Köchli shouted at the stunned faces and he, Mr Rampazzi, thought to himself that it doesn't help foreigners, us in other words, to have some crazy lady carry on like that, especially if she's got a sister who, from her size alone, is so intimidating. Mrs Köchli and Mrs Frueler, who then made the whole row stand up to let them out, left the room without closing the door behind them so that everyone heard Mrs Köchli shout one last time, we belong to this unfortunate community, too! and the sound of the sisters' steps echoed for a while in the sudden silence of the community room.

I, who picture the two sisters to myself, immediately want to disappear once and for all.

There are days that attract dark thoughts, I, who forget there are other people aside from the one who soiled the men's room, I want to forget there are others because I want to feel a focused hatred for someone who so clearly expressed his hatred of us yesterday, it was a declaration of war, I want to say on Sunday as we sit in the Mondial, it's autumn and we're discussing a special autumn menu that would feature venison, red cabbage, homemade *spätzle* noodles, I want to interrupt Mother, who is talking numbers, numbers that really aren't bad at all, the summer was slow but it was no different with the Tanners, I want to explode, I want to set myself against us, against our diligence, our constant struggle to improve, I don't want to listen to my professor who says he has nothing against foreigners, all that counts for him is hard work, I don't want to hear my professor when he speaks in my parents' voice, with their belief that by working hard, by always increasing your effort, you can achieve everything, you can push reality aside, put the shit-covered underwear in the plastic bucket, in the rubbish can, and no one needs to wonder what that was, what it's supposed to mean; listen to me, I want to say, should we maybe register a complaint against an unknown perpetrator, how do you draw up such a complaint, that's what we should discuss, instead of roast venison, pears with lingonberries, glazed chestnuts. Mother, who had opened the door, what is that? she asked, underwear with a load, I answered, what? Mother, as white as a sheet and with a panicked look, someone probably lost them, I said, Mother, who picks the rubber gloves up from the floor and starts to pull them on but I stop her, I've got it, I said as the waitress, I wrapped the underwear in toilet paper, one hundred per cent cotton, I said, trying to make Mother laugh, this will stay between us, what? yes, there's no point in making a big deal out of it. Is there no other alternative than making a big deal out of it or hushing it up? I asked, an isolated incident, Mother said, it won't happen again, and again that sentence—we haven't got human status here yet, we still have to earn it—exactly, and today, on this Sunday, as we sit in the Mondial, smoke, drink coffee, Father has propped the front door open with a wooden wedge and Mother opened the doors to the toilets to give the Mondial a breath of fresh air before Monday is here again, but today I want to talk about this isolated incident, not about the numbers that really aren't bad at all and that Mother has underlined in pencil, she is immersed in the numbers more deeply than anyone possibly could be on a Sunday, I want to talk about this isolated incident that's obviously connected to our status here. Father, who wrinkles his brow, gives me a measuring look, says, what's the matter, Ildi? I need Nomi, but Nomi isn't here, she had apologized and explained she'd come later, later is too late, I think, drinking my coffee without any grounds, in other words concentrating only on the present, I wish my Mamika were here, she could read my future from the coffee grounds and the future was never grand and weighty and significant, tomorrow you'll have an unexpected visitor, a stranger will bring you a gift, or, look here, you see this line, it says we have to give the chickens more feed tonight. What's the matter with you, Ildi, I look into the bottoms of their coffee cups, I'm talking with the dead, I say and raise my head, I look at Mother, at Father, then again at Mother, who lays her hand on the list of numbers, from now on, I'm spending my time with the dead, I say because Father and Mother are silent, are you tired, did you not sleep well last night? Mother asks, her beautiful eyes looking troubled. I know perfectly well you can't talk with the dead, but they listen, they like to listen, they like beautiful voices, the dead love anything beautiful. Father, who starts to cough, Mother, who slaps his back between his shoulder blades. Where am I? Father asks when his coughing fit is done, can someone tell me what is going on here, Ildi, what on earth are you talking about? and I get up and disappear behind the counter to make a coffee and I stay there behind the green counter, Mother and Father exchange puzzled looks, I don't want to work here any more, I say, Father, who takes Mother's hand, shakes his head and says, can you explain my daughters to me?

It's all my fault, Mother says after a short pause, she is furious with me and I, taking a sip of black coffee, am surprised that Mother knows exactly what it's about. Go on, Ildi, tell him already, that's where you want to take this, isn't it? No, you tell, I say and notice how still it is in the Mondial today. The refrigerator case isn't humming, the air conditioner isn't on and I see my future in front of me, in imaginary coffee grounds, a tiny apartment in the city, in a crooked, green house, the old nameplate that I don't cover with my name, or if I do, then only after a long time with I. Kocsis, Ildikó Kocsis or just Kocsis on a little scrap of paper and I won't leave my apartment for weeks, I'll just sit in the kitchen, the kitchen with a pantry, a sink, a beautiful window. I will sit there and watch the light shining through the beautiful window.

Yesterday, someone, how should I put it, left some filth in the men's room, and Mother gestured towards the toilet, Ildi, don't you want to come back and sit with us? No, and Father fiddles with his moustache, what kind of filth? Someone went next to the toilet, Mother says—someone didn't just go next to it, he took off his shit-covered underpants and laid them neatly and carefully next to the toilet, more than that, this someone smeared shit all over the wall, I say and place each word after the other. That I didn't see, Mother says, you didn't, I answer heatedly, because I'd already cleaned the wall by the time you came in. I see, Mother says and I announce, tomorrow I'm not going to write up the menu on the board, but will register a complaint against an unknown party.

I anticipate all sorts of reactions, but not what happens next. Father, still fiddling with his moustache, doesn't swear, doesn't light a cigarette, he sits in his chair at the staff table and looks at me, at me or the counter or the glasses behind me, I can't tell, and he stands up, slowly, leans on the back of the chair, runs his fingers through his thick hair and takes a few steps towards the counter, pauses, and for a fraction of a second it looks like he's going to sway and fall forward, but Father doesn't fall, instead he keeps walking and glances at me briefly before going into the kitchen, no curses, no imprecations, no questions, probably no memory either of the time when he was considered an enemy of the system, my counter-revolutionary Father, as I sometimes secretly called him, not without pride, I think, and now? Father, who rummages in the deep freeze, shifting packs of frozen meat, looks for the right cut of meat to prepare on Monday, Father, who even turns on the radio as he starts to clean the combi-steamer, I stand in the doorway, completely at a loss, watching my father, how his head disappears into the steamer.

Sit down, says Mother, still sitting at the staff table, I need to talk to you, and I remain standing in the kitchen doorway, stuck to the door frame, I want to stop eveything, my studies, my Russian classes, Saturday nights in Wohlgroth, but most of all to stop working here, in the Mondial, I want to disappear from this community, to finally

268

shake off the nice waitress (thank you and goodbye!) to stop fading into the wallpaper, the carpet, the wall clock, the display case, and the food doesn't taste like us any more, no, I don't want to sit down, or to write up the special autumn menu—Ildi, who has such beautiful handwriting—I want to leave behind this divided life, the daily routine in which the service industry is my fate, the word 'muzzled' pops into my head, I feel muzzled by sentences like—we want you to have a better life than we did; we're only working for you. Sit down, Mother says in a conciliatory tone, she watches me with that look I know so well, something opens up in her eyes, an endless corridor with echoing footfalls, nightmarish figures whose bodies advance inexorably, explosive footfalls that pierce my temples, Mother, who desperately tries to keep the gold-green-brown wallpaper from tearing, my train of thought won't follow the usual path—and what if I don't want a better life? what if I want to live in a crooked old house with a gas stove, a water heater, and a stone sink? Built-in closets? no, I don't have any because they're so practical and ugly. Mother and Father, who will stand in my spartan apartment, this is how we lived twenty-five years ago, when we first came to Switzerland, how can you do this? look here at the window, isn't it beautiful, the way the light shines through it? (all I really want is a beautiful window), Mother waves her hand at me, Ildi, did you hear me? and Father opens the two kitchen windows to clear out the cleaning solution's noxious fumes, if we don't defend ourselves now, if we don't at least try to do something, then we're nobody any more, I say to Father, to Mother, the door frame that stiffens my backbone (you can't look back when you go, when you leave your homeland, you have to advance with determination, be ready to take everything that comes; who said that?), Father takes hold of the spray hose, aims it into the steamer, the back of his head might be telling me something, but what? I'm asking for an answer, I say, can't you please look me in the eye? Mother, who stands up, takes a few steps towards me, you want an answer, fine, you can have one! Father, who puts down the spray hose, starts scouring the sink with a special sponge, a soft melody on the radio and the cold autumn air make me shiver, Mother, who sits on the stool next to the dishwasher, says, what now? and I keep standing in the doorway.

And then I go in to the restaurant dining room, stop briefly at the counter as if I wanted to order something, I continue on, past the tables, I stop and say goodbye to tables two, five, ten, eleven and fifteen, I shake hands with Mrs Köchli and Mrs Freuler and with Mrs Hungerbühler, my favourite guests, and to the construction workers whose names I don't know, I nod as I pass, my steps make no sound on the carpet, the green varnished front door, standing open, invites me to leave, I go down the three steps and pause on the pavement, just briefly, then I go over to the chestnut trees, a few leaves are already lying on the ground, and from the chestnut trees

I look into the Mondial, I hardly recognize anything because of the reflections on the panes of glass, and I'd like to sing a song but can't think of any, I bend down to pick up a leaf, would anything be different if this leaf weren't here? and I walk quickly to the underpass, the dry sound of my sneakers, and have I ever imagined how it would be if we lived in the Vojvodina now, in the middle of a war, what our daily routine would be like then? Mother asks me, her voice, echoing in the underpass, sounds solemn and loud, my head automatically turns to the right and the left, towards the window displays, a few skeins of wool, knitting needles, a sweater labelled 'handmade', a few spotlights illuminating the small scene, we certainly wouldn't be worried about trifles, everyday would be a struggle between life and death! Mother, who makes the sign of the cross, is it a trifle when someone takes a handful of his own shit and smears it on the wall of a public toilet? I ask the display window to my left in which a few school notebooks are arranged next to coloured pencils and compasses of various sizes, the difficult question is how to display paper persuasively, a knapsack hangs from a nail, two orange reflectors glow behind the glass, children can't go to school because their parents don't have enough money for a bus ticket, and you, Ildi, you almost certainly couldn't finish your studies but would have to help in the pigsty and milk the cows, you'd probably even have to do men's work, you know what happens to the men. And I keep walking, I leave behind the question of whether or not an underpass is a suitable place for a display window, Mother's eyes beg me not to misunderstand her bringing the war up now, but she's doing it because I'm losing sight of the bigger picture, she needs to remind me that we live in safety here, and after all we run a business and for that you can't let everything get to you, otherwise we'd have left a long time ago, Mother says. What do you mean by that? and I climb the stairs, two at a time, cross the car park with only a few cars taking up spaces, Sunday in a village, a dead Sunday morning in a village, and I drop a coin into a parking meter to hear the pleasant sound it makes when the red arrow drops back to zero. How many times do you think we had to work twice as hard as our co-workers, for less pay, and clean up the still-warm vomit left by little dogs, and that wasn't even the worst of it, it was all part of your father's daily routine when he worked as a waiter in a fancy restaurant, Miklós, you should tell Ildi about it! Your only chance to get ahead is to work your way up and that, believe me, won't happen if you don't present yourself as deaf and dumb. I shouldn't misunderstand her when she says I'm not used to making sacrifices, sacrifices? Yes, keeping quiet, putting up with things, and if you do have to listen, then do it with only one ear; if your father and I had proper educations, then we might have been able, then we might have had an opportunity to speak out, but in our situation? Do you actually know where we started? the face-less days, almost four entire years, when days had only one purpose, for us to function like robots, to work, Father as a butcher for Mr Fluri and at the slaughterhouse, and I as a cashier, a nanny, and Sundays we cleaned banks together. I never dreamt in those days, Ildi, not once or I would have been lost, and I keep walking, past the pharmacy, across a street, on my right a shopping centre, on my left a clothing store, then a newstand, a hosiery store, a hotel, is there a sacrifice that's too great? and someone waves to me from the other side of the street, I keep going and don't return the wave, past a shoestore, a store window with eyeglasses hung on invisible threads. When the two of you, Nomi and you, were separated from us for so long, that was an enormous sacrifice—was it too great? and I lift my head, gaze up at the clock on the Protestant church's steeple, the golden hands glow; Father, who turns to me holding the sponge, water drips on the linoleum, you were in good hands, Father says without moving his lips, the Lion Restaurant, closed on Sunday, and I stop and study the menu in the little case, the prices, the choices, what does 'Horse Tenderloin Delight' look like, I wonder, and I keep going, raise the collar of my jacket, in front of me the village hall, the police station, the Protestant church, that's true, I say, we were in good hands! the two fir trees that tower above the steeple, evergreen trees, I think, the village square, where farmers from the surrounding region probably once sold their goods and where there surely used to be a linden tree that turned the heads of even the strictest guardians of order when it bloomed in June, and, standing alone in the village square, I hear the fountain's constant plashing, maybe the sacrifice should have been greater, maybe it would have been better if you'd waited a few more years for us, Father, who looks at me with penetrating eyes, Mother who gets up from her stool, what do you mean by that? Nomi and I never decided to come here, that's all; and Mother, who undoes her hairclip and clamps it on her shirt pocket, Father, who tosses the sponge into the sink behind him, there we have it, Father says, your mother was right to remind you about the war, try with your thick skull to imagine for just a moment what that would mean, and I tell him that that's not the point, I want to understand how we're different, and for the moment I can't think of the Hungarian word for 'different', but suddenly it's clear why, in German, when someone dies you say he is *verschieden*, which means both 'different' and 'departed', the difficult condition of having departed, I think and go up to the police station, bars on the windows and doors, hello, is anyone there? I call out absurdly, I knock on the glass behind which a few wanted posters and official announcements from the local and cantonal police bureaus are fixed with magnets, and I picture Mr Bieri and Mr Brunner, the two village police officers who also work for the public health authority, hiding behind the metal curtain, spinning on their upholstered desk chairs, their cheeks red, showing each other the most attractive mugshots, exchanging information about certain people in the stillness of a Sunday afternoon, why is it called 'registering a complaint'? Mr Bieri and Mr Brunner, who could surely answer my question, hello! my voice echoes across the empty square, in front of the police station my rage has a face again, the Schärers or Tognoni, or someone else, I hear Mother say, it doesn't do any good to wonder who could have done it, besides, we're a family business, when someone makes a mistake, it falls on all our heads, and, don't forget the customers who like us, who support us—I haven't forgotten anyone! I say in a loud voice, and we huddle together in our mutual incomprehension, we have to assimilate, Mother says with that look I don't want to see any more, assimilate to shit? I scream and where does resistance begin? Sometimes you bring your good sense to the wrong place, Ildi, Father shouts back and comes up to me abruptly, grabs my hand, pulls me through the kitchen, past the counter, he scatters his Hungarian oaths throughout the dining room, just so you can see things clearly, he shouts as he yanks open the office closet, reaches for his jacket, here, read this! Father holds a letter out to me, a slim envelope, and his hands tremble, a letter from your sister! I look at the stamps, at Father's thick fingers for which the envelope seems to be too heavy, what has happened to Janka? how is she? I ask Father in a toneless voice and I don't look at him, I don't take the letter. How is she? good, excellent, in fact, how do you think someone is doing who has had to give up her entire life from one day to the next? She fled to Hungary with her husband and child because her husband was about to be conscripted into the Yugoslav People's Army! and because her work at the radio station was constantly being censored! Father, who puts the letter away again, no, I don't need to read it, the most important thing has been said and the second most important, Ildi, nothing is the way it used to be in Yugoslavia, men are conscripted to fight, anyone with a brain and a chance to flee has left and what do you think things look like in a city when so many people no longer live where they belong? Every third house is empty, do you know what it means when the graveyard is the only thing that grows? And I go to the fountain, take a gulp of water, wash my face, I still have to do something, I take a few steps until I feel like I'm in the very centre of the village, I look at the fir trees one more time, at the steeple, I reach into my bag, my hand on the cold aluminium container, and draw huge letters on the village square with the whipped cream dispenser, beautiful, white, delicious, correct letters in heavy cream, my harmless childish prank for us, the Kocsis family, before I finally disappear from this village for good.

NOVEMBER

I live in the city centre, near a highway, my tiny apartment is on the western bypass, a thousand automobiles and a hundred trucks drive past every hour, towards Chur, and I, sitting on my bed, think of words like 'stream of traffic' or 'traffic flow', my boiler rumbles in the kitchen, the electricity meter in the hallway is one tick too loud, why 'western bypass', actually, if the cars on it are coming from the west and heading east, when you're driving you always think in terms of the direction of travel, don't you? The 'Nation's Exhaust Pipe', that's what they call the street that borders the western bypass and is named West Street.

Several children's faces with noses pressed flat look at me from a double-decker bus that stops right in front of my window; I wave, they laugh and wave back, a child, who holds a drawing up against the bus window, a sun, a rainbow, clouds and in the middle of it all, a rabbit gnawing on a carrot, and I stand up and go to the window, stick my head out towards the traffic to see if I guessed the children's nationality correctly, no, I'm an attraction at the window, eyes, pitying, amused, curious, look at me and sometimes the glances are irritated, probably because it annoys them that I live here where everyone wants just one thing—to drive on, to drive by. And the fuzzy tree-shaped air fresheners or the dachshunds that decorate the rear windows, whose heads bob with every bump in the road. I look brazenly into the pinched faces of drivers getting upset because the traffic doesn't move, it is just stalled, already, at eight in the morning; me, I admire Kurt, Hans, Pavel, Rüdiger, and whatever their names are (the one exception—Cindy), the lorry drivers, sitting lonely and massive in their thrones, good luck charms dangling from their rear-view mirrors.

You should close your curtains, advises Mrs Gründler, the building's caretaker, it's a bit much to have everyone staring in your bedroom window, isn't it? it would bother me; Mrs Gründler, who visits almost every day, knocks briefly and the next moment is standing in my hallway with her little dog, Suriname York Hamshire, I could sew some for you if you'd like, I mean, if you've got *kei Stutz*, no money. It really doesn't bother me, I answer, when I'm asleep, I'm asleep and when I'm awake, I stare back at them or I sit in the kitchen. Well, fine, we'll see how long that lasts, at least until you have a boyfriend . . . and Mrs Gründler tosses her hair, drops her dog on the ground, Suri, who is used to negotiating sudden and drastic changes in altitude, stands up and wags his tail, I laugh, would you like a coffee? Oh, Ms Kotschi, only if I won't be holding you up, and Mrs Gründler walks briskly into the kitchen, your place looks really homey now, she sits, wheezes, milk and sugar? I ask. Black coffee today, Mrs Gründler answers and I pour the coffee, not into everyday cups, but into the two lovely little espresso cups, the only ones

I own. You're a treasure, and Mrs Gründler takes a sip, sips again, then starts to talk, what those boys got up to again last night, Ms Kotschi, I can't even begin to describe it! Mrs Gründler, who reaches into her coat pocket, here, I made this myself, not that I'm a rocket scientist, it's pretty simple, and the caretaker hands me a slingshot, I got one of those drunks with this last night, on the leg, goal! I yelled, bull's eye! By the way, Ms Kotschi, you didn't hear me?

Of course I heard the caretaker, you can't miss her foghorn of a voice, as she says herself, Mrs Gründler, irate over the guys who stumble out of the Glarnerstübli, the bar next door, after midnight, and before they can figure out which way they're headed what with their *bimbe*, their heads completely pickled, they've got to piss on the linden tree and in the morning, as soon as the rest of us step out of the building, we've got the smell of their piss in our noses, is that any kind of greeting? (Suriname York Hamshire starts in with his high-pitched bark that sounds like the screech of a bird when his *mommy* lets loose and I laugh so hard I cry); I already gave the owner of the Glarner the business this morning, I told him I'll shoot those boys' nuts off if he keeps letting them drink themselves senseless! And the caretaker puts the slingshot back in her pocket, takes a last sip of coffee, says, now that is better than aspirin, and Mrs Gründler stands up with an unexpected burst of energy, all right then, let's go?

I carry the caretaker's shopping bags and we climb the stairs, Mrs Gründler, who stops after just a few steps, pants, puts a hand on her hip, you know, Ms Kotschi, that Freddy is a born egotist, each time I struggle up the stairs, he stands there, in the flesh, always two or three steps above me, grinning at me, and I tell him it's a disgrace, I show him the wallpaper peeling off the walls, right here, Ms Kotschi, take a look! and here, in the corner, look at the cracks! the water stains! and Mrs Gründler takes my hand, shows me the worst spots, tell me, don't you think someone like this deserves reproach for his entire existence, he owns a house and leaves it to rot like an overripe fruit, but the fruit wasn't always rotten, that much I know. You know how long I've lived here? Since 1965, back then West Street was a gem, a beautiful neighbourhood street with trees and open space; why do you think I fight so stubbornly to defend that linden tree down there? Despite everything, I still love this neighbourhood, this house . . . I'm sure you understand, Ms Kotschi. Absolutely! and, deeply touched, Mrs Gründler pats my hand.

Before we reach the top floor, Suri patters past us countless times, up the stairs and back down, slips between our feet, you fresh little mutt, Mrs Gründler scolds him goodnaturedly, by the time we reach the caretaker's apartment, I've once again learnt a few things, not only about the owner, Freddy the Capitalist (who sure as hell is speculating that traffic will be diverted at some point and he'll be able to sell his old house for a fortune), but also about the owner of the Glarnerstübli, who's most likely in on the two bars 'up that way', where the girls shake their rear ends; I know that my neighbour on the floor above is from Romandie, a nice guy but not quite right in the head, who has some temporary job but otherwise doesn't know how to do anything with his fingers except run them over his guitar, you must have heard, right? All in all, there soon won't be any tenants who know what kind of food *Hacktäschli* and *Wurschtwegge* are, not that she's got anything against *ćevapčići* or *börek*, but, Mrs Gründler says, I eat everything, preferably something I've never tried before, but I spend half my days trying to explain with my hands and feet how the washing machine works to my Yugos, Albanians, Turks and Spaniards. I'm not an interpreter, Mrs Gründler says, as she opens her door and Suri slips into her apartment. So, sit down for a moment and get your breath back from all that hauling and clear my gabbing from your ears and I'll make us some refreshments. I, as always, have to look around the caretaker's living room, full to bursting with paintings and framed photographs hung in a crazy pattern on the walls, potted plants in every corner, a ficus, a begonia, cape-stock rose and ivy framing the bookshelf on which books are stored but also dishes, figurines, purses in all sizes and materials, letters stuck everywhere between the books; I sit across from Suri, who has hopped up onto her chair, the seat raised with two cushions, between us a little bistro table, Suri and I, we look out the window, four storeys below us the traffic rolls slowly forward; from up here it almost looks agreeable, Mrs Gründler says, pushing a serving trolley through her living room, she sits next to Suri in a wing chair upholstered in dark green velvet. I'm always amazed at how different almost everything looks from above, I say, and the caretaker answers with a laugh, you can open the window if you don't believe we're still in the same building and she hands me a plate with little canapés and Suri springs into the air, snaps at a piece of ham. Ms Kotschi, the caretaker says after applauding her dog and praising his powerful jumps, can I ask you a question, I'm a very curious person, may I? OK, you're always home, when I barge in . . . but you're young . . . don't you ever go out? What do you do on a day like today with all twenty-four hours? I'm setting up my apartment, at the moment I've got some time off, so that's why I'm at home so much. And you don't travel when you have a vacation? and Mrs Gründler swallows her last bite, pulls a tube of lipstick from her handbag, purses her lips, paints them lavishly, and says, darn make-up, but without this cherry red I feel so pale, and Mrs Gründler rubs her forefinger over her teeth, because they always get a bit of red too, but I don't do it for the boys, I tell them that right to their faces, most of them don't have any taste anyway . . . boys today, they travel halfway around the world with that . . . what's it called again, that's it, InterRail. I decided to take my time setting up my apartment, I tell her, so my things can gradually get used to the new environment, and I stand up and offer the caretaker my hand. The way you say that, you probably need to as well, not just your things, and Mrs Gründler juts her lower jaw forward slightly and shakes my hand. Yes, of course . . . thanks very much for the refreshments and stop by again soon, I'm almost always there for you, I say with a laugh and I'm gone.

Just three weeks ago I moved out, whatever that means, I stood for hours with Mother, Father and Nomi in the living room, in the hallway, then in the kitchen and in my room, Father shook his head, looked at the boxes with uncomprehending eyes, then at me, but we have enough place here, he said softly and looked so small, Father with reddened eyes, but I cried too, we all did; and Father kept wanting to take pictures of me, me, then Nomi and me, me and the drawings I made when I was little, me with my furniture which, except for the bed, I wanted to take with me. What good is furniture without you, Mother had said and Father was suddenly almost enraged, you can't do this to us, that's a terrible reminder, furniture that no one uses any more, and Nomi answered, we can bring it all down to the basement, right now, there's enough room there and if anyone comes to visit, then we'll be happy to have the furniture. Oddly, Mother and Father agreed with her right away, together we carried down the wardrobe, the bookshelf, the desk and the dresser, all four of us for each piece of furniture after a lot of back and forth about how best to carry it, about what would be easiest. Then, when Father saw the furniture in the air-raid shelter, covered with white sheets, he cried out, no, no, I can't look, we've brought ghosts into the house! Now, stop it for goodness sake, Mother said, it's just Ildi's furniture waiting for visitors!

Here in Switzerland, it's normal to move out, everyone here moves out young, at sixteen or seventeen, rarely older than twenty, it's part of growing up, Nomi and I often tried to explain to our parents, in German and in Hungarian, and we both knew Mother and Father would never understand why anyone would move out before getting married, would prefer to live in a 'hole' when they could live in a place that has everything. But only on the day I packed up my things did I understand there was much more to it—a profound sense of shame that Mother and Father felt about my moving out, what would our relatives say? In their eyes I could read that for them, my moving out was a rejection of family and they felt they were responsible, not just in part, but completely (Mamika, who whispers in my ear, don't look at a situation from just your point of view, but from all possible angles), and I looked at my parents and tried one more time, it really has nothing to do with the two of you. . . I told them then fell silent because I realized that no words could soothe them, what was most essential couldn't be translated.

Mother cooked my favourite dinner—roast chicken with paprika potatoes, cucumber salad, and crêpes for dessert, and because no one had any appetite, Mother packed it all up so I wouldn't have to cook for the next two days. I asked Father to make coffee because I like the way he makes it best, I watched him grind the coffee, place the paper filter carefully in the holder, pass his thumb over the measuring spoon, Father's patience as he poured the hot water in circles onto the grounds; we won't be able to visit you for a while, Father said as the coffee dripped into the pot, you must understand.

At midnight I put my jacket on, open the window, air out my apartment. West Street is closed from midnight to six in the morning, I look to the left along the street, watch the cyclists heading in the opposite direction, sometimes without holding on to the handlebars, sometimes singing at the top of their lungs, and I smoke a cigarette in the cold November air, the owner of the Glarnerstübli, who shoos his regulars outside, usually the same five men who need to hang on to the banister to make it down the three steps in one piece; and when they set their sights on the linden tree, my building's caretaker immediately starts scolding, I close the window and hear my neighbour, Laurent Rosset, who is still practising and whom I met on the stairs in the week after I moved in, we had barely introduced ourselves before he revealed his life's ambition—to be able to play the guitar like Jimi someday. Jimi? you don't know who Jimi was, there's only one Jimi in the world, and Laurent invited me that evening to his place, showed me his record collection, his pots of grass on the kitchen balcony, a few books on Georges Bataille and of course on Jimi Hendrix, sit down, I'll play for you! How am I? Laurent's question after playing Jimi's hits for me, *Foxy Lady*, *Wild Thing*, *Hey Joe*, *Voodoo Child* and all of them a second time because he wasn't warmed up the first time. I think you're already better than Jimi, I told him. *Comment? impossible!*

was I taking the piss, Laurent asked, he would never be better than Jimi, he knew that; and my thoughtless answer embarrasses me because I really hadn't taken Laurent and his adoration of Jimi Hendrix seriously.

I butter a piece of bread and sprinkle it with salt and paprika, I always eat something before going to bed and, as I chew, I wonder if I should unpack another box and my neighbour from across the way, one of the people I see every day from my kitchen window, is a delicate woman I call my Pale Heroine because she's always doing something—cleaning, washing, cooking, hanging up laundry and now that it's strangely quiet (a silence I can't really take in, probably because the sounds of engines, of braking, of honking, of tires squealing still ring in my ears), she's ironing in her kitchen and the timeless exhaustion in her face is visible no matter what she's doing; I stand up, open a box (unpack at least two boxes each week, that's the goal I've set myself), and on top is the yellow envelope in which I keep my photographs; I, who've never wanted to put up or frame pictures, pick out a few, pin them above the head of my bed, I don't have a plan for arranging them, I just make sure their edges touch. When I was fourteen, I started collecting the photographs my parents wanted to throw away, 'discard' is written on the yellow envelope, cut heads, unrecognizable pictures, and one very wrinkled and faded picture I particularly like of Nomi and me turning away (a gust of wind had blown sand in our faces), our postures reveal our sudden movement;

most of all the picture reminds me how we laughed with the sand in our eyes, noses, mouths, laughed and laughed.

I sit on my bed, eat another slice of buttered bread, doze off with the pictures newly hung above my bed, I wake up, hear Laurent still playing and fall back asleep.

We've switched roles, you never used to oversleep, Nomi says after pounding on my window on All Saints' Day. Startled awake, I opened the window with bleary eyes, why didn't you ring the doorbell? I did, Nomi answers, but you obviously didn't hear me, I pull on a sweater, pants, open the door and quickly run my hands through my hair before Nomi and I hug each other, come in, and we sit in the kitchen, here, this is from Mother, and Nomi reaches into her bag—pickles, paprika sausage, garlic ham, noodle soup, acacia blossom honey, poppy and cheese strudel, all the rest I left at home and to console Mama, I told her I'd be visiting you again soon, how are you? Nomi asks. My tongue is still asleep, I answer. I'm out of coffee, I'll freshen up and we'll go to the cafe around the corner, OK?

El Zac is the name of the cafe run by a Spanish couple and their three children; Nomi and I stand in the entrance, silently agree which free seats are best, sit down, order two double espressos, examine the room, the furnishings, our eyes wander towards the coffee machine, a piston-driven machine, not an automatic one! in a matter of minutes we know if the ventilation system is good, what's on the food and drinks menus, did you see how much they charge for a cappuccino, yes, fifty rappen more than we do; and of course we test the coffee to see if it's good and if so, who their supplier is—we dive into a world we shared for a long time—are you awake now? Nomi asks after we've finished our coffees and paid, yes! and we stand up, wave to the owners and stop briefly on the doorstep to check their opening hours, they've got a long day, we say, the rent is probably too high! Nomi and I take off across West Street, look at the window of a glazier shop and are amazed at how precariously the fragile wares are displayed, the owner is probably a former tightrope-walker, I say and we continue, and I show Nomi what I've discovered in my neighbourhood, the lovely kindergarten, the antique shop on Ida Square, run by a glum but friendly Czech, the neighbourhood health-food store that carries everything even though it's tiny and in the flowershop on Berta Street, we buy a bouquet of autumn flowers, I point out the Ämtler School to the right where they set out the urns on election Sundays and Nomi pauses for a moment, looks at the November sky, a blue November day, she says, a beautiful exception, and we walk on, past the Japanese cherry trees, we bend right onto Goldbrunnen Street and after a few more steps we've arrived.

I'd never have found it on my own, says Nomi, who called me up to tell me her boyfriend told her there was a communal grave in the Sihlfeld Cemetery and we could bring flowers for our dead to this kind of cemetery commune; instead of always avoiding this holiday, we could try to recapture its meaning, besides, we don't know how long it will be before we're allowed to return to the Vojvodina, and I, with the receiver in my hand, at first don't know if I've understood Nomi, did you hear me?

We walked through the Sihlfeld Cemetery, so beautiful because it's unusually large, we admired the trees, how much room they have to grow, enormous oaks and plane trees, all kinds of chestnut trees that had just lost their leaves, an avenue lined with graceful birches, we even found ginkgos, their yellow-gold leaves scattered over the gravel path; on our way to the communal grave, we gathered the marvellous, colourful shapes that fall from the trees when they are most beautiful and laid them on the gravestone with our flowers. On this blue November day we thought of our dead, our great-aunts and great-uncles, the grandparents we never met, Mother's mother and Papuci, and for you, Mamika, we sang a song and in your name we prayed that the living not die before their time.